DAYDREAMS OF ANGELS

DAYDREAMS OF ANGELS

STORIES

HEATHER O'NEILL

FARRAR, STRAUS AND GIROUX

NEW YORK

Farrar, Straus and Giroux
18 West 18th Street, New York 10011

Library of Congress Cataloging-in-Publication Data
O'Neill, Heather.
    [Short stories. Selections]
    Daydreams of angels : stories / Heather O'Neill. — First American
edition.
        pages ; cm
    ISBN 978-0-374-28042-0 (hardcover) — ISBN 978-0-374-71122-1 (ebook)
    I. Title.

PR9199.4.O64 A6 2015
813'.6—dc23

                                                        2015010134

Farrar, Straus and Giroux books may be purchased for educational, business,
or promotional use. For information on bulk purchases, please contact the
Macmillan Corporate and Premium Sales Department at 1-800-221-7945,
extension 5442, or write to specialmarkets@macmillan.com.

www.fsgbooks.com
www.twitter.com/fsgbooks • www.facebook.com/fsgbooks

1   3   5   7   9   10   8   6   4   2

CONTENTS

DAYDREAMS OF ANGELS

THE GYPSY AND THE BEAR

One afternoon in 1946 a child was telling his toy soldiers the tale of a certain tall, menacing-looking Gypsy who was walking down a road in rural France. He had a trained bear and he played the violin. Something magical was meant to happen to him, naturally. However, in the middle of the tale, the child was called to lunch and never returned to the story.

The Gypsy stood there, contemplating his existence. He wasn't even a real Gypsy, not a member of the great Romany people, but more like the fictional kind, like the ones that you see in old-fashioned storybooks. He had on a pair of black leather boots, a pinstriped suit and a hat with its brim pulled down over one eye. He had a twinkle in the eye that you could see and a violin case under his arm. At least the boy must have thought that Gypsies were the most handsome men in the world, because he was darn good-looking. He was just a stereotype, a collection of spiffy attributes and flashy characteristics. He was one-dimensional in that sense. He had no depth.

And he was stuck with a bear that wore a jacket and followed him around and talked nonstop. The bear had tiny, deep-set eyes that looked like buttons in an armchair, and spiky black hair. What a nuisance, he thought. How could he travel by train with such a monstrous creature? The bear was actually quite gentle and kind and was oddly erudite. The child's father was a university professor, and the bear seemed to have been modelled after him. But despite the gentilesse, the bear informed the Gypsy that he would raise his great paws and slap him to death if he would dare to try to abandon him. He had no intention of being a bear without a Gypsy. He would be shot to death immediately, and furthermore, he had absolutely no plans to return to the wild. Quite simply, he did not have the constitution for it.

They were stuck together in the country. Why had that idiot child put them out here on this road? He was at home in the kitchen, drinking *chocolat chaud* out of a fancy teacup while his maid wiped his cheek with a napkin. Then he would be tucked into bed under a comforter filled with goose down. His rocking horse would never have any idea what it felt like to have gravel under its hooves.

Where had he seen this country road? The field next to them was filled with cats with bells on their necks, and a donkey with a straw hat on its head. A line of hens marched past them, single file. This boy really knew nothing about country life. And he had created two characters—a Gypsy and a bear—who equally knew nothing about country life.

The boy hadn't even had the wherewithal to put any money in the Gypsy's pockets and they were forced from the get-go to earn their own keep. From the presence of the Gypsy's violin and the bear's jacket, they could safely assume that they were performers, but they needed a town to ply their trade. They needed an audience. They couldn't just stand on the road, waiting and waiting for random passersby.

You could not have adventures in the country. Actually, you could have adventures in the country, but not the kind of adventure that the Gypsy wanted to have. He swiped a bicycle from the side of a farmhouse. The Gypsy allowed himself a small moment of joy when he discovered that the bear was quite good at riding a bicycle. With the Gypsy balanced on the handlebars, the bear rode the bicycle all the way down the road that led to a big city.

* * *

As soon as they got to the city, the Gypsy thought, This is more like it. There were so many buildings, as though all the blocks in a toy chest had been piled up one on top of the other. People stuck their heads out their windows to get a look at the pair of them. Much as the citizens of this town were interested in the Gypsy and the bear, these new arrivals were just as absolutely amazed by the city. They tried not to act like tourists—in awe of everything that they saw and eager to take it in. The Gypsy slyly nudged the bear in the side to make sure that the animal was seeing what he was seeing. The bear nodded, indicating that he most certainly was.

There were all these rows of stores to look at. There was one with prosthetic limbs that hung in the window, looking to complete a person. There was one that had beautiful ladies' hats. There must have been a thousand apples for sale at the fruit store. The Gypsy turned his head and noticed that there were pigeons exploding off the side of a building, as though a mortar shell had hit it. The street they were on was so narrow that it almost seemed as if two people on opposite sides of the street could lean out of their windows and kiss one another. Children stood on their balconies, looking down at the Gypsy and the bear, and called out to them. One little boy leaned over the railing with a pot and a wooden spoon and banged them together. They had their own marching band.

As soon as they entered the town square, they were happy. The bear liked it because it gave him the sensation of being little. Everybody on the road to the city had looked at him as if he was huge and as if they had never seen anything so enormous in all their lives. When he was in the square, it made him feel innocent, like he was a little beloved kid that everyone would be kind to.

The Gypsy liked being in the square because he was a protagonist, and thus he had to be the centre of attention. When the Gypsy began to play his violin, both he and the bear were taken aback for a moment. The musical phrase did cartwheels across the square like a tiny Russian gymnast. He had known that he was able to play, but he hadn't expected to be quite so talented. He was suddenly thankful that the boy who created him had been spoiled. He had obviously gone to quite a few musical presentations and listened to all sorts of wonderful records. Perhaps he had recently begun taking lessons himself and this was what he wanted to be able to sound like someday.

For his part, the bear was able to do all sorts of amazing things that you would never in your whole life imagine that a member of his already highly regarded species could do. These were feats that had never even been performed in any of the venerable European circuses before. The boy had seen them in an illustrated storybook about bears or maybe he had even seen them in a dream. The bear was able to roller-skate with his arms behind his back and his feet pushing out behind him. He was able to ride a unicycle and juggle, spinning the balls around as though he was God deciding where to put what in the solar system.

The Gypsy continued to play his violin in a strange way as the bear performed. When people listened to him playing the instrument, they fell under his spell. Watching their big eyes and their nodding heads, he realized that he could persuade anyone, through the music, to do whatever he wanted. He knew all sorts of tunes that weren't even really tunes per se—it would be safer to call them magical incantations. There was a repertoire in his mind, although he didn't know how it had come to be there.

He cast an eye around the crowd to see what kind of tune would get him the most money. He could play a tune that made you feel so guilty about past deeds that you would feel the need to pay amends. There was another that would make you fall head over heels in love with him. The girls would drop their coins into his hat, hoping that it would somehow get him to notice them long enough so that they might entice him.

He had a tune that made the listeners feel ashamed. And when he was done, he would look them in the eyes and people would give him their coins in order to get him to look away. He had a melody that made you feel as if life was so short that there was no point in holding on to anything. It was silly to hoard their money and not give it to the young violin player, because the truth was that they didn't even know if they were going to be here the next day.

Instead, he played his most beautiful and inscrutable tune, one that provoked people to look deep into themselves, and the audience couldn't bear for it to end. They threw all their money onto the ground and screamed out, "Encore, encore!" And the Gypsy kept playing until nobody could afford to give him any more money. Then he feigned terrible sadness and began to pack up his instrument.

The people in the square were left with a profound feeling of loss when the Gypsy and the bear walked away. That feeling of emptiness would follow them around and haunt them, and as there would be no way to ever hear that tune again, they would always feel incomplete. Some stopped to stare in the window of the prosthetic store, to see if their missing part was there.

The Gypsy, in turn, was left with the feeling that he was better than everyone in this town. He had a huge talent, after all. It belonged to him and it was the only thing that he cared for, the rest of the world be damned. All that he wanted from them was money. He had looked at the faces in the crowd, and his only relationship with them was how he could manipulate and get precisely what he needed from them.

He liked being cold, he thought as he and the bear walked along the narrow streets looking for lodgings. He didn't see a single reason in the world why a person shouldn't be hard-hearted. You got sad and depressed when you started worrying about what the fuck other people were thinking and whether they liked you or not.

"Wasn't it amazing?" the bear said.

"Yes, we were fantastic," the Gypsy agreed.

"All the marvellous looks on the faces of the children," the bear said. "They were enraptured. It made me feel good to bring a little bit of wonder to everyone's life like that. Doesn't it make it all worthwhile?"

"What on earth are you talking about? We do it for the money and that's the only reason."

"Oh, I thought the audience members were so lovely."

"Your persecutors! Who would put you in a cage?! You're terrified that they're going to put a bullet through your brain one moment and then you're calling them lovely the next. We'll see how lovely they are when we're trying to get a room in any of their one-star hotels."

"They don't know. It's not their fault. What are they supposed to do when they've been told their whole lives not to believe in fairy tales?"

* * *

They ended up renting a room on the top floor of a brothel, it being the only establishment that would let to a strange good-looking man and a bear. It was a small, dingy room with a window so high up, you would have to climb on a chair to look out of it. All that the Gypsy could see was the big fat moon, which looked like the bald head on a gentleman who sat in front of you at the movie theatre, blocking your view.

The bear plopped himself down on the double bed, filling it up completely. There wasn't room for the Gypsy to squeeze in anywhere. But he didn't mind, because the boy had created him to be a romantic. The Gypsy wanted to go out into the town and win over the heart of a schoolgirl.

But the bear told the Gypsy that if he tried to leave the brothel, he would find him and he would kill him. He would chase him right onto the street and murder him with everyone watching. He then hooked his jacket neatly onto the bedpost, getting comfortable.

The Gypsy looked at the bear, surprised. He and the bear had made pretty good money. They had a solid act together for now. Why would he leave the bear now that there was clearly a benefit for him in it?

"You know," said the Gypsy, "if I have to continue living cooped up with you, I might consider the possibility of blowing my own head off."

"You're being insensitive," answered the bear.

The bear propped himself up on some pillows and began reading a copy of *Anna Karenina* as the Gypsy slammed the door.

* * *

The Gypsy had wanted to seduce a virgin and instead he was stuck in the whorehouse. This wasn't a challenge whatsoever, as anybody with a wallet could win the heart of one of these girls for the evening.

He walked down the hallway and toward the stairs. There was a carpet of roses running along the stairs that had been stepped on so much that the floral patterns in the middle had worn right off. Many men had been on this path before. He was a Gypsy. If there was one thing that he was supposed to do, it was to take the road less travelled.

And these girls had all been through a war. The servicemen had been lined up around the block. Their pretty little toes had probably all been broken from having to dance with men in army boots. He was probably going to get a vicious strain of Canadian clap that no doctor would be able to cure. His loverboy days would be over before they had even begun.

The madam was sitting on a purple couch with thin legs that seemed as though it was about to give out from beneath her any minute. She was wearing a low-cut dress that exposed her unbelievably enormous cleavage. The boy, you see, had quite a vivacious grandmother. She leaned forward and pinched the Gypsy's cheeks.

Seeing that this did not change the boy's dissatisfied expression, the madam promised the Gypsy a very special lady.

"She's an orphan. Both parents are dead. I can show you the death certificates. I'm not going to sell you some phony goods. Oh, you should try her. All the men come in here looking for orphans. They have great pillow talk. For an extra dollar they will tell you their tale of woe."

Ah, of course there was an orphan in this story, because the boy had read so many stories about them. The Gypsy walked down the narrow corridor, with rooms on either side of it, with trepidation. When he opened door number 5, the

Orphan was lying on the bed. She was wearing such giant bifocals that he couldn't even see half her face. But since her nightgown was very pretty and she was slim, he settled on staring at her.

"Are you the one with a bear in your room?" she asked.

"I am."

"You are really handsome. Are you really a Gypsy?"

"I have no idea how to begin to answer that question."

"Do Gypsies make love in a certain way?"

"No." He paused. "Look, I paid for a tale of woe."

"Do you want it before the sex or afterwards?"

"I don't know. What's the difference?"

"If you want to hear it before, it's usually so that you can feel as if you've come to my rescue. If you want to hear it afterwards, it's because you want to feel sad and lonesome. Some men like to feel sad and weep after sex, and to feel intimate and tender and like they too are a lost little kid."

"Which do you recommend?"

"Afterwards, definitely."

* * *

The Gypsy had never had sex before. He hoped that it was something that the little boy had imagined that he was skilled at, the way that he had made the bear so wonderful at tricks. It was probably too much to ask, since the boy had already thought to make him a musical virtuoso. And the boy was still so young. He didn't know anything at all about being good in bed or performance anxiety.

He stood in front of the bed for a moment, not even knowing what to do with himself. The Orphan took off her enormous glasses and put them on the little table next to the bed. And for a second he was the one who felt that he wasn't seeing straight. Or at least it was safe to say that he couldn't believe his eyes.

She had round cheeks and pouty lips. Her bangs hung down almost to her small, upturned nose. Her eyes were blue. And they were the most innocent eyes that he had ever seen. He didn't care how many men had made love to her before. He didn't care if an entire regiment of Canadian soldiers had made love to her in one afternoon. She was so brand-new–looking that he couldn't imagine that anyone had ever touched her before.

She curled her body and sat up on her knees, and she looked like the white flower that had suddenly bloomed. She was wearing sheer pink stockings that went up to her knees. Her tiny white nightie covered her private parts, but if she were to do something like reach up to a top shelf, everything would be revealed.

She unbuttoned his shirt and took it off. She pulled his undershirt over his head, and he smiled as she patted down his fancy hair that had been mussed up. He couldn't believe how good her hands felt on him. He'd had no idea that that was what it felt like when another person put their hands on you. It made your whole body feel alive. It made you feel loved. It made you feel wanted. It made all the cells in your body seem to glow in the dark.

Out of his element, he let her do all the work, as if he

were sitting on a chair, watching this strange man and woman. Who knew how much better it felt to have someone else unbuckle your belt? He was moved in the same way that people were moved when they heard his violin playing. He was as completely undone as they were. He was at her mercy when his pants fell to the floor.

* * *

When it was all over and the Gypsy was lying on his back, sweaty and wiped out, the Orphan began her tale of woe. He had forgotten all about it. He was glad that he was getting it now, almost like a bedtime story.

The girl's first memory was of her mother dying. She was standing under an umbrella in the rain, next to a grave, as her mother's coffin was lowered into it. Her boots were covered in mud. The raindrops were heavy, like coins being tossed into a hat.

As they walked away from the funeral, the girl's grandmother told her that her mother had been a whore, so it was probably better that she was dead. The girl didn't know what a whore was. She did know what an orphan was though, because she had read about them in books. They were unhappy, they often met talking animals and they could never, ever trust any of their relatives.

She packed up a tiny suitcase. The Gypsy knew this part of the story well. It was the type of story about orphans that was in dozens of books. He knew exactly what the Orphan was wearing without her having to tell him. She had on a little pair of black lace-up boots whose soles were worn thin. She had a pair of black tights that had been mended dozens of times and still had holes in the knees. She had a grey-and-blue-striped dress that was frayed at the bottom, and a wee skimpy coat that had gone to seed.

The Orphan's grandmother drove her to a huge stone building in the middle of the city. There were massive wooden doors that should have been impossible to open without three people pushing together, but they swung open easily. Such are the improbable physical laws that govern a world created by a child.

The Orphan walked into the dormitory and saw that there were sad, skinny girls all over the place. They slept in rows of squeaky beds with cast iron frames whose white paint was peeling off. They often ate little bowls of gruel. It never tasted like anything at all, and there was never enough of it. The orphans were hungry all day long. They often thought of going up and asking for some more, but the young boy must have known that it would be a cliché.

All the orphans looked tired and worn out. It was clear that they were not staying at the orphanage for free but had to earn their keep. One of the principal things that the girls did to keep the orphanage up and running was laundry. They would hurry up the back stairs of houses to collect baskets of dirty clothes and then pull them back to the orphanage in their wagons. They would sit at buckets, scrubbing vigorously all day long.

They were beaten all the time for their misdeeds. No matter how much they toed the line and tried to be good, they were children and so they would make mistakes. They were beaten for spilling a glass of water or for losing a sock from their basket of laundry. Their laughter would be quick and furtive and frightened, and then disappear, like a mouse sneaking briefly out of its hole. And they were even beaten for laughing after the lights were out—although this was a very rare occurrence indeed.

The Orphan often found herself having to lean over, with her dress lifted up, while she was viciously pounded with a wooden panel. She couldn't sit down at all. And she wept whenever she had to have a pee.

The orphans were also expected to perform in the Charitable Children's Orphan Orchestra, which played at various functions in order to raise money from wealthy citizens. The orphans would ding triangles and bang cymbals. It made the noise of cash registers being rung up. There was one girl who played the trumpet a little, sounding like someone yawning first thing in the morning. They didn't have to be particularly talented. Their job was mostly to look pathetic and adorable. Many of the girls liked it because it got them away from the orphanage and work for the day.

The Orphan chose to learn the violin. She practised every evening. She practised when she had finished all her laundry. She poured all her energy into playing the instrument. She wanted to have a skill more than anything else because she knew that it was the only thing that could take her far away from the orphanage, not only for the day, but forever. It could save her from a life of servitude. If she could play the violin properly, she thought, she could have a whole different kind of life story. She could be a whole different kind of character.

The priest who was the musical instructor was particularly violent during his lessons, but she didn't mind. She was glad that he slapped her when she made a mistake. She thought that the sooner she was able to master this tempestuous piece of wood, the sooner she would be out of there.

Her playing sounded horrible at first. All the other girls covered their ears and made fun of how badly she performed. The neighbours who lived in buildings around the orphanage heard the music but did not know what it was. It sort of sounded as if there was a little girl crying for her mother under their window, and they so wished that she would go away. Why should they have to deal with her stupid problems? They had enough of their own without having to deal with this. It sounded like a cat in heat. They prayed that the animal would hurry up and get laid. That some tomcat would put the silly slut out of her misery and knock her up.

She knew that she would be good one day—she knew that all her pain had to translate into something. Because where art is concerned, pain can be transformed into magic.

The Orphan did not like being a girl one little bit. As she walked down the street, pulling a wagon of laundry, she didn't like the way the men looked at her ass, knowing that she was poor. She didn't like the way they all thought that they might be her Prince Charming.

Once she went to a house to collect some laundry and a woman gave her an old suit that had belonged to her father, who had recently passed away. She told the Orphan to throw it away or sell it to the rag dealer. The Orphan brought it back to the orphanage and tried it on in the closet. The old man had been tiny and was practically the same size as her. It was the first time that the Orphan felt comfortable in clothes.

She found a pair of glasses in the breast pocket. The little boy had obviously recently started wearing glasses and thought it only fair that everyone should. She put them on out of curiosity and found that she could see much better. She knew that she looked ridiculous in the glasses, but it was better than being blind. She kept the glasses on and hid the suit in the closet. No one seemed to bother her about the glasses at the orphanage, or notice that there was anything different about her appearance.

Then one day the Orphan did not tuck her sheet in properly after she made her bed. It filled the Headmistress with so much rage that she went after the Orphan, who was so busy scrubbing away with a bucket between her feet that she did not notice her coming.

Swooping down behind the Orphan, the Headmistress grabbed the back of her hair with her fist and forced the girl's head right into the bucket of water. She yanked her up for a breath, and the Orphan's body shook and she gasped uncontrollably. The Headmistress pushed her back under the water again. She let her up and the Orphan collapsed, writhing and puking on the floor. Lying prostrate, with her little finger splayed beneath her on the tiles, the Orphan knew that she could sink no further in this world. And so she slowly rose up, straightened her tiny spine and knew for the first time, and without a doubt, what dignity felt like.

That night, when the Orphan picked up the violin, she began to play a concerto by Mendelssohn. The priest looked up, surprised. He could not master such a tune. She was playing better than he had ever been able to. She was fourteen years old and she had surpassed him. Actually, her playing could even be described as miraculous, and everyone in the orphanage stopped what they were doing to marvel.

Realizing that the orphanage now had a soloist, the priest's head was filled with plans. Their Charitable Children's Orphan Orchestra would be able to play all over the country, and perhaps they might even be invited to perform for diplomats. They would surely be rewarded financially for delivering to the world a child who could create such sounds!

But this was not to be, because the very next morning the Orphan decided to run away. She put the suit and the violin at the bottom of a laundry basket filled with clean underwear that she was supposed to deliver. She carried the basket out the door and down the street, as if she was an ordinary woebegone orphan going about her godforsaken task. In any case, it wasn't terribly hard to escape from an orphanage. All orphans who are the heroes of stories are able to escape from their orphanages.

She changed into the suit in an alleyway. Only a black cat saw her, but it was too busy saying witty things to alert anyone.

"By the time a child is eleven years old, it's all too late," said the black cat. "They've picked up character traits that will plague them like fleas for the rest of their lives."

The Orphan pushed her hair back and then reached into

a parked car and took a hat off the dashboard and pulled it down over her head at a jaunty angle. She put the violin under her arm, and when she stepped out into the street she was no longer an orphan, but a travelling Gypsy.

The Gypsy sat up, dumbfounded by the tale. He got out of bed and looked into the Orphan's closet. There was his famous suit hanging from the coat hanger. He looked in the corner and there was a dark burgundy violin case, that was none other than his own.

Turning back, he saw that the Orphan was gone. The Gypsy avoided looking into the mirror, frightened of whose face he would actually see. The Gypsy knew something about himself now. He was only putting up a front to the world. He had to put a distance between himself and other people. It was because of his childhood that he couldn't trust anybody. He had grown up relying on himself and being independent. He had never learned how to let other people into his life.

As the Gypsy walked up the stairs to his room, with his shoes in his hands and his belt buckle undone, he was overcome with empathy for the bear. It made him feel sad that the bear was up in his room, reading paperback novels and trying to put himself to sleep.

And of course the bear had been right. The Gypsy could never travel without him. And even though it was a monster, a beast that people had all sorts of preconceived notions about, the bear was really his own great big heart. The bear was who he would have been if he hadn't had a difficult childhood. The bear was everything that was good and decent about the Gypsy, and it would follow him whether he liked it or not, everywhere he went. It would never let him just look at the world coldly. It would always magically make him notice that everything was full of wonder.

THE GOSPEL
ACCORDING TO MARY M.

Jesus and I were pretty good friends, and after he disappeared from our neighbourhood and all those TV reporters started showing up on our street, I was a pretty hot property. My mom would freak out and call them vultures when they tried to ask me questions, but I'd try and chill her out. "Be cool," I'd say, and it wasn't just that I liked being on TV; I truly liked talking about Jesus. I still do, and to this day, people are always asking me to tell them everything I know about him.

Jesus and I were in Grade Six when we first met, and back then not everyone was allowed to hang out with me. A part of the reason was the way I dressed. I was the only girl in class who had a pair of high heels, and for my birthday my mother bought me a ton of black bracelets with studs on them. Other people's parents said I looked like a whore, and they didn't want their kids to get my whore cooties or something. But my attitude has always been to just be who you got to be. A part of this way of thinking comes from me, but a good part of it also comes from the stuff that Jesus taught me, but more on that later.

Jesus first showed up in the middle of the school year and sat at the back of the class. On that first day, when our chemistry teacher put on this movie about molecules, Jesus held his hands up in front of the projector and made a shadow puppet of a dove. That's how I first noticed him.

It was about a week later when everybody started to notice Jesus. In moral ed. we had to give a presentation on a social concern, and Jesus did his on world hunger. He went up to the front of the classroom, without a loose-leaf paper or anything, and started going on about how there wasn't such a thing as world hunger, which, as well as being a downright weird thing to say, was also factually incorrect. We had all seen pictures of Ethiopia on the news and those poor kids were definitely hungry. Jesus said that if God fed the sparrows and butterflies, then he would also feed humans.

The teacher pointed out that a lot of animals had gone extinct because the environment hadn't provided for them, but Jesus shrugged and went back to his seat, so we all figured he was really stupid.

* * *

A lot of the kids in the class tended to not like Jesus very much. This, of course, was not helped by the fact the teachers thought he was nuts. I know teachers aren't supposed to think stuff like that, but you just knew they were thinking it anyhow. Like when we went on a class field trip to the zoo,

Jesus went over to the lion's cage and stuck his hand through the bars. The teacher was still screaming at him the next day in class, going on about how not only could he have lost a hand, but he'd also have been forced to go from school to school, giving lectures about it.

"Why would you do something so stupid?" she demanded.

"I knew that the lion wouldn't have bitten me," Jesus said. "I could just feel it in my heart."

You know he became the talk of the teachers' lounge with that one.

But you'd think bravery like that would impress kids, right? Well, you're half right. Feeding your hand to a lion is cool, no doubt, but it's just that he was also relentlessly lame. So lame that it undid all of the good. For instance, once when we were all in the back of the schoolyard and Judas was explaining to us where babies came from, Jesus positively spazzed out.

Now, I knew about all that baby stuff, even then, and I knew that Judas was fifty percent full of crap, but if I piped in with my corrections, he'd be all "*Excusez-moi*, Professor Been-Around-the-Block," so I made sure to keep my mouth shut.

But Jesus, on the other hand, started having a complete breakdown. He said that Judas was a liar and that if a woman hears someone whispering in her ear in the middle of the night and if she sits up and looks around and no one is there, she'll be pregnant by the morning.

"If you think that's the truth," said Judas, "then I have some magazines for you to look at," and everyone laughed. I'm sad to report that even I did, a little.

* * *

Since Jesus and I lived on the same block, we'd walk home from school together. One day, on our way home, he invited me over to his house to play with his Ouija board. I hadn't played with one of those since I was a kid. Ouija boards reminded me of my mom's creepy boyfriends, but since I didn't get a lot of invitations, I accepted. Plus, in all honesty I've always liked weirdos into the occult. It's just the way I'm built.

As we walked to his house, Jesus told me that his father didn't really love his mother. He didn't believe that Jesus was his child. He told me that while swinging his lunch pail. He told me that the same way you'd tell someone that you liked apples. When someone tells you something like that, all casual, it sort of takes the pressure off. You don't have to start rocking them in your arms and stuff. I appreciated Jesus for going easy on me like that, since we've all got our troubles.

His family lived in a building that had a huge billboard advertising beer on the roof and there were dogs walking around in the stairwell like they owned the joint.

We went into his room, turned off all the lights and set up the Ouija board on the bed. As soon as we touched the marker, it started zipping around like a cockroach high on roach poison. I had never seen such a thing before. Jesus and I took our fingers off the marker but it kept sliding around all the same. It spelled out, "I-AM-WITH-YOU-JESUS." Jesus and I screamed our heads off. We jumped off the bed and ran right into the apartment hallway. Under the stairwell, I let Jesus put his hand under my shirt and on my chest to see how hard my heart was beating.

* * *

After that, things started getting weirder and weirder. Sitting in the cafeteria one day, Jesus put his juice box down and turned to me.

"Tell me if this apple juice doesn't taste funny to you," he said.

I took a swig. It tasted exactly like wine. I recognized it as wine because I'd had some at my cousin's wedding the year before.

"Why did your mother give you wine?" I asked.

"I don't think she did," he answered.

Word of the wine spread like wild. Pretty soon everyone in our class was lined up at our table, asking for a sip. Jesus passed around his box and everyone got some.

When there was none left, we all sang this crazy fast version of "Don't Worry, Be Happy."

After that, everyone started letting Jesus hang out with them, and since I was his friend, I got to hang out with everybody, too.

The socializing seemed to be doing Jesus wonders. He really came out of his shell, doing all kinds of really daring things, like one time, during recess, he made his way onto the school roof and jumped right over the alley to the next building. We stood under him on the ground and watched as he sailed over us.

A lot of boys in class took to following him around, anxious to see what he'd do next. The boys started calling themselves "The Holy Ghosts." Jesus got mad and embarrassed when he heard about it, though. He didn't think the gang should have a name. He didn't even think that they *were* a gang, although that's obviously what they were fast becoming.

* * *

Jesus showed up one day at my house. He was wearing no shirt and little red Adidas shorts. My mom said that, in general, guys who were as skinny as Jesus were embarrassed by how they looked without a shirt on, but Jesus didn't seem to care. My mother said that that meant he had inner strength—a real screw-all-of-y'all attitude.

I never invited people over, so I was a little put off having Jesus in our house. Once, I had Judas over and he said he found my apartment depressing. He said that the postcards of KISS on the wall in the living room made him want to off himself.

"I like your place," Jesus said, leaning against my bedroom windowpane. "You have a great view from here—right out onto the record store. It probably helps you dream of music. We have the best neighbourhood."

"Wouldn't you rather we lived in Westmount?" I asked. Westmount was the fanciest neighbourhood in the city, and my mother was always going on about how if she won the Lucky Seven, she'd set fire to the building and move us there in a smoke cloud of glory.

"Being rich is stupid," he said. "It's way better to have less. It makes you cooler. No one from a rich background can ever really be cool."

He said all of this in the same way that he dropped the news about his dad. Very matter-of-fact. Maybe that was why I bought it. It seemed to somehow make sense, like he was saying something that I had already thought myself but had never actually gotten around to putting into complete sentences. Jesus' words made me feel like no matter how much there was something deep down wrong with you, there really wasn't anything wrong with you at all.

I was sitting on the side of my bed, listening and thinking, when Jesus remarked on the cut on my arm. I got it when I crashed into a telephone pole while running and looking into people's windows. Jesus held my arm and kissed it, and then, just like that, the cut turned into a scab. It was like I was in a dream, where funny things happen and you don't try to question them.

It was then I had a brainstorm. Our washing machine hadn't been working for months, so I brought Jesus over to it and it turned on. It still made the same old awful clanking sound, but still, it *was* working. I brought my mother over to see and she tried to get Jesus to pick a lottery number for her, but he wouldn't do it. Finally she gave up on getting it out of him and settled on using the numbers in his birthday and she won thirty-three dollars.

* * *

When the weather became nice, Jesus and I started hanging out in Jerusalem Park. There was a fountain there with a golden spout. The only problem with Jerusalem Park was all the older bums who hung out there and were always coming up to you. Sometimes they wanted to hit you up for change or smokes, but mostly they really wanted to mouth off about their hippy-dippy ideas.

It was at the park that Jesus and I first met Jean-Baptiste. Even though it was spring, he was wearing a big brown fur coat and eating from a jar of honey with a plastic spoon. His legs were folded and, judging from his bare knees, he didn't have anything on under his coat.

Jean-Baptiste came up to us and said that seeing Jesus gave him a real déjà vu. Déjà vu was big among the hippie bums, it seemed.

"It's like I recognize you from when I was a kid," said Jean-Baptiste, "but that would be impossible. I'm twice your age. Plus, I grew up in Winnipeg."

Jesus smiled politely. Jean-Baptiste looked at him in a knowing way.

"We were born for terrible things to befall us, weren't we?" said Jean-Baptiste.

He kissed his palm and put it on Jesus' forehead.

"Are you wacko?" I shouted at Jesus. "Don't let him do that. You're going to get hepatitis."

"You think this boy is afraid of germs?" Jean-Baptiste laughed. "He has a pure spirit. He wants everyone's germs."

"I don't know, Mister," I said. "Not everyone likes to roll around in the dirt like you do."

"*He* sure does. He's got a Messiah complex. He'd put it on the line for anyone, anywhere, anytime!"

For some reason this made me sick and scared. And angry. I was angry we had even stopped to talk to him.

"If you're so smart," I said, "go find yourself a job."

And then I grabbed Jesus by the hand and together we ran out of the park.

* * *

That was the last time I ever saw Jesus. He had karate lessons with Judas that night and they were supposed to take the bus downtown together like they usually did, except that night Judas never showed up. His mother gave him a lift and he figured Jesus would put two and two together and head downtown on his own once he saw he wasn't coming, but Jesus probably just stayed sitting on the bus bench, waiting. Judas always said he really regretted that.

The story went that Jesus was abducted, but nobody can really say for sure. The thing is, he would have been really easy to kidnap. Jesus trusted everyone. He probably walked right into the kidnapper's car without any hesitation.

There were pictures of Jesus plastered to every telephone pole in the city, and practically the whole school had to be treated for post-traumatic stress syndrome. It seemed like no one could get the image of him walking into that kidnapper's car out of their heads.

This one kid in our gang, Peter, said he saw Jesus in the park three days after he vanished, walking across the kiddie pool. But you couldn't believe what Peter said. He'd become totally obsessed with Jesus after the disappearance. Every composition he wrote in class was about him. The teachers said that it was his own way of coping with the stress.

I guess I was dealing with some serious stress of my own, because one day in art class, when the teacher told me that little girls who wore black tank tops didn't get into college, I stood up and yelled, "What makes you so perfect, you jerk! You've done too many lousy things yourself to be judging children!" And the teacher got all red in the face because he knew it was the truth.

I knew that Jesus would have loved that one. It was the kind of thing that he would say, and it felt good to say it.

SWAN LAKE FOR BEGINNERS

It all began with a very young scientist named Vladimir Latska, who lived and worked in Moscow. He had graduated from university in 1949 when he was eleven years old, and for a time he was often seen on television and heard on the radio, babbling prettily about cells and biology. He had big blue eyes and he would tilt his chin up to the heavens when he lectured, as if to accentuate his concern with lofty spiritual matters. His hair stuck straight up in the air, which was all the rage among young geniuses at the time, and he wore the same shabby suit covered in soup stains for three years straight, as he was too profound to bother changing his clothes. He waved his hands excitedly when he spoke. It was as if he was a conductor and the world was his orchestra, and he was trying to get it to perform a magnificent concerto. He almost danced when he spoke about science, lecturing at times on his tippy-toes. It made him beloved by audiences even when, at times, they didn't understand a word he was saying. They would line up after his lectures on genetics to have an opportunity to pinch his cheeks.

After several years in the laboratory, he went to the government and announced that he had discovered a way to clone animals. To prove it, he had with him a cage filled with white kittens that he declared were identical and were all named Boris. The kittens were all curled up together, like a pile of snowballs that had been patted together by small mittened hands in preparation for a war. Latska quoted dozens of poems, explaining the wonders of cloning and the beauty of multiplicity. Of course no one believed him, and they weren't sure why they had arranged to have a meeting with this teenager. The officials held up the kittens and claimed they saw subtle differences. Latska offered to take them to his laboratory outside the city, where he had thousands of additional cloned Borises running around on his property. They laughed because there didn't seem to be a point in having three thousand kittens named Boris, and what with the Soviet Union being what it was in 1955, they were very busy.

Never living up to his early potential, Latska began to be seen more as a flamboyant entertainer than anything else. The world had all but forgotten him when, years later, in 1961, Rudolf Nureyev, the country's most exciting young dancer, ran screaming to the police at an airport in Paris, demanding to stay. Nureyev defected, much to the government's and the Soviet people's dismay. It was considered so damaging to Soviet propaganda that it was kept out of the national press, and the government tried to pretend Nureyev had never existed. "Rudolf who?" was the official party line.

The rest of the world, however, went batshit crazy, in a manner of speaking, for Nureyev, celebrating his every movement, putting him on the cover of magazines and catapulting him to fame. That was when Vladimir Latska chose to return, approaching the government this time with a proposal that they found intriguing. Latska claimed that through cloning, he could deliver back to Russia a new and improved Nureyev.

The government decided to give Latska a chance. They gave him a vial of blood that a nurse had collected from Nureyev during a routine checkup, and almost unlimited resources for the project. Ordered to keep the operation absolutely top secret, Latska and his men, a group of unemployed scientists and unlicensed doctors from the countryside outside Moscow, got into planes and headed to a small town in northern Quebec called Pas-Grand-Chose. In addition to being a desirable location because of its isolation, its proximity to tundra, and the fact that it had not had a tourist in a hundred years, the town was also singled out because of its high unemployment rate. It had been the country's largest manufacturer of bloomers, and when they went out of style after 1941, the citizens of the town found themselves in dire straits. The area had the broken, random look of a train set that a child had abandoned years before. The Canadian government turned a blind eye as the town welcomed the project with open arms, hastily constructing a makeshift enclosure around Pas-Grand-Chose in preparation for the arrival of the covert scientists.

Banned from most universities, Latska's team of misfit scientists was also wildly enthusiastic about the idea of regular work. Vladimir Latska believed that the only worthwhile scientists were the mad ones. Other scientists asked too many questions about the implications of their research, never taking the irrational leaps of faith necessary for true discovery. Latska believed that the Nureyev Experiment was really a magnificent project, certain to be a shoo-in for the Nobel Prize and to reestablish his credibility. Latska put an ad in the newspaper looking for homes for his three thousand kittens named Boris. He took only one Boris with him, though, that being all he really needed. Perhaps he should have taken it as a sign that we only really need one of a good thing.

There was a parade in Pas-Grand-Chose for all the mad scientists when they got off the plane. They were a curious sight with their hair sticking straight up in the air, their bottle-cap glasses and their briefcases that had smoke coming out of them. They had cardboard boxes filled with beakers and Dungeons & Dragons sets. None of them had girlfriends.

With a bunch of Nureyevs, the Soviet government would be able to open shows every night in every major city in the world. They could even have two or three of them touring together so that they wouldn't get tired. They could do three-month engagements, and if one broke an ankle or had a nervous breakdown, it wouldn't be a problem in the least. They had put a spacecraft on the moon, and now this! Nureyev would be sorry that he had thought himself unique. He was replaceable. It was the Soviet Union that was unique.

* * *

There were twelve Nureyevs cloned in 1961. The scientists and indeed the whole town were reverent of the handsome little Nureyev boys. Everyone was in awe of the fact that these children were actually the greatest dancer of the twentieth century. The boys walked around town in fancy little suits, carrying red balloons, and everyone kissed them and told them how wonderful they were.

The scientists were determined to give the Nureyevs happy childhoods. Whereas the real Nureyev had only been able to join a professional dance school when he was seventeen, these Nureyevs had dance classes starting when they were five years old. They would learn both Russian from the scientists and French, which was the language of ballet, from the inhabitants. They wouldn't have a father who would be away at the front for most of their childhoods and who hated their dancing. They wouldn't have to wear the same shabby velvet coat for a decade, go hungry on a regular basis and live during a devastating war. This way, the carefree clones would be even greater dancers than the actual Nureyev had ever been. The scientists shivered with joy when they imagined the results.

These first Nureyevs were raised in happy, middle-class, two-parent families who adored them and showered them with praise. They were given puppies, had fairy tales read to them and were given holidays on the banks of the Saint-Laurent River. They went to puppet shows. An effort was made to paint everything pink and blue and green.

Cartons of butterflies were brought in from Brazil and were let loose in the town square. It looked as though someone had opened a window while a nerd was working on her stamp collection and the wind had lifted them all up in the air. The children ran around with their arms stretched out in joy. The butterflies died of shock and fell to the ground hours later, but they were quickly swept up by groundskeepers. The townspeople made the boys crowns of dandelions and daffodils to wear on their heads, telling them that everything was always going to be all right.

However, to the scientists' dismay, when this generation of Nureyevs became teenagers, they had very little interest in dance. They were sensible and well balanced, and so they wanted more reliable careers, ones that promised economic security. They wanted to become political attachés and commodity traders.

Those who could dance did so with proficiency but had no edge. No one would be throwing underwear at them, let's put it that way.

One of the boys was given a biography of Nureyev to read. A scientist thought he would be inspired by the glory and fame that Nureyev had achieved. Instead, the young clone was horrified. He shared the book with the other clones, who were equally shocked. All they took away from the biography was how rude and irritable the dancer had been, how miserable and conceited, and how difficult and unpredictable life as an artist was. They slammed the book shut, like a folk dancer pounding his foot on the floor to announce the end of an act.

* * *

With the next generation of Nureyevs, the scientists decided they'd try a less hands-on approach. They hired local childless women to raise the Nureyevs. The scientists allowed them to be raised unsupervised, in order that they might have normal childhoods.

But it was found that the mothers had too much influence on the Nureyevs. One of the mothers spent all her time watching medical dramas on television. This boy grew up wanting to be a surgeon. He wore a white bathrobe around the neighbourhood, carrying a clipboard and insisting on checking other children's pulses. Another mother was very good at making cupcakes. To the scientists' consternation, her little Nureyev announced that he was going to open his own bakery and name it Jeannette's Delight, in honour of his mother.

Then, rather disturbingly, one of the clones opted for a career playing the accordion. The scientists tried to account for this abnormality. After questioning his mother, they found that she had sung a Parisian ditty about the Avenue des Champs-Élysées to him when he was a little boy. Now he wore a black beret, smoked all the time and had changed his name to Pierre Gaston. His cigarette smoke wavered above his head like a French philosopher's thought bubbles. The shock of this forced the scientists to reexamine their methods altogether.

When the Russian government read Pierre Gaston's self-published volume of poetry, called *A Lonely Winter on the Seine*, they withdrew significant funding.

* * *

Exasperated, the scientists decided to make one group of young clones dance like Nureyev by force. These young boys had to endure eight hours of training a day. The dance instructors humiliated and hit the boys when they messed up their steps. The callous teachers threatened to murder their dogs if they didn't execute their pirouettes perfectly. They wouldn't let them eat unless they managed a grand jeté. Half-starved Nureyevs would crouch in the corner, massaging their aching legs and whimpering unhappily. So joyless was this group that they barely resembled boys anymore.

This was indeed a dark period. They practised so much that they didn't even have a chance to change out of their leotards. You would see a sixteen-year-old Nureyev, in a black leotard with little red sequins and boots, standing outside for but a moment, trying to figure out who he really was. His sequins glimmered like a distant galaxy whose constellations were emitting their tragic messages in Morse code.

Nonetheless, the scientists achieved some surprising successes with this group at first. As a whole, this generation was composed of remarkably skilled dancers. But by the age of seventeen, when they should have been ready for an adoring public, they hated dancing with a fervour. So repelled were they by the thought of spending their lives on stage, they began to sabotage their dancing careers. They were known to jump off the roofs of two-storey houses. This wouldn't kill them, but it was almost certain to break both their ankles. They threw themselves out of cars. One ate hamburgers all day, and he became so fat that he couldn't jump at all any-more. One would close his eyes when passing ponds, so that he didn't have to look at swans reaching about gracefully with their necks. He ended up falling in and drowning.

It is almost impossible to believe that these dark events took place. It is hard to get anyone to admit to having taken part in these Nureyev years. Participants explain how their own jobs and livelihoods were on the line. The events scarred everyone, especially Latska, who was known for wanting to bring whimsy back to science. This project was turning into something ugly.

* * *

The government threatened to withdraw funding anytime one of these generations of Nureyevs didn't work out. The project was diverting money from Olympic teams, the circus and outer space. It was with some level of desperation that Project Siberia was launched.

Project Siberia generated the most press in relation to what *The Globe and Mail* referred to as "the Nureyev Debacle." It is always brought up in documentaries about the subject as evidence of the insanity of the project as a whole. There was, however, a very clear method behind the mad-ness. The scientists were, in essence, looking for the missing link that would turn Nureyev the man into Nureyev the dancer. They weren't quite sure what they were leaving out, so they decided to omit nothing whatsoever. A large-scale effort was put into place to more accurately simulate the conditions and main events of Nureyev's actual childhood. Nureyev was famously born on the Trans-Siberian train near Irkutsk, Siberia, and he often cited that as being the most romantic event of his life and symbolic of everything that followed. He had been raised in the town of Ufa, south of the Ural Mountains. The scientists tried to make the part of the town where the clones were cloistered resemble the time and place where Nureyev had come into this world, opened his eyes and decided who he was going to be.

The Nureyevs were told that their country was engaged in a great war and that all the men were at the front fighting. The scientists had citizens walk around with crutches and with their heads bandaged in order to appear as if they had recently returned from the front. Everyone wore sheepskin hats and leather boots. Citizens were supposed to dress up as soldiers. It didn't seem to particularly matter what war they were supposed to be taking part in. Teenagers opted to wear red military band jackets with gold buttons and piping, looking more like members of Sgt. Pepper's Lonely Hearts Club Band than soldiers. It became trendy for girls to wear grey caps resembling those worn by Confederate soldiers in the American Civil War.

In order to re-create the harsh poverty in which Nureyev had been raised, the boys were only allowed to eat gruel. They couldn't find the recipe in *The Joy of Cooking*, but one of the town's cooks improvised with some watered-down Quaker Oats. Under strict instructions from the top, the groundskeepers air-conditioned the Nureyevs' bedrooms all the time. In summer, the foster parents were told to keep the lights on in their rooms while they slept—in order to re-create the white nights in Russia, when the sun never sets. All the little Nureyevs had dark rings under their eyes from trying to get some sleep under eight lamps with one-hundred-watt bulbs glowing around their beds.

They weren't allowed to go to church and they had to tear the story of Noah and his ark out of their French textbooks. Their reading primer was called *See Citizen Spot Run*. All Monopoly boards were burned. They were given classes in Marxism and told to hate the bourgeoisie. When they asked who the bourgeoisie were, they were told they were property owners. One group of Nureyevs smashed the window of a hardware store with rocks, thinking that the owner was an Enemy of the People.

They walked home in their oversized men's boots and scratchy cable turtleneck sweaters. They curled up on their hay-filled mattresses, kissed their pet rock good night and then went to sleep. They fantasized about one day washing their hair with shampoo. They were a cantankerous group of little boys.

Indeed the citizens of Pas-Grand-Chose began to complain as loudly as the Nureyevs about some of the implementations of Project Siberia. All the inhabitants of the town were having their comforts curtailed, which was natural given the fact that they were supposed to be living in Ufa in the 1940s. The post office was shut down, as there was to be no communication with the outside world. Some of the town children wept bitterly. One girl had a subscription to *Canadian Geographic*, which she would never be able to get.

Another boy was awaiting a shipment of sea monkeys that he had sent away for.

A row of new buildings was shoddily constructed. They had roofs that made them look like soft ice cream cones, like those of the Kremlin. This part of town became affectionately known as Little Moscow. This area became the closest thing that Pas-Grand-Chose had to a red-light district. Villagers, including the Nureyevs, would buy modern Western music in some of the shops in Little Moscow. The shop owners served hot dogs inside to regular citizens under the table, although they were supposed to be only serving borscht. Citizens squeezed in there to watch Eddie Murphy films and drink Coca-Cola at an underground theatre. They watched *Rocky IV*, in which Rocky defeats the Russian. They didn't know which side to root for. They didn't know what side they were on. The citizens didn't even know where exactly they were.

Speaking today with some of the town's residents about the past, however, you will note a marked nostalgia for life in the make-believe Soviet Union. Indeed, some aspects of life in Project Siberia seem quite lovely. There was a snow machine blowing snow year-round, and it was apparently wonderful to lie out on a beach towel on warm summer nights and watch the flakes falling like blossoms off a cherry tree. A reindeer would sometimes stroll by, the antlers on its head looking like the arms of a skinny diva, supplicating the heavens.

Almost every resident you speak to will mention the wolves. A scientist had read that Nureyev's mother had to trudge for miles through the snow to bring back potatoes and she was surrounded by wolves one terrifying night. A group of three hundred large grey wolves was rounded up from rural Quebec and set loose in the town in the middle of the night. They lurked around town, behind trash cans and telephone booths. The villagers were all terrified of the wolves and regularly petitioned for their removal, but the Nureyevs seemed to take to the animals. One witness described seeing an eight-year-old Nureyev walking the most terrifying-looking wolf down the street on a leash, calling her Susie. The skinny wolf had a rib cage that resembled a xylophone.

The Nureyevs left out bowls of Kibbles 'n Bits for the wolves. They tried to teach them to sit. None of the other children were allowed near the wolves. Their mothers put little cans of pepper spray in their lunch boxes, in case they encountered a wolf on their way home from school.

Then, in a move that seems strange even in light of all the other extraordinary occurrences, the scientists decided they couldn't re-create a distinctly Siberian awakening without a Siberian tiger. It took quite a bit of paperwork to have one of these endangered tigers delivered. They wrote a three-hundred-page grant proposal detailing their need for the animal. Nobody in Moscow wanted to read the ridiculously long proposal, so they put a tiger on a plane and sent it over.

The townspeople had to build a cage that seemed to be the size of a castle just to be able to contain the measurements of the beast that was coming.

There was great excitement the day the tiger arrived. For some reason everyone thought that the Nureyevs would finally feel the grandeur of their original's past and begin performing. Everybody cited the day when the tiger came as being a happy one. The cage was taken off the plane, loaded onto a truck and driven through town to where they had built the makeshift zoo. Everyone who lived there had come outside onto the street to watch the procession. The children had written signs on pieces of paper that said the French version of things like "Go Tiger Go!" and "Welcome Home!" It was as if the tiger were a victorious football team returning home.

The hype surrounding the arrival of the Siberian tiger was almost religious. Everything else about Siberia seemed to entail some sort of deprivation. In this case, they would be granted something amazing. They were entitled to this tiger. It was their birthright.

Whenever a young Nureyev was feeling low or uncooperative, the school psychiatrist would send him home with a note saying that he should spend thirty minutes with the tiger. The Nureyevs would whisper things to the tiger through the bars of the cage. Or they would go and sit on one of the little chairs positioned in front of the tiger's cage and cry in frustration. The bright-orange tiger looked like it had been covered in gasoline and set on fire, always in flames.

The Siberian tiger seemed to always be escaping. One witness saw a dozen young Nureyevs running down the street, being chased by the tiger. They were all laughing hysterically and clapping their hands and leaping off the ground, almost making sautés.

"They all had a dark, wicked little streak," the witness said. "They were always plotting to let the tiger escape."

This statement reveals the growing strain that the citizens were feeling toward the clones. How much of a burden it was to live in a place filled with so many Nureyevs began to be apparent to everyone. Many of the clones didn't work. Some living off disability cheques they'd received after a class lawsuit was launched against the Russian government by the generation of Rudolf Nureyevs who had been forced at gunpoint to dance. Although they didn't share the real Nureyev's desire to dance, they did seem to share his temperamental and tempestuous nature.

Since there was no work for them in the town, many of the Nureyevs turned to crime and the jails were filled with them. There was some confusion over the matter of sentencing them, for identifying them in a lineup proved hopeless. They were forced for a while to carry passports and papers everywhere. This seemed to fit in with the aesthetic of Pas-Grand-Chose. But once again, they were indignant, and they all flushed their papers down the toilet.

After a while, the police tried their best to simply ignore the Nureyevs and their antics. It simply wasn't worth the hassle. So the Nureyevs basically got away with all manner of things and terrible behaviour. Sometimes they acted like children provoking their parents, trying to see how far they could go. They would walk into a store, take a bottle of vodka off the shelf, hold it up to the clerk and say something like, "Mind if I take this? No, I didn't think so," and then walk out the door, laughing. One got on a bus, and when the conductor asked him to pay the fare, he simply told him to bugger off.

There was graffiti all over the town, which the Nureyevs had written. They would walk their wolves off the leash, although this was clearly against the law. They all seemed to engage in all manner of inappropriate conduct and public displays of indecency.

You can still see the graffiti today: "Even the birds are free." "Will we be charged to take a shit next?" "I am not what I could have been." "Are you going to measure how much my shit weighs, Mister Scientist?" "BEWARE OF FREE WILL!"

The little girls in Pas-Grand-Chose proved to be terrible dance partners for the Nureyevs. The Nureyevs would insult their dance steps, yelling that, furthermore, the local girls were too fat to hold up in the air. They had no intention of lifting peasants up toward the heavens. The little girls spun awkwardly above their heads as though they were satellites that had fallen out of orbit. The boys decided that they were going to go on strike from dancing until suitable partners were found. Female dancers were brought in from Montreal to be their partners. The scientists looked for older partners because the real Nureyev's favourite had been Margot Fonteyn, who was nineteen years his senior. A whole airplane filled with retired ballerinas arrived and settled in Little Moscow. They were underweight, self-centred and chain smokers.

They hung around drinking coffee and complaining about their arthritis. Their skin seemed as thin as rolling paper. Applying layers and layers of pancake makeup and staring into a hand mirror, they'd say, "What happened to me?" One read detective novels. One would not stop talking about her recent divorce and how if she hadn't had such a lousy alimony cheque, she wouldn't be here. They loved gossiping about one another. There wasn't a lot of chemistry between these dancers and the young Nureyevs.

In life, Nureyev, with his mop of blond hair, his steely-blue eyes and pouty lips, was considered quite magnificent-looking, but in this town he wasn't considered beautiful at all. Beauty is supposed to be rare and unequalled. For them, looking like Nureyev was commonplace.

The Nureyevs didn't enjoy one another's company much either. There's nothing worse when you're experiencing self-loathing than looking around and literally seeing yourself sitting at the other end of the bar. They were only able to feel like individuals when they were somewhere alone with the doors closed. Whereas the original Rudolf Nureyev had an *amour fou* with the dancer Erik Bruhn, the clones all remained single.

* * *

The project was not abandoned because of the unhappy Nureyevs crowding the streets and bars. Oddly enough, the project was abandoned because of a little Québécois boy named Michel who lived in the town. He was the son of one of the caretakers at the zoo. He and his father had previously lived in a tiny town where virtually everyone was employed by the local underwear factory. Michel had never seen ballet before he had arrived.

Michel had dark hair and brown eyes and a welcoming,

sweet face. He was an ordinary boy. He collected hockey cards, he had a German shepherd named Samuel and his mother had died of cancer.

Shortly after his arrival, Michel was walking down the street when he saw a Nureyev who was dancing *Swan Lake* in the middle of the road. He had on an Adidas headband that he had Krazy Glued some seagull feathers onto. He was inebriated and was dancing in a farcical manner. Some of the workers and a couple of scientists were shaking their heads sadly at the spectacle. But Michel, on the other hand, stood transfixed. He thought it was the most beautiful thing he had ever seen.

Afterwards, Michel often expressed his interest in learning dance, but he was never given any classes. Nobody bothered to encourage any of the other children in the town to dance. What would be the point? The trainers didn't want to waste time on children with regular physiques. Michel learned all his dance moves from television. He was able to exactly re-create the audition scene in *Flashdance*, which he'd seen at a secret viewing. Michel went on to master routines from *Star Search* and Dr Pepper commercials.

Michel's dancing began to be a common sight in the town. His neighbours found themselves dragging over milk crates to sit on in his yard and watching him dance for hours. Word would spread down the street that Michel was performing and the other children would stop their games of kickball and come to watch. Mothers would stop hanging up their laundry and old men stopped playing cards. There was something new about his dancing. Something that nobody had been able to imagine before. It opened up their minds in a way that only art can.

His father made a contraband videotape of Michel dancing and they sent it to the National Ballet School in Toronto. After Michel got accepted, his father quit his job. They piled all their things into the back of his truck, and they rattled off into a future that was completely unknown and bewildering to them. And it was as much to their surprise as it was to anyone's that there was glory on the road ahead for them.

When Michel was interviewed later on television, he was asked the unanswerable questions people always ask artists: How does it feel to be you? When did you realize that you were you? How is it that you do what you do? What makes an artist an artist?

Only individuals, all on their own, can decide to dedicate their lives to expression. Art comes from some mysterious place that cannot be located by science. Scientists could make a human, but they could not make an artist. The scientists themselves decided to end their project.

* * *

After the project was abandoned, the town suffered a major recession. Almost every citizen had worked for the Nureyev project at some point in their lives. Many of the residents left, having to sign strict confidentiality agreements before departing. The Nureyevs, en masse, wanted to get as far away from the town as possible. Their visa applications, however, continued to be rejected.

The Nureyevs were always trying to disguise themselves as travelling salesmen and get aboard charter planes that were departing from Little Moscow. They would try and get neighbouring farm girls to fall in love with them to help them escape. One Nureyev dressed up as a woman and tried to escape past customs that way. At night you could always hear voices coming out of the sewers, because they were always down there, trying to find a path out of the town. If you were leaving the town, you would have to pop the hood of your car to prove that there wasn't a Nureyev hiding in there. One was even found crouched in a box of leaf-shaped bottles of maple syrup that was being exported to the United States. That's something that they had in common with the original Nureyev: the desire to defect from a place that suffocated them and impeded their civil liberties.

When the Berlin Wall fell, the Nureyevs were finally permitted to leave, and leave they did, moving to all sorts of places. They never went public with their stories, however. They were actually terrified of anyone finding out that they were genetically identical to Rudolf Nureyev, as they would be subjected to relentless experiments by Western scientists this time. And quite frankly, they were exhausted of the constant scrutiny and limelight they had experienced in Pas-Grand-Chose. They led simple lives, trying not to draw any attention to themselves.

Their childhoods had been public. There were rooms filled with file cabinets detailing every aspect of their lives: how many times they had peed, their caloric intake, their nightmares, the crayon drawings they had made in elementary school. If there was anything at all that you needed to know about the Nureyevs, it was right there. But they argued that no one knew them. They wanted privacy and a sense of solitude where they could figure out who exactly they wanted to be. When the original Nureyev passed away, they watched the five-minute segment on the news, impressed by the accomplishments of that extraordinary man who thought that real life only happened when he was dancing, but then they turned off the television, knowing he was a stranger to them.

If you ever see anyone on a subway who looks incredibly like Rudolf Nureyev, you're probably actually looking at one of his clones, but just don't say so to his face.

* * *

As for Latska, he still lives in Pas-Grand-Chose. Lately he has been working on something on a much smaller scale: making phosphorescent snails. He can be spotted at sunset, wearing a long sort of kimono that goes down to his feet, wandering around in a melancholic trance. He will ignore you when you call out to him, as he has become a recluse, like his clones, eschewing the public gaze. As the sun goes down in Pas-Grand-Chose, the lights of all the snails begin to glow. They are like the lights on top of taxicabs stuck in traffic in Times Square. They are like the little TVs lit up at night in the hospital rooms of terminal patients. They are like the Indiglo of watches being checked in a movie theatre during a really long film. You feel as though you are standing in the Milky

Way and you could scoop up the stars with a butterfly net. It is so utterly charming and wonderful that you will never feel quite the same after looking at it. Does it have any great goal? No, it is a strange miracle. It is art for art's sake. It proves that the universe is full of surprises.

And as for the Siberian tiger, it is known to creep up fire escapes, slip into bedroom windows and crawl into the single beds of children. Snuggling up to the youngsters under their blankets, with its mouth next to their ears, it tells them not to be afraid of their revolutionary dreams. It lets the children know that it has their backs.

THE HOLY DOVE PARADE

Dear Piglet,

The thing that bothers me the most about all the newspaper stories is that you are reading them. And it worries me that you don't ever get to hear our side of the story. I have so much time on my hands these days that I want to just tell you about how things happened, baby step by baby step.

I met Edward when I was seventeen years old, outside the grocery store. He had just gotten out of the juvenile detention facility that was on the other side of town. It was his eighteenth birthday. He had a jacket tied around his waist, and a plastic bag with some paperback books in it. I took one look at him and I thought, Hallelujah. We drove my parents' car to Montreal and I did not see them again until the trial.

The newspapers and my family and old acquaintances are always going on and on and on about how much I changed. What they don't mention is that it was a good change. Because I don't care what anybody says—nobody wants to go through their whole life being nothing but a pipsqueak afraid to speak up and afraid of their own ideas. And I might still be that girl if it weren't for Edward.

We are brainwashed from when we are very little to have the thoughts that the government wants us to have. We think these are our own thoughts, but they are not. They are like frozen-dinner thoughts. We buy them already made and then heat them up in our brains a little and then think them. As if they are our own. As if thoughts didn't take any effort.

You have to create thoughts from scratch, Piglet. And as for the ingredients, you need love, wisdom, terror and acceptance. You have to put all these emotions together in order for them to be big and bold and gigantic ideas that you can be proud of and truly call your own. These are the kinds of thoughts that are free and original and can change the world.

After you spent time with Edward, he would teach you how to have all these amazing ideas. You would realize how limited your thoughts had been before.

Those were my favourite days. The days when it was only me and Edward and before we had anybody else with us. We ditched the car and were sleeping in the park in the city. Edward would talk about his ideas and his visions. We didn't have any money or jobs, but we were so young that we didn't even know how to worry about them yet. And so for the moment the two of us had achieved our goals in life. We were free. Once we got a can of beer and when we opened the tab it sounded like a flashbulb and like someone had taken an old-fashioned photograph of us.

I was always running up to cars that were stopped at red

lights, trying to clean their windshields. I would beg everybody for a little change. Sometimes I sang outside the door of the metro. You should have seen me then, Piglet. I was wild.

Edward was really good at dumpster diving. He could really live like a bum and it didn't bother him at all. Edward never worried about germs from other people. He would pick up a cup of coffee that was on a bench and was half filled and drink from it, or sit at a table at a food court and eat whatever was left. While he ate, he would be reading the newspaper with his legs crossed. There was something really dignified about him always. He was above material possessions. He really was. (And, whew, did I find him handsome!)

He got us two half-eaten Monte Carlo potatoes out of the garbage of a fancy restaurant. He would say that I had nothing whatsoever in the world to worry about because we were living like kings. He said that he always wanted to live like a sparrow in the city. He said that he would eat garbage that was left behind for him and he would build a nest anywhere. But he knew that he had to find a place to stay because of me. Even though he couldn't pay for it, he signed a lease for an old storefront that had been abandoned for ten years on a block that was filled with rundown tenements. It used to be an ice cream parlour. There was still a sign for ice cream painted in gold lettering on the window. Edward said that it was the perfect spot for him to start a church.

We filled up the ice cream parlour with chairs that we found in the garbage. There were all these mismatched kitchen chairs for all the wild variety of people who came to sit in on Edward's lectures.

It's a funny thing. When you are a little kid and people ask you what you want to be when you grow up, you don't say, "I want to be a prophet," or "I want to be a visionary," or "I want to be an apostle." But these are all things that you can be. A bright kid born into horrific circumstances is what marks the birth of a prophet.

* * *

Edward was put in a group home when he was six years old. He was beaten and mistreated by the staff for years. He had cigarette burns up and down his arms. There were marks on his back from straps.

Edward often walked around without his shirt. He wasn't ashamed or self-conscious of all the marks on him. He wasn't proud of them either. He simply didn't seem to think about them that much. But just because he went around acting as if they were nothing but some marks—no different than moles or acne scars—didn't mean that they didn't somehow get below the surface.

Edward said that he didn't mind having a bad childhood. Edward said that someone had to have that childhood. He said that somebody had to be born on that day, in that house, to that family, in that town, in this province, so it might as well be him. And one thing that made him happy was knowing that since he was having that shitty childhood, it meant that there was someone out there who wasn't having it.

Edward always had the loveliest way of thinking about things. Edward never felt sorry for himself. Edward always thought that who we are is so much bigger than our circumstances. Certain people, if they found themselves in Edward's shoes, would be bitching about everything they had been through for their whole lives.

He said that it was generally the state of childhood—to find yourself in a home that you didn't like and to be subjected to the random laws of ignoramuses. Parents go through their children's psyches looking for contraband ideas the way that guards toss apart prisoners' cells looking for items that they might have smuggled in. All children were being raised in prisons of one sort or another, according to Edward.

His defence attorney wanted to bring up details from Edward's childhood during the trial in order to elicit sympathy or to come up with an excuse for what had happened. Edward didn't see the relevance. He didn't see how anyone could bother saying that they had so little power over themselves that they would let nonsense that had happened to them when they were children dominate them now.

He, of course, wanted to take full responsibility for his actions.

Anyway, he had started sermonizing when he was in the group home. He said that these ideas all started coming to him. Whether it was God, or maybe some sort of divine common sense, he couldn't rightly say. He thought that we were all part of a big family. He did not believe that biological ties were the true basis of what constituted a family. You had to treat everyone you met as if they were your child and you were responsible for them.

The kids who had their television privileges taken away

and had nothing to do would listen to him philosophize. He had this captivating way of saying things too. Even if he didn't have a powerful message, you may have just ended up listening to this guy shoot the breeze.

* * *

Jimmy came in one night to the ice cream parlour and never left. Jimmy was just about the clingiest person in the universe, he was impossible to shake. He was the same age as us. He had had a bit part in a made-for-television movie when he was fifteen years old and it had driven him insane. I never met anybody who was as proud of his looks as Jimmy was. He had been raised by a single mom who would leave him alone for weeks while she was off with her boyfriends.

He used to spend all his time picking up girls in bars. In the morning he would tell them that he didn't want to have anything to do with them. Of course, this would make them cry. It sort of made him feel powerful and successful.

As soon as he met Edward he decided to change his path in life. He wanted to be Edward. He was crazy about how everybody would hang off Edward's every word. Jimmy also wanted to be able to say things that might change the world and how people think. People were always quoting Edward, so Jimmy wanted people to repeat all the dumb stuff he said too. There wasn't a chance in hell this was going to happen, though.

He was always looking for approval. If he was going to throw a crumpled-up piece of paper into a wastepaper basket, he had to make sure that everybody was looking at him. He liked to talk about how popular he was in high school for like half an hour straight. And he was always mimicking the way Edward spoke. And he started wearing shabby old suits like Edward.

I told Edward that I sometimes thought Jimmy was missing a personality. Edward said that if someone looked at Jimmy, he could see everything he needed to know about himself. Jimmy was different things to different people. If you were a thief, you thought that he was stealing from you. If you were full of grace, then when you looked at Jimmy, you saw a saint.

"I guess that means I'm a dick," I said, and we both laughed.

At the trial, Jimmy had all sorts of lawyers and experts coming up with a million different reasons to explain away why he did what he did. Jimmy didn't have any shame whatsoever. He didn't care what happened to the rest of us. He only wanted to get out of having to go to prison.

Edward said that that was Jimmy's prerogative. He said that it was in Jimmy's nature to try every which way to get out of a trap and that we couldn't do anything but stand back and let him act out his performance. He said that Jimmy was by nature an entertainer, so his trial was going to be more of a circus than anyone else's. Although Edward did also say that Jimmy was a lot like an insect stuck in a spider's web.

Jimmy's court-appointed lawyer tried to say that he had a personality disorder and that he had fallen under Edward's spell. He said that he believed that Edward was Jesus Christ.

This was sort of funny because once Jimmy said that

the only thing that he remembered from Sunday school was Jesus giving everybody chores and giving everybody advice that they had never asked for. So even if it was true that Jimmy thought Edward was Jesus, this didn't seem to mean very much, seeing as how Jimmy didn't think very much about Jesus.

* * *

A girl named Nikki ended up living with us not long after Jimmy. Nikki went into the same group home as Edward when she was twelve, after her father had been molesting her for seven years. She was three months younger than Edward. She always liked the things that Edward used to lecture about in the common room. When she got out, she came looking for him.

Sometimes that girl was too much for me. Once we were at a restaurant together and she was acting wild. She was wearing these busted-up shoes with butterflies made out of sequins at the toe. She kept crossing and uncrossing her legs neurotically.

She took the flower that was in a little vase on the table and stuck it behind her ear. She said that when she was eleven years old, she used to rob gas stations all the time. When she started talking about how bad she was as a kid, you couldn't get a word in edgewise.

Finally, a perfectly ordinary waitress came up to serve us.

"Will you bring me some ribs, please?" Nikki asked. "And don't skimp out on the portion because I'm a girl and you think that I can't finish it. Bring me a portion as if I was a big fat fucking dude with a giant moustache who likes to eat pussy."

The waitress blushed and walked away.

"Now you've gone and made her think that we're weird and creepy," I said.

Nikki held up the napkin dispenser and started applying her lipstick while looking at her reflection in it.

"Oh, sweetie. There's nothing wrong with being weird and creepy whatsoever. Don't let anybody tell you any different. You were raised in a box, all coddled and shit. I always forget."

Nikki used to fight with Edward all the time. Once he wouldn't loan her twenty dollars and she lost it. She went and pushed all the doorbells that were outside the building and screamed, "Fuck you, fuck you, fuck you," into the speaker when people answered.

Once she was jumping up and down on the sidewalk in her knee-high boots, calling Edward every name in the book. "You low-life, skinny-butted, self-destructive, drug-addicted asshole." I can't even remember why. The police came over to see what was wrong, because from the outside Nikki and Edward seemed like a prostitute and a pimp arguing.

When I complained about Nikki, Edward said that she was another version of himself. He said that he could just as easily have turned out to be Nikki.

Edward said that Nikki went around reminding people that their pasts were going to haunt them, reminding them that they couldn't only look out for themselves. And that the whole city had to deal with the sound of her crying now because no one had bothered to come when she was in her crib.

There was testimony about Nikki's murderous tendencies for days and days. The prosecution wanted to prove that Nikki was not under the hypnotic influence of a charismatic leader. She was a ticking time bomb. She was a crazy bitch on the loose. One of these women who is bound to go from one abusive boyfriend to the next until she finally stabs one in the chest.

* * *

Why did we stay with Edward? the papers always asked. They always came up with these ugly reasons. They said that we were brainwashed and that we had been programmed by thought control. You will have heard about this theory, no doubt, because any book now that is written about cults has a chapter that mentions Edward. You will find Edward in all sorts of textbooks where he does not belong, sort of like a pressed flower in a car engine manual.

* * *

Edward became a real asset to the lower-class community that lived in the derelict tenements around the storefront. Everyone who lived there knew it. He would be walking through the park and he would meet somebody whose mind was all mixed-up. Someone whose mind had grown all wild like weeds in a garden and whose notions were all tangled up in knots and who could not get out of the labyrinth of their own mind as they ran around and around, always arriving at dead ends, always coming to the same signposts over and over again. Edward would talk to them and calm them right down.

There was a little boy who was having trouble seeing out of his right eye. Edward went over to his house and asked to see the boy. And Edward took the bandage off the boy's face and the boy was able to see perfectly. His mother said that it was a miracle.

She brought over an enormous rhubarb pie. We couldn't get over how delicious it was. We were all so low on cash and we were hungry. We kept declaring how good it was. The little boy's mother sat on the other side of the table and wept. Sometimes she would go ahead and dab her eye with a napkin and then other times she would let out a violent sob. We were all so happy. Edward swore to the woman he had nothing to do with it, but she told everyone otherwise.

Edward went and sat next to a child molester on a park bench. He did not think that there were evil people. He thought only that there was evil inside of people and they needed help to have it removed. He spoke to the man on the bench for nine hours.

That was another thing that was incredibly comforting about Edward. He would never be the first to tell you that he had to go. He always stayed with a person until they didn't need his company anymore. He would end up in these smelly old ladies' apartments for hours and hours. He always said that time was the most precious thing that one person could give to another. You were giving them some of your life.

This old woman got Edward to go and talk to a drug dealer who was going to kill her son because he had stolen a bag of weed, or had smoked it all, or something like that. And Edward made the situation okay.

There is a solution to every problem and Edward seemed to know them. God wouldn't have created a world full of problems if he hadn't also created an answer book.

Jimmy found an ad for a minister at the back of a magazine. I thought that Edward was going to think it was a stupid idea. But to my surprise, Edward filled it out and sent it in with a cheque.

He said that a lot of the older people in the community would be comforted knowing that he was an actual minister. They didn't feel easy knowing that a skinny eighteen-year-old in a ratty jacket could offer words of wisdom and had the power to heal people. They had never, ever heard of anything like that before. There had to be a name for someone like Edward. They were so thankful when he got himself a card with a little dove on it.

We had picked up a couple of secondhand bibles that had pages that looked like they were made out of moth wings.

Nikki said that we should call the church the Holy Dove Parade. I thought this was a ridiculous name, but Edward said fine.

* * *

There were more and more people coming to the ice cream parlour every evening to hear Edward's sermons. There were always different characters showing up. I really liked them. They were the type of people that my dad always put down. There was this fat cat that was always hanging out there who always felt like he'd just come out of the dryer.

We were always starving, though. All the money that we made was from passing out a collection plate around the church after Edward's sermons and from selling pamphlets that Edward had written with his ideas on them. And let me tell you that this was not a lot!

Still, we were young and carefree. It seemed like it wouldn't be such a bad thing at all if we just continued the life we were living. During that period, we all got pretty much accustomed to eating very little and doing without. Except for Nikki. She would get all crazy when we were broke. She didn't think life would be worth living if she couldn't go to Nickels Deli sometimes. She would go and turn tricks and then spend her money on food and cigarettes and going to the movies. We disapproved, of course, but she would bring home big jugs of wine and chocolate and we would stay up late having a good time.

There was a roll of photos taken of us all one day when we went to Oka beach. We ate some mussels and french fries and filled our pockets with pretty stones. Edward and I were messing around in the water, splashing about. He was wearing a straw cowboy hat and cut-off jean shorts. I had on a bikini and heart-shaped glasses.

There is one photo where Edward has his arms around

me and his chin on my shoulder. This photo was really popular and was in all the papers. The thing that confused people was that we looked so happy. And if we were so happy, then what on earth motivated us to do what we did? And why did we go and throw away our lives if they were happy ones?

* * *

Then we started to make money. Sometimes I was shocked by the amount of money that was in the collection plate after sermons, especially considering the average income of people in our neighbourhood. But there were people who believed in Edward so much that they insisted on giving him amounts of money that were quite large for them—even twenty or fifty dollars. When I sometimes tried to give it back to them, they held my hands in theirs and told me that I did not understand the value of what it was that Edward had done for them.

There was one guy who won the lottery. His winnings were $250 and he insisted on giving $125 of it to Edward. He told Edward that his life had, without a doubt, become incredibly lucky ever since he started going to the church.

We started to see more and more well-dressed people showing up. Some had fur coats and three-piece suits. I kid you not. They came from different parts of town. I mean, you would never see that type of person down there. I don't even know where they were parking their cars!

I had to open a bank account. Jimmy and I even built a website together that received donations. It was the first

time that Jimmy and I got along. It was amazing to be working on something that mattered like that. We couldn't believe
that we got to be a part of something important.

Nikki went around handing out flyers and ranting and
raving to people about the church. She would go knocking
on doors. She had to be a big part of this too. Edward and
Jimmy and I laughed because we thought that surely she must
be driving people away. But a lot of people showed up with
her flyers in their hands. She was very proud of herself. I guess
she had a right to be.

* * *

And then you started hanging out at the church. We never did
take away the gold letters on the window of the store, so every
now and then a little kid would come in with a fist full of
change, asking about the different flavours. There were a lot
of kids in that neighbourhood. There were always little girls
skipping rope on the sidewalk, like they were popcorn kernels
exploding on a frying pan.

In the paper it said that one of the reasons that we ran an
ice cream parlour was so that we could lure children into our
trap. But who thought like that? We weren't sinister. We liked
kids. We acted like kids who had no rules ourselves. There
was this aura of wildness about us then and that was why
children were always drawn to us. There was no ice cream
for sale!

When you first came in we thought that you were full
of light. (Is your hair still so blond? No one will ever send

me a picture.) You came in with a shoe box that had a sparrow with a broken wing in it. You wept and wept. Edward had never seen a child so full of compassion. And when that bird's wing was mended and it was brought back to life, you declared that it was a miracle. And we liked that you believed in miracles. And we all thought that you sure fit so well into our world.

You were so daring. Once you stood up on a chair in the back row in the middle of one of Edward's sermons and you called out, "Hallelujah!" We loved that. Everybody in the ice cream parlour cheered. Edward said that you were going to be a powerful preacher one day.

You probably don't even know how wonderful you are. You were always offering to help out. You even got along with Nikki. She rode you on the handlebars of her bicycle while you shouted through a bullhorn, "The Holy Dove Parade is the place to be on Sundays!" There was the sound of a card in the spokes of the wheel, like machine-gun fire. A police officer told you guys to knock it the hell off.

Maybe we just liked having a kid around. Then it really felt like we were a family. We could all do away with the memories we had of our other families. They were nothing to us. And you were always so sad when you had to go "home" to those horrible people who claimed to own you.

Your parents did not worship you properly. They were not very spiritual or enlightened people. One day you came in with a black eye and Edward just about went crazy. He went to speak to your father, but he wouldn't listen to Edward. He slammed the door in his face.

I had never seen Edward lose his temper the way he did when he came back from your apartment. He upturned the kitchen table. He didn't like me seeing him like that. I was staring! He went into the bathroom, turned on the faucet and screamed. I think that it had reminded him of things that he was pretending not to remember from his own childhood.

* * *

Why did we go along with Edward's final plan if we hadn't been brainwashed? the newspeople asked. Nikki and Jimmy came along with us because there was no way to get rid of them. Jimmy generally didn't give a shit about anybody's feelings, so long as he was doing good. And Nikki had been breaking the law since she was in diapers. And the only meaning that they had in their whole lives was the Holy Dove Parade Church. So if Edward said that we were picking up and moving, then they were picking up and moving too. They couldn't imagine a life without Edward. Although I guess that's what they have now.

And why did I get into the van? everyone wanted to know. Why did I even hook up with such a character to begin with? Well, he made my life exciting.

There was something else too. Edward said that we could never, ever have a little kid of our own because he didn't believe in biological families. He thought that the root of capitalism was that when we were born, our parents owned us. And he said that biological families had a knack of teaching people to band together and hate outsiders, which was essentially just getting them prepared to wage war against others. It taught us that we had no responsibility to anyone that wasn't related to us and so we could go around treating everyone like dirt.

If we were ever going to have a child together, this was the way that we were going to have to do it.

* * *

You got very upset about being taken away from your parents that first night. The moon was light brown like a slightly roasted marshmallow. And there were so many stars.

I was surprised that you started crying when you were separated from a family that treated you so badly. But that was probably because you were so confused. Sometimes we cry and it's only because we are bewildered and not because we are sad at all. When we told you that your parents had said that it was okay for us to take you, you stopped crying. I know it was a lie. But you see, you weren't really missing them. You were only worried about their feelings because you were sweet and compassionate.

You were happy in the country. We rented a big house in the middle of nowhere. We stayed up at night collecting fireflies in a jar, and it was like those bugs were writing gold letters in the air. You had never even seen fireflies before, and it was wonderful to watch your expression. I had never seen anyone look that way before: you were bewitched. We made a big collection of butterflies that we pinned behind a frame. We had always been so busy in the city that we never had time for all of that.

We once saw a baby deer and it looked like it had just learned to walk, like it was wearing leather cowboy boots that it hadn't had a chance to break in. The raccoons were all wearing their sunglasses.

In a funny way, we were all having the kind of childhood that we had wanted through you.

* * *

Your photograph was everywhere! You were on the television. You were on the front page of every newspaper. Everybody in the whole province was wondering where on earth you were. Everyone thought that you must be dead.

Edward said that this was exactly as it should be. Because when you reemerged, it would be like the original Jesus coming back from the grave. People would think that you were the Second Coming and, oh my goodness, they would listen to your words then. And they would be the words that Edward had taught you. He became convinced that he was going to teach you to be a much, much better preacher than he was. He had such high hopes for you.

I was lying in bed once and I woke up and Edward was staring at me. The light from the kitchen door behind his head made him look like he had a halo. And he was looking at me with so much love. He was happy. He didn't care about anybody in the whole world except me and you.

Maybe it was because it was the first time that Edward had ever had a family of his own that he became protective of it. He became defensive of us all in the way that he had always criticized other fathers for being. He bought himself a rifle and began staying up all night keeping guard. Then Edward began stockpiling weapons. He had the whole area rigged with explosives. It was crazy. He spent every cent we had.

Maybe it was his childhood abuse that was pushing him over the edge, even though he always swore black and blue that it was nothing to him. He had spent his entire childhood locked away. I guess it was only natural for him to think the enemies would be coming back to put him in prison. How could he not figure that it was only a matter of time?

Nikki went around with a holster and a gun on her at all times. Even when she was singing in the backyard while hanging up laundry, she still had a gun hanging around her waist. I began to find her terrifying. Jimmy was always practising with a rifle at blowing the head off a scarecrow. He was a really good shot, which figured, seeing as how he was a jock in high school. I guess judging by their actions out in the woods, it might be accurate to call them sociopaths. But who am I to judge?

I didn't have anything to do with all that. I would bring you down to the river to swim and read you a copy of *Winnie-the-Pooh* that I found in the house. (You used to say that you were Piglet and I was Pooh Bear. Remember? You must.) But I was probably the most delusional of all of us, because I believed that we were safe and that no one was going to come find us. I thought that we could live that way forever.

* * *

We were running low on money. And then Nikki was caught soliciting a police officer while she was in town. They found a shotgun in the trunk of her car and your little sweater in the backseat. Two police officers were blown to pieces by booby traps when they surrounded the place. Three others were shot dead.

* * *

Why I'm writing all this to you now is because you are a little bit older, and I thought that maybe there's some possibility that you would want to carry on Edward's teachings. Because whatever the papers say, he had some wonderful, wonderful ideas.

The world needs more preachers. And if Edward saw that in you, then it probably was inside of you. Because Edward was never wrong about what he saw in people. Edward always saw the best thing about a person.

But even if you don't want to take over the Holy Dove Parade Church, you could just carry around some of his ideas in your heart. They will make you live in a much bigger way. No matter what other people are saying.

Love, Pooh Bear

DOLLS

The rummage sale was set up in the church basement. All the dolls were put together on one table. They started chit-chatting immediately. Dolls are social. That's what they were invented for after all, to always be up for playing with children when no one else is.

Humans can barely make out their voices when they talk. They make an almost inaudible sound that is similar to that of hair burning. It's a small noise that you assume is coming from someplace far away.

None of the dolls here were in particularly good shape. Everyone had lost their shoes. They wore dirty socks and their dresses had chocolate-milk stains. There is no laundry for dolls to go to. Once you are dirty, you are dirty forever. You are stuck with a bad haircut into eternity.

The marks of ballpoint pen were on most dolls. But the worst is what the dogs had done. There was a doll whose red jacket and matching trousers had been taken off. Without these, she was almost certain not to be bought. The worst thing is to be a naked doll. She was terrified that she would be mistaken for garbage.

There was a doll that used to be named Mary. The doll with four fingers. She had been operated on by a child with a pair of blunt scissors and black yarn. Her intestines were filled with hidden things, a key to an old diary and a few coins from Poland.

She was fifty years old, but she had the face of a baby girl. She once came in a marvellous box filled with trinkets. There were postcards of the Eiffel Tower and bottles of perfume and powder. There was a pill bottle filled with baby teeth. There were porcelain teacups with zebras and birds with winding tails on them. She came from a good time.

Now she wore a dirty white coat and a blue nightgown that she had borrowed from another doll twenty years before. She liked to talk about the war, about how it made everyone feel so alive. "What we would do for a pair of stockings!" she cried. Her hair had gotten into a mass straight up over her head and had a plastic barrette with a duck stuck in it. She had long eyelashes drawn around her eyes by a child with a ballpoint pen. They gave her a misty-eyed drunk look.

* * *

Next to Mary was a doll in a black dress named Clemente. Clemente had a faded, faraway look about her. Her eyebrows and lips, which had once been painted carefully on her face, were worn off. She had been left under the snow for an entire winter once. She claimed to have had an affair with a rat at that time. The rat's name was Charles. They ate cake all night long. Often he would set the tip of his tail on fire to please her.

Once she was brought back inside, she became friends with a taxidermied rabbit in the hallway. They were always pretending that they were married. He had a little piece of paper with his Latin name on it written in black ink. He thought this was his ticket to a museum. Clemente had once believed she might end up in a museum just like some other dolls she knew, but she had been wrong. She had ended up here, at the rummage sale, with a price tag for seventy-five cents on her wrist.

* * *

Then there was a doll with fancy clothes named Marguerite. She was from England. She had been bought for a child by an aunt while on vacation. She had once had a parasol, but her accessories had all long since been lost.

She came with a book that described her. According to the story, her father owned a manor, where she had a horse named Phillipe. She was given French lessons on Wednesday by a tutor. The little child who owned her believed all of this, but Marguerite knew it was a lie. She had come from a toy shop in downtown London. She had always felt guilty about her forged identity. She hoped that she would be able to start all over with a new kid.

* * *

Then there was Esta. She was a rather cheaply made doll. She hid the information on her behind that said her date and place of birth. She couldn't have anyone know that she was only five years old and had been made in China.

* * *

There was a German doll named Karmen. She talked about how in Germany all the dolls wore black boots and were given their own beds. They were driven in baby carriages down the street. She used to go to a tea party every day of the week. She was not ashamed to admit that now she was addicted to tea. She had spent the past few nights going through withdrawal.

* * *

One doll named Ella had an eye that fell into the back of her head. You had to shake her violently to get the eye to go back into its place. But she claimed that when her eye was in her head, it had visions. She was able to see the little girl who used to own her standing on the back of a bench, waiting for a bus. She was able to see her wearing a long black coat at her mother's funeral.

* * *

And then there was a doll in a blue dress named Hannah. She claimed she had been owned by a lonely child with no other toys. All the dolls became quiet to pay attention to this story. To have a child who has nothing and is miserable without you is a rare treat indeed.

"She lived with her grandmother and her grandmother did not buy her any gifts," Hannah told them. "The little girl used to pray that her mother would come and visit her, but she never did. The little girl was always hungry. She never had anyone to play with after school. She had ugly clothes. She never went on holiday. She had one seashell that she would dust."

"She must have loved you," Mary whispered.

The dolls all knew how it went. You were taken home and told you were special. You were defined by being loved. Love exposed you to loneliness. Love gave you a personality but damaged you, too.

None of the dolls at the rummage sale wanted to see themselves as trash. Each one knew that once, she had been special. Once, she had been loved.

WHERE BABIES COME FROM

My brother and I became experts at knowing when the next trip to Grandmother's was coming. The signs started popping up weeks ahead of time, with Mother's notebooks piling up on the kitchen table and her records getting louder and louder. She had rough drafts of her poems thumbtacked to the wall above her desk, which kept spreading out until they were wallpapering the room. And the business of doing dishes started to slow down and eventually ground to a halt, forcing us to start drinking orange juice straight from the carton and eating Chinese takeout almost every night. All in all, these were pretty good days.

But then we'd hear it: "It's time you kids had a visit with your grandmother. She's a wise woman and you have much to learn from her. So pack your suitcases, my darlings."

There was no arguing with Mother when she was in one of her creative moods and needed to be alone. We loved seeing our grandmother, but we couldn't help but feel a little left out of our mother's life, too, and so my brother and I gently sobbed as we stuffed our clothes into our bags. And then that very night we found ourselves at Grandmother's house, sitting in our pyjamas on the chesterfield, sipping hot chocolate.

"Mother says you have wise things to teach us," my brother said, making it sound almost like a challenge.

"That's true!" Grandmother said, laughing. "What can I teach you about tonight? Shall I tell you where babies used to come from? Well, they weren't delivered by storks. That's the silliest idea anyone ever had. And cabbage patches? Don't make me laugh. When I was a girl in the 1940s, we all got our babies at the beach."

"At the beach!" we yelled. She put her fingers to her lips to quiet us down and then she began the story.

"Back when I was a girl, babies were washed up from the ocean when the tide went out. You would see their little bottoms peeking up from out of the sand, and if you dug them up quickly, they would be yours to keep. You had to wake up and get to the beach very, very early if you wanted a baby, because there were always loads of girls at the seashore looking for them.

"There was quite a commotion, girls running around frantically, because once the sun went down and the tide came back in, the babies were loosened from the sand and were swept back out to sea. Then it was pretty much all over and you had to go home empty-handed.

"Girls would take the train out there, with little baskets of boiled eggs and bottles of white wine, and I was right there with them. The clouds were like wedding veils that had been whipped off the heads of brides.

"We were still so young that it was exciting just to be riding the train alone, to have the wind in our hair and no parents around. Once you had a baby of your own, no one would ever tell you what to do again. You forgot about working at the factory. You forgot about not being pretty, or not being able to type quickly enough, or how much you hated all the household chores. We thought this was what being an adult was like. It was going to be all wine and roses and making babies.

"But in truth, the train ride was the last time we would ever be so carefree. Everyone had warned us before we went down that being a mother was really, really difficult, and some of the older mothers knew it from experience. But when you thought about it on the train, you could only imagine the baby with little rain boots, playing at the beach and saying it loved you."

* * *

"Although you rode on the train alone, the proper thing to do was to have a fellow waiting back at home for you. Some girls chose wisely when it came to picking fathers, paying attention to what a man did for a living and what his character was like; but other girls were complete fools, choosing a man because he was good at pool, or looked good in a fedora, or because other people liked to be around him because he laughed and made jokes. That he was temporarily out of work and had a criminal record was of no immediate concern.

"Sometimes a girl got so excited about meeting a bloke she particularly liked that she rushed off to the beach to get a baby before she was even married. There were a couple of these girls on the train when I went. They hadn't packed any lunch or made any preparations for the journey. All they had were the hickeys on their necks and their heads full of dreams. They wandered the shore, kicking up water, with stars in their eyes.

"There were a couple of girls riding up front in first class who'd married really well and wore fancy shoes and expensive tailored dresses. And they had nannies with them who were going to help with the babies the minute they got them out of the water. But still, in spite of all this, they were going to have to take off their shoes and tights and get their feet wet in the sand like all of us.

"I remember one girl, just having found her baby, suddenly starting to cry because she realized that one day her little baby was going to die. Another girl started crying because her baby was going to be raised in a world where there was war. One girl was worried that her little boy would fall in love with someone who didn't love him back.

"There was a mother who didn't even seem to really want a kid. Her mother-in-law had to come with her and kept nudging her to go on. She would look back and claim that the water was too cold, that there were no more babies in there. She would get distracted and start collecting seashells and disappear behind the rocks, claiming to see some baby bottoms over there. When her mother-in-law went to check on her, she found her sitting on a rock and reading a paperback novel.

"In the end she found one in the moonlight. A baby with

dark, dark, dark brown eyes. The baby looked at her suspiciously and she felt as if neither of them particularly wanted to belong to one another. She didn't especially want to be a mother and he didn't particularly want to be a child. He hadn't asked to be born, yet there they were, all together, a new family boarding the last train of the night back home."

"Wait," I said, interrupting her. "You could still find babies at night?"

"Yes," said Grandmother. "These were the night babies. You see, although some girls didn't want babies, most of us did, and some of the unlucky ones who hadn't found one yet grew desperate and refused to go home empty-handed. And that's how they found them, by stepping out farther and farther into the water, looking and looking, knowing that there had to be a baby out there somewhere; but the only babies you could catch at that point were the babies swimming around in the ocean.

"People often said that it was better sometimes to leave the children alone in the water after a certain point. Once they had had a taste of the sea, it was hard for them to ever really adapt to ordinary life."

"But what's so different about night babies?" I asked.

"Well, after a whole day of swimming in the night ocean, they had had too many extra hours of dreaming, perhaps. They had already got it into their heads that they weren't going to be discovered, that they were going to be absolutely alone in the world, left to sleep with the fishes and be sealed up inside a clamshell forever—to never have to work or weep or be married or pay the rent, or look for children themselves.

"The first people these children saw were the riffraff who haunted the beach at night: drunken men cursing on the boardwalk, teenagers writing dirty poems in the sand with black paint, indiscreet couples making love against the rocks, and forsaken lovers with stones in their pockets, wandering out to sea.

"And in the sea, the little colourful fish flitted around these babies as if a piñata had been split open in front of their faces and there were candies falling from the sky. The fish whispered their secrets to these babies, telling them tales about drowning sailors and women who fell overboard in lovely dresses that opened like umbrellas—how the women sank to the bottom of the sea with their eyes closed and their mouths open, as if waiting for kisses.

"As the babies floated through the water, the octopuses reached out and put their arms around them. That feeling of being wrapped up in eight arms could never be duplicated, and once they'd been rescued, when they were full grown, these babies could never be satisfied by only two arms. They always wanted more when they were hugged and so they were always lonely. When they went out dancing, they held their partners too tightly and wept.

"They had a tendency to drink too much at weddings and birthdays as well. They liked that feeling of the room rocking back and forth and of losing control and tumbling over. Being under the sea was like always falling down the stairs except that you didn't get hurt. They stayed out late, for there was no morning or night under the deep, deep sea. They were always trying to convey that which can't be conveyed. They chose to do things like play the trumpet for eight hours at a stretch and name their dogs Baudelaire.

"Looking back, I realize that I myself was too young to be going down looking for babies. I was married at nineteen, you know, and completely clueless about everything." Then Grandmother sighed. "Maybe that's why I ended up with a night baby."

My brother and I leaped off the couch.

"You had a night baby?" we yelled. "Mother was a night baby?"

My brother and I jumped around with a million questions.

"Did you ever regret getting a baby later than the other girls?" I asked.

"Never!" Grandmother said. "I liked having a little brown-eyed girl who was obviously a poet. And that's why your mother weeps when she hears music she likes on the radio, and why she waters flowers in the middle of the night and is always doodling stars on the margins of her paper!"

"Is it a bad thing?" my brother asked nervously.

"Oh no. Whether your baby was found during the day or at night, you loved it just the same. You see, all mothers think they've magically found the perfect baby, and they are all convinced that their baby is more beautiful than all the others. And they give them their very favourite names. They name them after grandfathers and mothers and saints and movie actors and lovely flowers and military generals. All sorts of new names for all sorts of new people. Most of the fathers, like the mothers, fall in love with their babies at first sight. They weep and love them madly with a love that lasts the rest of their lives. It's amazing, when you think about it, how much love a single soul requires."

And then we were all quiet. It was so sad and sweet to imagine Grandmother as a young girl looking for a baby down at the beach, with her stockings all wet and the sun going down. And then Grandmother beckoned us to her side, telling us our mother would be back in good time, and both my brother and I hugged her with all of our might. We hugged her just like we were little night babies too, reaching out for human arms from under the waves.

THE MAN WITHOUT A HEART

Andrea and her son lived in a big building on a busy street. There were loads of small doorbells in the lobby. There were fluorescent blue tiles that had been put in a long time ago when the building was fancy. Some of the tiles had come off the floor and had been replaced by different-coloured ones, and the floor looked like a Rubik's Cube that was never going to be solved. And now the building was filled with all sorts of lower-class people who couldn't afford to live anyplace else.

Michal was ten years old and was small for his age. He had a short afro and enormous brown eyes. There was supposed to be an *e* in his name. But Andrea didn't know about it when she was filling out the birth certificate. She thought that happened to be the way that you wrote *Michael*.

Michal didn't have any friends. He was so shy that other kids forgot that he existed. He would sometimes sit quietly near a bunch of kids, hoping they would notice him and invite him to play. He was terrified of them, but he longed for their company.

Andrea was a hard worker. She worked ten hours a day at the grocery store. She had big boobs and a pouty mouth and dark skin. She brushed her hair violently every morning and pulled it into a tiny little ponytail at the top of her head. But the elastic was always popping off and her hair would be sticking straight up by the time she got home. She was still pretty adorable.

She had the face of a little girl. It sure as hell didn't stop men from being mean to her. She went out with just about anybody who asked her. And for some reason, it was only the lowlifes who asked.

She went out with a guy who made deliveries for the corner store on a bicycle with one of those huge baskets on the front of it. He wore a black leather vest without a shirt on underneath. He told her that he couldn't ever be tied down to one woman. For a long time she put up with a guy who used to beat her. One guy only ever came over after ten o'clock at night.

She was always loaning her boyfriends money. They were always coming over and eating her and Michal's dinner. They would never, ever take her out to a restaurant in exchange. One of her boyfriends would scoff at the food she prepared. When she served Hamburger Helper, he said that when he was growing up, his mother would never, ever prepare him something like this. And he kicked over a chair and walked out.

Michal always kept his distance from the men his mother dated. Most of them didn't seem to mind. Some of them resented Michal. If she was going to have a kid, at least she could have had a really fun one. Michal just skulked around, looking at the floor. No siree, they thought. When they had their own sons, they were going to be much better than this kid. They would be tall and outgoing and good at sports.

And these guys all ended up leaving Andrea at the drop of a hat.

* * *

Then Andrea met Lionel. He was buying a package of Twizzlers at the store where she worked. Lionel was tall and had sharp features and was good-looking. He looked like those statues that the Romans were always making of gods, except he was black. And Lord, was he smart. For a while, Andrea finally thought she had struck gold.

She could talk to him about Michal too, and he was interested.

"He's so shy," Andrea told him. They were lying in bed after making love. "He's been like that since he was really little. I worry about him. I mean, how are you supposed to get anywhere in the world if you can't even bring yourself to ask for simple instructions on the subway ride?"

"Where's his pops?"

"Nowhere. He left me when I was pregnant. I was nineteen years old and I had nothing."

"You must have been foxy as all shit when you were nineteen and pregnant."

"You're crazy."

"I would have gotten all romantic poet on you, if I had

seen you pregnant. Seriously. I would have been resolute in my endearing affections."

Andrea laughed.

* * *

Michal was sitting in his small room at the end of the hall when Lionel walked right in. He was wearing a pair of silky shorts that Michal noticed looked way too small for him. They had a print of roses on them and were the bottom half of a pair of pyjamas that belonged to his mother.

"Do you know how to play chess? I see you got a board."

Michal looked at his hands and nodded. Lionel set out the chessboard between them on the single bed.

"The best way to play chess is in silence. You can't say a word, brother. If you do, it'll upset my equilibrium. I'm going to be playing seven moves ahead, okay?"

When Michal took Lionel's knight, the man yelled out.

"What kind of move was that? Wow! Where'd you learn to play like that? Are you Russian?"

Michal put his finger over his mouth to indicate that Lionel had broken the Rule of Silence.

Lionel continued in a whisper. "Do you have like a little earphone on and that Vladimir Stanislavskovitch is whispering in your ear from St. Petersburg? Man!"

Michal laughed. Much to Andrea's amazement, Lionel and Michal bonded.

Lionel would go into Michal's room and she could hear the two of them chatting away incessantly. Michal would babble excitedly. She never heard him talk like that with any-body. They would walk together to the store to pick up some milk. She would see them out the window, waving their arms about in discussion.

But it turned out that Lionel was probably the worst of all her boyfriends. He had been addicted to heroin and he started using again. He sold their television set for drugs. He stole money from her wallet, her jewellery and some of her dresses. He even stole her bus pass and then sold it to the neighbour for five dollars. Andrea worked hard for the little she had. So Andrea threw him out forever.

* * *

Lionel went into rehab and they didn't hear from him for a couple of months. When Lionel called up, wanting to see Michal, Andrea was sure that it was some sort of lame-ass excuse to keep her in his life. But she wasn't going to turn Lionel's offer down. She was so exhausted and overwhelmed that she would take whatever babysitter she could get, even if he was an ex-junkie.

But Lionel was only allowed as far as the lobby. Andrea wouldn't let him in the apartment ever again. It wasn't that she was doing it to be mean, she was only using common sense.

Lionel agreed to pick Michal up from school and walk him home in the afternoons and refused to take money for it. They passed by the homeless who were out rooting through the garbage to find parts for time machines.

"What are you wearing?" Michal asked.

He was wearing rubber boots, a pair of denim shorts that were pinstriped, a blazer that had seen better days, and a light blue undershirt.

"People look at me because I am a damn bona fide original, my little friend. I have an original style of dressing. I dress in the manner of a pimped-out Edwardian gentleman."

Despite being on welfare, despite not having a high school diploma, despite living in the crappiest boardinghouse in town, Lionel generally thought that he was superior to everybody. He could not be bothered under any circumstances to care what people thought of him.

As he and Michal walked down the street together, Lionel nodded and greeted everybody.

"You've got to be sociable. You can't be afraid of people."

People would glance at Lionel strangely because of his getup. Some people looked nervous, others gazed straight ahead as if he was about to ask them for money and some went ahead and said hello back. Michal laughed every time Lionel greeted someone. He cringed, his shoulders up, embarrassed. He put his hands over his face.

"You do it. Just make eye contact and smile at any of these jokers."

Michal smiled and waved at a middle-aged woman. He couldn't believe he was doing it.

"Hello, sweetheart," the woman said.

"See! You like people. That's why you're shy. It's because you care so much about what people think. You've got way more regard for these fools than I do. And it comes to you natural-like. I was bitter even as a little kid. I was like this character from Shakespeare named Iago."

"The parrot in *Aladdin*."

"No. I'm not talking about a bird. I'm talking about the immortal bard. The greatest writer who ever lived. And he had this character who messes stuff up for everybody. And they put these scholars on the case in order to figure out why Iago did all the stuff that he did."

"What's a scholar?"

"Scholars are like therapists, but for books. But none of them could figure out Iago's motivations. Why he would fuck everything up."

Lionel paused a second as if reflecting on his own words. The cars were honking at one another behind him on the street.

"Hey, whatcha got left over from your lunch?"

Michal reached into his school bag and pulled out a Ziploc bag with half a peanut butter sandwich in it.

"There is nothing like a peanut butter sandwich that was made by someone's mama. I could make a sandwich like this, but it wouldn't taste good at all. This is like manna."

"What's manna?"

"Food that the gods delivered."

* * *

The next week they were doing Michal's math homework together at a picnic table at the park. A crow opened its wings, like a man opening a trench coat to exhibit some stolen jewellery that he had for sale.

"How can you not understand this?" Lionel asked. "This is simple basic shit."

"I'm an idiot. I can't do anything right."

"No, no, no. You've just got a mental block. Let's go over this all careful-like, okay. We can do this."

"Everybody thinks I'm stupid."

"Who's everybody? Come on. You're afraid of what's going to happen if you let yourself be able to figure all this shit out. I was like that. I was scared of all the ideas that were in my head. I couldn't accept the responsibility that comes with being smart. So I went and started doing all these drugs because they made me numb. And I destroyed myself just so that I couldn't be great."

"Subtraction makes no sense. How can anything be less than zero?"

"You're right! You're right. Everything stops at zero. Zero should be as low as you can go. The government invented negative numbers. Why? Just so that people can go into debt and then never get out of it. But we're going to have to play their game. Then when you learn to play their game, you can challenge them. I tried to reject it all and look at the sorry-assed state I ended up in. Okay?"

"Okay."

* * *

The next weekend Lionel and Michal went to the amusement park together. Lionel was wearing a blazer and a long striped silk scarf and a pair of track pants. He had on a pair of shiny leather shoes.

Lionel had a plastic bag filled with Coke cans. They had coupons on the sides of them. You could trade them in for a dollar off at the amusement park. He had been looking through the trash for them all week. So when Michal pulled out the twenty-dollar bill that his mother had given him to pay for both their admissions, Lionel told him to put his money away.

They walked around the park, checking out the fanciful structures.

"Once, when I was a little boy, I was trapped in a hall of mirrors. The configurations rattled me. I've never really been able to think properly since then."

Michal didn't want to go on any of the scary rides. He held Lionel by the sleeve of his blazer, pulling him away from the roller coaster. He begged and whined, but Lionel insisted. On the ride Michal squeezed his eyes shut. He wrapped his arms so tightly around Lionel's waist that the man started having a coughing fit.

"We're going to ride this thing until you are no longer afraid."

By the end of the day, Michal was able to put his arms up in the air. He was fearless. He was alive.

Michal was too short to go on the pirate ship.

"I hate being a midget," Michal yelled.

"Don't worry about being so little. You're a late bloomer. Anyways, it's what's on the inside that counts. You know how your mom puts marks on the inside of the doorframe, showing your height? Well, you're going to get to a certain age where you don't get any taller. But your insides never stop expanding. That is limitless."

* * *

Lionel almost always had a paperback book somewhere on him. He loved to read. He took Michal to the Children's Library every Saturday. It was a building made of red stone with squirrels and birds carved into the stone arches around the doors.

He had a pair of reading glasses that he got from the pharmacy. He took them out of his breast pocket and put them on as he was going through different books that were on display.

"Here's a book about peeing on the potty. The great theme of man versus himself. It's bound to win the Pulitzer."

"This book about the owl looks really good," Michal called back, holding a book over his head.

"Damn! Check this out! It is an abridged children's version of *Don Quixote*. You've got to take this out. It's all about madness and the inability for anybody to ever really be heroic. My man Cervantes was prophetic. He foresaw the modern age coming."

Lionel sat in a little armchair that made him look like a giant. Michal sat on the carpet on the floor, which had a cobblestone pattern and was meant to look like the yellow brick road.

They always took out the maximum number of fifteen books. Michal walked down the street with the pile right up to his chin.

"You have got to read, Michal. Every time that you read a book, it is like depositing money in the bank. You spend every weekend reading a pile of books this big, I swear to you that you are going to be a rich man."

"No, I won't. How?"

"Trust me on this one. This is the only thing that is going to make you into a rich man. No matter how hard your mother works at that grocery store, she is never going to be a rich woman. There is nothing that your mother can do to get out of that building in this lifetime. And that is the class divide, my friend."

"Will I always be poor?"

"No, because we are going to have a revolution. The odds will be against us, because it's going to be Michal against the whole fucking structure. The whole country."

"The whole country!"

"Yes, but don't worry. I got your back. We are going to outwit the motherfuckers."

* * *

One of the neighbours was over drinking coffee with Andrea. The roses on the wallpaper behind her head looked like the tomatoes thrown at the opera singer that had missed her head.

"I know he's been spending some time with Michal lately, but I stand by my statement that he is a heartless fuckup. One thing that he has going for him is that he will never have a heart attack, because you need to have a heart in order to have a heart attack."

Andrea laughed really loudly at her own joke.

"He needs somebody to listen to his prattle. And about the only person that's buying what he's selling is an eight-year-old. Michal needs some sort of male in his life. Notice I said *male*. Not *man*. I won't go that far."

And once again she started giggling at her own humour.

"He's all flash and shine and razzmatazz. He stole my paycheque right after I cashed it. It was the holidays. I had to take Michal down to eat at the food bank. You gotta be heartless to do something like that. Stealing from a single mother. It's disgusting."

"Heartless," the neighbour said.

"That's what I said."

"You think it's safe, Michal going out with him? I'm not saying this to be mean, but I wouldn't let my kids around him."

"What choice do I have? It's funny, but I know that fool is good for Michal. The Lord puts everybody in your life for a reason. There's some reason that fool's in my life."

The declawed kitten tiptoed on the table in just its stockings.

* * *

For Michal's birthday, Lionel got him a big black journal to record his thoughts in.

"Your ideas are important. Learn to articulate. The more you formulate your thoughts—the more you write them down or say them out loud—the more powerful they will be. Ideas change the world. Everything that you see around you originated with an idea. Bad ideas and grand ideas."

They were on the bench on the corner. There was an aging black cat that had dyed its fur with a cheap bottle of dye from the pharmacy, but it wasn't fooling anybody. Michal took out an envelope that had been sealed with what looked like electrical tape.

"I got this in the mail from my grandma. My mom said not to open it in front of her 'cause she's mad at Grandma. She always sends a card. It's got this tape all over it though. Can you help me?"

Lionel took out a pocket knife and slit open the envelope while Michal flipped through the page of the big new book and held it up to his face to smell the new pages. Lionel took out the card that had a dog dressed up in a clown outfit and carrying balloons. He was about to comment on the decline of the fine arts in civilization when five twenty-dollar bills slid out and landed on his lap.

It would have been nothing to put those twenty-dollar bills in his pocket. It would have been easy to get up and split with that money. He held out the bills.

"You have hit the jackpot today," Lionel said, his voice cracking a bit.

Michal took the money and whooped. He stood in front of the bench and did a chicken dance of joy. There was a bald man sitting at the bus stop whose scalp and neck and hands were all covered with tattoos of birds.

"You are just asking to get us mugged, my man."

He hadn't taken the money. But it had crossed his mind. It was always with him, that wickedness. It was unpredictable like the weather, and he knew that.

* * *

Lionel was waiting outside the building for the little boy. He was wearing a box that he had cut a hole in the top of to poke his head out of and holes in the sides for his arms to go through. It was painted silver. He had a plastic funnel on his head. He was taking Michal trick-or-treating in a more upscale neighbourhood, where they would get better candy.

Michal came out dressed in a brown lion suit. He had a mane around his head and some whiskers drawn on his cheeks with grease paint. When Michal saw Lionel, he laughed and laughed.

"I used up a whole can of silver spray paint on this thing. I almost asphyxiated myself. My lungs probably glow in the dark."

"You look ridiculous!"

"What do you think you look like?"

"I won third place in the costume contest at school."

"Well, la-di-da."

After two hours, Michal's pillowcase was full of candy and he couldn't walk another step. They sat at a picnic table, eating tiny Mars bars. The pigeons all around them had heart murmurs.

"Excellent. State-sanctioned panhandling. I love it."

Some kids that Michal knew from school walked by. Michal immediately got quiet.

"Don't be afraid of anybody. That's the number one thing that keeps people down in this world. This idea that other people are better, scarier, more intimidating. Fuck that, Michal.

There ain't nothing a rich kid knows that you don't know."

Lionel looked at Michal to make sure he was getting his point across.

"What do they know that we don't know?"

"Nothing."

"Who are we intimidated by?"

"Nobody."

"That's right. No-fucking-body."

Then Michal started to laugh.

"What's so funny?"

"You have a funnel on your head."

* * *

Andrea was working late and couldn't go to Michal's open house at school. Lionel showed up with his hair combed back. He had on a gold dress shirt with diamonds on it and a pair of dress pants that were too long and were scuffing on the floor. He had a long black coat. He looked good. He sat in the seat and looked through all of Michal's reports.

"I think that the teacher secretly hates me," Michal said.

"I'll ask her some discreet questions and I'll find out for you."

Lionel went up and introduced himself to the teacher as a friend of the family.

"Michal is the light of our lives."

"I'm sure he is," the teacher said. "He was really shy at the beginning of the year. But he's been really coming out of his shell. He signed up to be in the school play. I was so surprised."

Lionel turned to Michal and winked. Michal smiled.

"What did you think of the Remembrance Day poem that he wrote?"

"I put it on the wall."

"I know, right? Wasn't it amazing! Like how does a little dude like that have so much compassion? I mean the sky is the limit for that guy. He could be a politician even."

"It's so nice of you to take an interest in him."

"Oh, it's a delight. What's amazing is the work you do with all these little weirdos. Those handprints you have on the wall that the kids turned into turkeys are hilarious! Where did you come up with something like that?"

The teacher was smiling. Michal's mother once told the neighbour that in certain lights, in peculiar moods and on rare occasions, Lionel could be quite the ladies' man. When she first met him, she found him so magnetic. If he wasn't such a fuckup, he could seduce any woman he wanted.

Lionel walked Michal home. The surface of the moon on a clear night looked all dented, like it had been out drinking and driving and had now lost its licence after a crash.

"You know what, little guy? When you're in doubt and you don't know what a person thinks of you, I want you to go with 'They're crazy about me.' Okay? Not 'They hate me.' Will you do that from now on?"

"Okay."

"Okay. You're really good about keeping promises. I notice that about you. You're a stand-up guy. And why didn't you tell me your teacher is hot?"

"I didn't know she was!"

* * *

Sometimes Michal would take out money that Andrea had given him to buy them both supper. Lionel would protest that he couldn't take any of her money, but he usually relented. What were they supposed to do, starve? They would go and buy themselves hamburgers and soda pop at one of the fast-food joints. One night they got themselves a window seat and watched all the lights of the world turning on one by one. It was the witching hour.

"Do you believe in reincarnation? I do. Because if you think about it, how else do you explain the fact that there are people out there who are sixteen times more intelligent than others? I think that I have lived dozens of lives. That's why I feel so weary, you know what I mean? I only have to mend my ways. Act in a more moral way, and then I can be born something else, you know. I'm sick to death of being human. It's a punishment."

Outside, a man who had been drinking wobbled around, as if gravity had suddenly lost its grip on him.

Lionel always had a ballpoint pen behind his ear. When they were finished at the restaurant, his paper napkin was covered in stars. He had a habit of doodling stars. When he had been dating Andrea, everything in the house started to be covered in stars. The borders of the newspaper and the phone bills would be covered in stars. The little boy thought there was something magical about Lionel.

As they walked home, every time the doors of a bar along the street opened up, the sound was like change spilling out from a slot machine.

"All great philosophical tracts were written at night. I have to stay up late. You have a bedtime now. But when you grow up, you can choose to be the type of person that has a bedtime or the type of person who does not. Everybody's got to figure out their own way to do good in this world."

There were cockroaches scurrying across the sidewalk. They shook hands and said good night.

* * *

Michal saw Lionel lying on the grass in the park. There was a dog sniffing next to him. Michal had to say hello to Lionel three or four times before he opened his eyes. Then it took Lionel a few seconds to figure out who the boy was. His eyes were all glazed over.

Andrea sat across from Michal at the kitchen table. She told him that Lionel was sick and that he would never, never, never be able to stop doing drugs. He had been on them too long. She had known boys like that since she was a little girl. Lionel would never be able to stop.

"I know that," Michal said.

"I don't know why he bothered to go out of his way to be your friend, just to start using again and abandon you. He's heartless."

"No, he's not."

"You certainly can't expect him to be here forever, baby, okay?"

* * *

Lionel got better again, and when he did, he took Michal to the park to teach him how to play basketball.

"How come you never had your own kids?" Michal asked.

"I'm an addict. I would never pass that gene on. Besides, I have you. That's way, way better than any sucker that would come out of me."

Michal smiled. He had a good feeling inside of him that he knew nobody could take away from him.

"Although some of my genes aren't so bad. I do have kick-ass hair."

When Lionel started about how handsome he was, it usually meant that he was in a good mood.

Lionel had been a so-so basketball player in high school. That day he was dribbling the ball around feeling like a superstar. Lionel moved about all graceful and was able to get the ball in the basket sometimes. A bunch of other kids came to watch Lionel and to ask if they could play. It was always an event if a cool dad or an older brother took a little bit of time off their schedule to come and play.

Michal looked at Lionel and he was proud of him.

* * *

Michal was so excited about going to the zoo that he was already standing behind the glass door to the lobby, waiting for Lionel to show up. Lionel had a bag of peanuts that he had gotten from the grocery store. He said the peanuts they had for sale at the zoo were an extortion racket.

They squeezed in together on a plastic seat on the subway train. He was wearing a green button-up shirt with polka dots, pinstriped pants and a pair of black army boots, the black of which had long since worn off the toes. Lionel didn't dress any differently on a weekday than he did on a weekend. He had long since ceased to be able to differentiate between the two. Michal was rocking back and forth because he was so excited.

Lionel picked up a newspaper that had been left on the seat next to them. The row of old men on the bench across from them sat hunched over like a row of buzzards.

"We have got to keep abreast of the news. Even if it makes us weep."

Michal tried to turn the pages of the newspaper while Lionel was reading it.

"Ah, ah, ah. We'll get to the comics in a little bit. I want to read the comics as much as you do, trust me. I'm itching to get to them too. But they are dessert, okay? We have to be worldly men. You don't want your life to be confined to this little neck of the woods."

"I like it here."

"Travel the whole world. And if after seeing everything that there is to see out there, you want to come back here, then be my guest. But I'll bet you five dollars that you will not."

"Five dollars!"

"Yes."

"You won't pay up."

They shook on it.

A few days later, Michal's mother found a map of the zoo. There were red Xs drawn with a ballpoint pen on the entranceways. The word *EXPLOSIVES* was written underneath the Xs. There were black arrows next to the words *EXIT STRATEGY*. It was clear what this was. Michal and Lionel had come up with a plan to liberate the animals from the zoo.

Lionel called from the telephone in the halfway house. She sat in the kitchen, listening to Michal's side of the conversation.

"Where will the animals go? Oh, oh, oh! We can put the wolves in the park. And then we can go and put up signs saying that there are wolves in the park. Keep out!"

Michal was quiet for a bit.

"What are we going to do with the tiger, though? It will walk down the street and it's going to eat children!"

Michal was laughing and laughing.

"We can't put hippopotamuses in the swimming pool! They'll get chlorine in their eyes!"

Michal was laughing so hard that he had to cross his legs so that he wouldn't pee himself. Andrea realized that she had been right about Lionel the first time she had met him: she had struck gold.

* * *

Sometimes, after Lionel buzzed for Michal to come down, Andrea and Lionel would shoot the breeze on the intercom in the lobby. Lionel could still make Andrea laugh. But she knew not to let him up. And Lionel knew that it was probably a good thing that Andrea kept him down there at the bottom of the stairs. Neither of them had ever been successful at romance. And the both of them knew that what Lionel and Michal had was bigger than what they could ever have.

Andrea didn't really have much of a family. Lionel's childhood had been different. His family had expected things from him. He had been so clever as a little boy. He knew that he had been born with possibilities that other people had not been born with. He was at the top of his class and his teachers said that he could get an academic scholarship to any school he wanted. He thought life was going to be a breeze.

That was before he knew that he was a drug addict. He went to parties like other kids. He did drugs like other kids. But lordy, lordy, lordy, all of that crap affected him in a different way than other kids. It possessed him. He should have known that he was cursed at birth. He was like Sleeping Beauty. Even though there were all these good fairies that gave him looks and charm and smarts, there was a motherfucking dick of a fairy who showed up and said that on his sixteenth birthday he was going to prick himself with a hypodermic needle and he was going to walk around in a daze for the rest of his goddamn life.

Lionel couldn't bear to be around people who knew what he was like before drugs had taken hold of him. Lionel's mother said that the way he had turned his back on the family was worse than his addiction. He was heartless.

* * *

"Read me something from your journal," Lionel said as he was walking Michal home from school.

"Today I had a conversation in class with a boy named Callum. He said that when he grows up, he wants to work on a ship. He says that he doesn't mind the sea. He also had a dog that died last year. They buried it in the backyard. He said that he thought that he was going to cry, but he didn't."

"Magnificent! You know what you did, my boy? You located an existential hero! You captured Callum in a nutshell. You know Callum in a way that Callum doesn't even know Callum. When you look at people, you know exactly what they are about. People are going to love that about you. Nobody likes to go about the world being anonymous and unknowable. They want to know that they are being seen for who they really are. You are a man of the people. You are going to be a leader, mark my words."

Michal started to skip next to Lionel because he was so happy.

"Yes sir, I am a lucky man to have found you, my little buddy. I never knew what the point of me was, you know that? Until you came into my path."

They passed a funeral parlour on their way, and inside it they were playing a corpse's favourite song.

* * *

Michal got a scholarship to McGill law school. He ran for public office. And later in life when he was a member of parliament, people always asked him how it was that he had come all this way. He had grown up with nothing. He had had a single mother who worked ten hours a day at a grocery store. Where did he find the courage to follow this road?

"His name was Lionel. He was a heroin addict. He died of an overdose when I was thirteen years old. He had the biggest heart in the neighbourhood. I still owe him five dollars."

DAYDREAMS OF ANGELS

On that day, God decided to send ten thousand angels down to a shore in Normandy as there was going to be a terrible battle. The soldiers would need every angel He had in His house. All His most magnificent and awesome angels stopped whatever they were doing and headed down to the seashore. Then God found Himself short of angels. He had to do what He hated to do. He had to send some of the cherubim down to take on some of the tasks that His more senior angels usually handled. It was a shame to have to use the cherubim, the angels that were normally in charge of romantic love. They were sleazy and ridiculous. But what else could God do that day?

One cherub was sent down to Montreal. He was walking around in a tailored suit, with his trumpet case at his side, when he spotted Yvette Olivier beside the merry-go-round and immediately found her lovely. She had on a black jacket that was tight at the waist and flared out at the bottom. She had a bouncy brown bob that she tucked neatly behind her ears. He liked that she had big brown eyes. Angels all had blue eyes, and brown eyes always seemed so simple and honest to him.

The girl's cheeks and nose were bright pink and her eyes glowed, but she was dancing about happily on her tippy-toes. She'd been feeling sick and feverish for the past couple of days and her mother had been fretting over her like mad. Her mother had been continuously saying silly things like this wouldn't be happening if she didn't stay out when the sun went down, and this wouldn't be happening if the girl's father was here and wasn't overseas in the war.

Of course none of her mother's assertions made any sense whatsoever because now Yvette was feeling better. Oh, and she had lost a few pounds, which was something that she had been desperately trying to do for a while. Feeling so good to be up and about, she swore she would never take being alive for granted again. She wanted to go by her friends' houses and tell them how much better she was feeling. She hoped that everyone would be up for going to a nightclub. She wanted to be picked up and swung so high that her skirt would fly up over her behind and when the boy put her down, she would feel his sweat dripping off his forehead onto hers. Since her body still felt a little bit tired and weak from having lain in bed for so much time, she thought that if she went out dancing, she might wake herself up once and for all.

She had taken a shortcut through the park as the shadows became as long as pulled taffy. There was a cute boy who worked at the merry-go-round and who had told her to come by to see him right before she had taken sick. She hoped that he hadn't found a new girlfriend, but it was entirely possible that he happened to be as fickle as she was.

Yvette always had a crush on about six boys at a time. That's just the way that she was. She was always sneaking out to go dancing with them. Her father had put an extra lock on the front door so that she couldn't escape. Undeterred, she would sneak out her window and would ride her bicycle down a back alley to find a hiding place where kids were playing records and smoking cigarettes.

She was the eldest child in her family and all the others were still very young. They were all crazy about her and they jumped around the house like wild little dogs when she came home. She was so easy to love, always throwing her arms around everyone and singing popular songs from the radio before breakfast. Her father yelled at her before he left that she gave him more trouble than all the other kids put together, but secretly, he had admitted to himself that she was his favourite. He had never in his life met someone who was so free.

She held on to the cast iron gate that surrounded the merry-go-round, waving and laughing at the boy. He didn't come over, though. She tried calling out to him, but there was no way in the world that she could be heard over the deafening music of the calliope. The sound of the calliope crashed over her voice like a huge wave.

Yvette started stumbling around with the back of her hand on her forehead, trying to pantomime that she had been sick. She looked like a tragic heroine in a black-and-white silent film, one who had found out that the evil landlord was stealing her home. The boy, who had the very important task of making the carousel turn around and around, still didn't seem to see her. Or perhaps he did but he wasn't in the mood to fall for her charms that day. The unicorns and zebras all looked straight ahead in their circular path, refusing to take notice of the girl either.

The cherub did, however. He started to laugh out loud at Yvette's little performance. He clapped his hands together in a smattering of applause. She was a breath of fresh air. He most certainly had a soft spot for girls who were brash. He hated shy and humble girls.

Yvette turned toward him. She suddenly forgot all about the merry-go-round guy. She considered him for about thirty seconds and then decided: Oh, what the hell. She was going to be in love with this complete stranger for the evening and she would see where it led. She thought he was quite handsome, although she couldn't put her finger on how old he was.

They walked down the street together. When the cherub told Yvette that he had liked her mime routine, she screamed in laughter. She told him that she went to the movies as often as she could and that her biggest dream, although she was sure it was impossible, was to be a movie star. She suddenly stopped in her tracks. Then she started fluttering her eyes as if she were blind, with her hands clasped at her chest. She slowly put out her hand and felt the cherub's face. She was reenacting a scene from Charlie Chaplin's *City Lights*. He thought it was one of the most beautiful things he had ever seen, and believe you me, he had seen a lot of things.

There was a little old lady wandering about in her nightgown on the sidewalk across the street. Yvette insisted they go help her. The cherub told Yvette that someone would be along to take care of her any minute now.

"Are you crazy! We can't leave the poor sweetheart there!"

The cherub waited while Yvette took the old woman by the arm and led her back to her building. The old lady jabbered away the whole time. She smiled at Yvette affectionately and they disappeared into the stairwell. It was a few minutes before Yvette came back down.

"Sorry!" Yvette cried. "I wanted to make sure she was okay. I put her to bed and gave some food to her poor mewing cats and straightened up a tiny bit. I'll swing by tomorrow to see if she needs anything."

"Are you done with your good deeds?" the cherub asked.

"I would hardly call that a good deed!"

The cherub took Yvette to a little bistro. He wasn't even sure what he was doing, taking this girl on a date! There were round mirrors on the wall like the windows of a ship. There were stains on the tablecloth. The menu was written in pretty handwriting on a chalkboard on the wall. Their knees were touching one another's under the table.

She wanted to hear words of love. That was okay. That was what he spent all day doing. He had notebooks full of them. He had been coming up with inspired and ridiculous things for men to say for years.

"You are the girl that I have been waiting to meet my whole life. I feel like I've known you forever. I feel like you can read my thoughts and can understand me better than any other human being can."

He was feeling a little sickened by his own words. He didn't think they were good enough for her. He suddenly felt dishonest.

"Wow! You do have a way with words."

"Thank you. I've been practising them for about a thousand years, but I've never had anyone to say them to."

"I've heard all those lines before."

"Of course you have, but only because I wrote them. I give them away. I want other people to be happy."

"What is it you do for a living? Are you an artist?"

"I do play a mean trumpet."

"You don't! I adore music! I mean it. I'm really truly crazy about it."

"Come, I'll show you."

He didn't know why, but he felt like he really wanted to bowl this girl over. He knew that he already had her eating out of the palm of his hand, but it wasn't enough. He wanted to impress her and impress her some more. He wanted to show her everything that he was capable of. He wanted to turn himself inside out for this girl.

He didn't have any money though, so she picked up the cheque.

As they were walking down the street, he took out his trumpet. Because he was a cherub, he played different types of tunes than, say, a seraph might. Although impossible to put into words, his melodies sounded most like a baby cooing in its sleep, a girl laughing under the covers, a moan escaping from someone's lips while making love. She clasped her hands together when he was done, in awe. The angel was out of line and he knew it. Humans aren't supposed to hear angels playing while they are still on earth. They are supposed to experience it in heaven, as part of their welcoming reception, so to speak, as a reward for a lifetime of being truly good. But that was what the girl was. She had the biggest, truest heart that he had ever encountered and she deserved to hear all the songs in his repertoire. If she wanted, he would stand there and play them one after the other until the very end of time, when there was no more planet or any people on it.

"That was the most beautiful trumpet playing that I have heard. Really! And I've been to all the downtown clubs! You could go to America with playing like that. You could have your own record. You should be famous really."

And if the angel were a human, he would have blushed. They walked down the street happily, arm in arm.

"I'm glad you haven't enlisted. My father's a major. He's overseas, but we get letters from him all the time."

When she mentioned her father, she took a tiny gold cross that was hanging on a chain underneath her sweater and gave it a little kiss. He supposed she thought that that would make her father safe. The sweet girl had no idea, did she? If she knew how many angels God had sent down to France that morning, she wouldn't have much confidence in her little trinket.

What a day, what a day, what a day, the cherub thought. Even though he proudly considered himself above human concerns, he was momentarily taken aback by the sheer solemnity and horror of what was about to happen.

Well, he was certainly going to have a more pleasant time because the girl was clueless. She had never known any real hardship in her life. Because she had no idea what it felt like to grieve, her face was an unreservedly happy one. The sun was setting as they hurried back to her place. He hid in the alley behind her brick house until she leaned out the window and gave him the signal. A black cat rubbed up against his leg. Its tail waved, like the hand of a magician's assistant exhibiting that there was nothing. Then, since Yvette had poked her head back inside, he opened his two wings, which were small like those of a dove, and they emerged through the slits in his jacket. He flew up to the landing of the fire escape and squeezed through the bedroom window to be with her.

As his wings folded themselves back into his jacket, the cherub paused for a second to take in the condition of the girl's room. It was cramped and messy and had pink wall-paper and a skinny bed with a brass frame. There were some pairs of dirty stockings hanging off the bed frame like the arms of swimmers holding up their bodies on the side of a pool. There were postcards of Boris Vian stuck on the wall above her bed and an aquamarine-blue record player at its foot. There were records lying everywhere with the faces of the singers on the covers, looking like they were crying out in pain, as if they were terrified of being stepped on. For a girl who was so tidy about her physical appearance, she certainly was a slob about other things.

She hopped from foot to foot, saying, "Shh! Shh! Shh!" Or else her mother would come in and kill them both.

Having sex was one of the few things that humans were good at. Lord, they made an entire production of it. He liked all the excitement. Her pulse was wild and she was acting as if it was a matter of life and death. He could tell that she didn't even really love him but, rather, was just mad about the whole game. He could almost burst out in laughter about how much human beings liked sex. She went behind the closet door and came out with a black lace bra with little pink bows on it and a pair of underwear that almost matched, and a garter belt holding up a pair of nylon stockings that had a hole in one of the thighs. How did they come up with this stuff on their own?

She bent over the bed with her ass in the air and she asked him if he would spank her just a couple of times. He loved it. He loved it.

* * *

As Yvette and the cherub rolled off of one another and fell into a happy slumber, the sun was about to rise on the other side of the ocean, in France. The armada crossing the Channel from England was quite something to behold. The ships were like buildings with hundreds of little windows and doors and populated by cooks and janitors and doctors. They were like a whole little city that had somehow drifted off to sea. It was a lot like Noah's Ark. Except there were no animals. Instead, two of every kind of young man had been piled onto each boat: two jokers, two jocks, two nerds, two ladies' men.

Major Olivier was standing in the landing craft as it pushed out onto the water ahead of the fleet. He and his boys stood in two lines, as though they were children waiting to be let back in after recess in a schoolyard. He was thinking about how his daughter back in Montreal would go crazy for so many of the young men here. These boys were her age and she would be able to find something good about each one of them. She was so pretty that she attracted all the most popular boys, but she gave all sorts of kids the time of day. He once saw her waltzing around the ballroom with a skinny boy with a lazy eye. She found some lovely quality in them all.

Lately he found that he was seeing all the boys in his company through Yvette's eyes. He laughed at all their jokes and each and every one of them broke his heart. It was terrible that some of them were going to die. Some of them were a pain in the ass and some of them weren't his cup of tea, but none of them were anywhere close to being rotten. Not one of them deserved to live or die more than the other.

You could not ask why now, Major Olivier thought. You could not pause to think about the bigger questions while you were at war. You had had time enough as a child to do that.

Instead, the major thought about how the little ship could possibly get to the shore with the waves being so wild this morning. The waves rose thirty to forty feet on either side of them. It was like a giant was making a bed and the sea was a great comforter, and the boat a tiny toy that was being tossed about on it. The machine-gun fire from behind him started its awful crackling, and the sounds of mortars exploding erupted. The world was going to pieces, wasn't it? It was like someone had taken the whole world and stuck it in the blender at the five-and-dime back in Montreal and pressed the puree button. He wondered if his hair would go grey early because of this. His father always used to say that if you went to war, your hair went grey early. He had always been so vain about his jet-black hair. He felt as if he would never be able to eat again because of the seasickness.

They all felt the bottom of the landing craft scrape against the gravel at the bottom of the shore and the ramp lowered. The men began to charge out and Major Olivier was right behind them when for a moment, at the edge of the ship, he was frozen in his tracks in a state of awe. What was he seeing on the cliffs? At first he thought that he was only seeing the smoke and debris from missiles that they'd launched at the shore, but as the smoke cleared, he saw it was something else. He slowly realized that the entire beach was covered with angels. They were standing on the sand, sitting on tree branches, perched on the rocks. You couldn't even begin to count them. There were some that were still coming down from the sky.

Some were holding up their gowns and walking with their feet in the water and kicking it about. One of the angels had made a beautiful pattern on the sand with clamshells. There was an angel with his arms stretched up in the sky, doing a backbend. One was juggling some stones.

One was looking at a little bird hatching out of an egg. Some angels liked the simple things. Some of these angels hadn't been down to earth in a while. One had caught a fish by the tail and was holding it in his hands so that the other angels could see how large it was.

There were others that looked like they had been waiting patiently for hours, sitting on the cliff with their eyes closed, enjoying the salty breeze on their faces. Their curly golden locks were being whipped into a frenzy and tangled into dreadlocks.

The angels didn't see that there was anything particularly alarming about going to heaven—or that there was anything for people to get worked up about. Anyway, that was their job, to remain level-headed about things, so that they could calm you down and tell you that this was actually, very soon, going to be the best day of your life.

The major saw more of them coming down from a parting in the clouds. He was amazed. Why was he the only one who could see them? He was absolutely certain that they were there. He had never hallucinated about anything in his whole life. He looked and looked and they were still there.

What did God know that they didn't know? Why would God be sending that many angels unless that many soldiers were going to be slaughtered? It could only mean one thing, and that was that they were all going up to heaven that very afternoon. He thought he had known that, but it was something that was impossible to grasp until the moment was upon you. Until death rings your doorbell, or tosses a stone up at your window from down below on the street, you never quite believe it exists, do you?

Major Olivier was filled with so much dread that he puked all over himself. He began to beg everyone to come back. He screamed, but nobody could hear him. The noise of the waves overwhelmed his voice. The wind blew out his words like they were matches.

He turned quickly, pointing wildly and waving his arm toward the shore. It was like he was in a dream, because nobody was paying him any attention. There was one soldier crouched against the wall to avoid the bullets. He crossed himself and Major Olivier could tell from the movement of his lips that he was supplicating to God and the heavens to come and protect him.

Major Olivier wanted to say no, no, no, no. You don't want to call on the heavens now. You want to tell the angels to go away. You should throw a stone at them, so that they will all fly up into the air like a group of pigeons. They're here for souls—our souls! There were angels that were hovering over the water, like kites on the end of strings. They were ready to take up souls that hadn't even got to the land yet. There were angels landing on the hulls of the landing crafts.

The bullets were coming quicker and quicker. He could hear explosions. What could he do? There was nothing that anybody could do now but storm the beach.

The praying boy headed out, and Major Olivier followed behind him. They were neck-deep in water and they were forcing themselves toward the shore. He ducked down because there was a volley of bullets whizzing over his head. He closed his eyes. He wanted to see his daughter again. He had no idea why on earth he had such a beautiful daughter. She would be sitting at the breakfast table with her curls all over the place, with one of her brothers on her lap, in a terrific mood. She would fling herself into his arms when she ran into him on the street, wrapping her legs around his hips and kissing him on the forehead. He felt blessed all the time.

When he opened his eyes again he was underwater. There, right in front of him, was an angel with his hair swirling around his head like a Catherine wheel and his enormous wings spread out like great penknives. Major Olivier felt so terribly warm. He put his hands on his chest to see where the heat was coming from and he realized that there was blood all over his uniform. It was going to be all right now, as he was already dead. He had been dead this whole time.

* * *

Yvette was lying on her bed with her eyes closed and the blanket tossed aside when her mother came in the room to check on her. Her mother crouched down in the kitchen by the stove and wailed and wailed. The other children gathered around the mother, terrified and simpering. The neighbours could hear Yvette's mother through the floorboards. The sound made them cringe and weep and cross themselves over and over.

The doctor came sadly to the door. Like everyone else in the neighbourhood, he had a soft spot for Yvette Olivier. He looked at the body of the pretty young girl lying under the covers. What a shame that this girl, who still had so many days of partying ahead of her, had to be taken from this world. He looked at the symptomatic red rash on her chest.

"Meningitis," he said. "What an awful night she must have had."

It was peculiar though: the doctor couldn't help but notice that she had such a happy look on her face. She looked as if she was still alive and was having the most fantastic dream of her life. She looked as if she was about to burst out laughing. Whatever else, the doctor seemed suddenly certain that that girl had gone to meet her maker in peace.

THE ISLES OF DR. MOREAU

Grandfather often enjoyed telling my brother about how, when he was younger, he was a ladies' man.

"I never had any trouble getting girls," he'd exclaim. "None whatsoever."

It was hard for my brother and me to picture it. The grandfather we knew sat on the couch all day, sucking on chocolates with his dentures out and cursing the TV. Who could picture him on a date?

Our mother didn't like him telling old girlfriend stories, saying that most of them only served to objectify women and feed his own ego, but whenever she'd leave the room, we would beg for one of his tales.

"Tell us about Dr. Moreau!" we yelled one evening when the washing machine had broken down and Mother had gone off to the laundromat. "Tell us about the Island of Dr. Moreau!"

Grandfather often claimed he'd had a job working for Dr. Moreau and said that the women on the island were unlike any he'd ever seen.

"No . . . I can't tell you that story," Grandfather said, playing possum. "Your mother would have my head."

"Please!" we yelled. "We won't tell her you told us."

Grandfather sighed and agreed to tell the story if in exchange we each rubbed one of his feet, at which point he gave in, proclaiming that all stories needed telling eventually and this one was a doozy.

"I was a slim, handsome devil back then," Grandfather said. "But it wasn't enough for me to seduce women. I wanted love. True love."

The story began, he said, one afternoon in 1945. He was out fishing in the Saint-Laurent River when a pompous fool in a white cardigan and sailor's cap sped by in a motorboat, causing his rickety rowboat to be pitched out to sea.

After two terrible days adrift, a large vessel pulled up and the sailors yelled for him to come aboard. Once he got on, Grandfather saw that the ship was filled with animals. It was like Noah's Ark! He had never seen so many kinds of animals in his life. The zoo in Montreal didn't even have a lion. All it had was a geriatric elephant that peed every time it sneezed. The sailors said that they were transporting the animals to the Isle of Dr. Moreau.

* * *

It had been years since Grandfather had heard a word about Andre Phillipe Moreau. Moreau had once been considered one of the world's most eminent scientists. At the age of seventeen, he had famously visited Saint Petersburg to present the tsar with a mechanical monkey he'd built out of clock parts. The monkey was trained to move its head from side to side when someone was talking, in order to give the vague impression of actually listening. It knew how to diaper a baby.

Of course no sane mother would leave her child with a robotic monkey, so the monkeys were purchased by orphanages, where they were wildly adored by the orphans. There was even footage that circulated of a little boy weeping and telling one of Moreau's mechanical monkeys about how he had been picked on at school that day. The image of the little boy talking so intimately to a monkey with glass eyes and steel teeth filled the public with so much dread that the monkeys were very soon placed in storage in a Romanian hangar, where they probably remain to this day.

Despite this setback, Dr. Moreau was still considered a young man of unparalleled brilliance, and after claiming in a medical journal that, given enough resources, he could cure male pattern baldness, a pharmaceutical company gave Moreau a massive endowment. He then moved to an island on the Saint-Laurent, where he used the money to commence work on his real project.

Moreau called the small island "the Isle of Noble and Important and Respectable Betterment of *Homo sapiens* and Their Consorts." Of course no one could be bothered to say this, so it became simply known as the Isle of Dr. Moreau.

Occasionally, you would hear people speak of Moreau—about a new lawsuit brought against him by the pharmaceutical companies, for instance—but more often than not, as he had not been heard from in decades, he was usually spoken of as an example of wasted potential.

"Some people said his downfall all began after he fell in love with a Russian princess," Grandfather informed us knowingly. "She was too cold and cultured to love him back and it made him want to turn his back on society."

* * *

When Grandfather first arrived on the island, he was eager to meet Dr. Moreau. The first time he saw him, the doctor was dressed in a three-piece suit and was reading a book of poetry. He smiled at Grandfather and said, "Welcome to this humble little piece of paradise, my child."

The island was undoubtedly the loveliest place that Grandfather had ever laid eyes on. There were lush flowers everywhere and monkeys and goats running all around. Moreau was in need of extra workers, and so when he was asked, Grandfather readily agreed to stay on.

It was only after weeks of doing menial chores in the laboratory that Grandfather came to understand the nature of Dr. Moreau's work.

Moreau wanted to create a race of humans who could love more freely—a race who, unlike the Russian princess, would be willing to give their hearts to one another without fear. He believed that somewhere along the line, the evolution of the human species had taken a turn for the worse, and he believed that, by combining the genetic makeup of humans with the right animal, love would no longer need to be a tragic thing, continually questioned and denied until it drove us mad, but it would be something simple, good and pure.

Moreau's first step, as a means of experimentation, was to begin combining DNA from different animals. The workers Grandfather met were always talking about those first crazy days. They spoke of the ill-fated union of a hippopotamus and a sloth. The giant hippo would try to hang from a bar in its cage and then collapse on the floor and vomit. They spoke of the half gorilla, half parrot and how it would get all up in your face, repeating what you'd just said over and over. In the workers' opinion, the worst combination was cows and bats. Eerily they flew through the night sky, dripping milk onto the heads of those below.

After years of mixing animals with animals, Moreau finally felt he was ready to begin his true work: mixing animals with humans.

* * *

Grandfather was advised by the other workers not to become too close with these animal people who now populated the island, especially the women; but he was young and searching for love, and the only women who were one hundred percent human anyhow were a couple of older cooks and some washerwomen.

"I had needs!" Grandfather cried.

The creatures were a bit odd in general, since their idea of what it was to act like a human was derived from watching Dr. Moreau, and he was a man who sipped cocktails during surgery and kept his laboratory filled with birds, saying they reminded him to always make sure that his ideas took flight. Moreau spent hours contemplating matters ontological and zoological. He always used big, complicated words and you could only ever understand half of what he was saying. Grandfather said that one time, instead of merely instructing him to open the blinds, Moreau had cried out, "Remove the impediments that curtail my lumination!" Grandfather stood there, shell-shocked, until Moreau pitched a coconut martini at his head and got up to do it himself.

So the half humans, in imitation of the doctor, could often be seen strutting about with walking sticks and saying nonsensical things like "Life is nothing more than a flickering candle. Troubled water that is not even water."

This is all to say that the island was afloat upon a sea of pseudo-intellectualism.

* * *

The creatures had such highfalutin ideas of what it was to be human that when Grandfather showed up, all the girls treated him as if he was a superstar. He had never been so popular in his life.

At first it was disconcerting for him that these women, even if they were very pretty and often looked completely normal, were indeed half animal; but after a while, it just became commonplace to see a vaguely pony-faced girl throw back her head and let out a good-natured whinny, like a happy horse.

His dating life on the island began one day while he was out for a stroll and ran into a half-swan girl.

"But if I had known that swans mate for life, I never would have started with her," said Grandfather.

He first saw her at a small clapboard theatre that Moreau had ordered built to expose the animals to art. She was on stage, dancing the lead in the ballet *Swan Lake*. Grandfather thought he had never laid eyes on anyone so gorgeous in his life. She had such long legs and incredibly graceful movements. She was nothing like the girls he'd known back home in the lower-class district where he lived. She was the kind of girl that you could introduce to the Queen even.

Licking his hands and smoothing his hair back, he walked into her changing room and handed her a daisy he'd picked from the shore. As soon as she saw the flower, she became hysterically happy, clapped her hands delightedly and threw her arms around his neck.

Grandfather was amazed at how easy it was to win the swan-girl's affections. They saw each other every night and couldn't get enough of each other. She would ask him if he thought her neck was too long—which it was (it made her look like she was perpetually peering over taller people's heads at a parade), but Grandfather told her he loved her neck. And to confirm this, he would lavish it with kisses, which, because of its great length, was no mean feat.

Although Grandfather found her endearing, there were aspects of her personality that got on his nerves. For instance, she would often point out children on passing bicycles and say that they looked like what their children were going to look like. And after having dated for only a few weeks, she showed up at his door with her suitcase in one hand and her houseplant in the other, declaring that she was moving in.

Grandfather was almost relieved when she met a half-swan man who brought up marriage five minutes into their first encounter. Grandfather realized that she didn't really love him anyway. She would have had anyone who came along and that wasn't what he wanted.

"To love everyone is to love no one," he said. "My ego wouldn't allow it."

* * *

After that he decided to wait until the right girl came along, and not immediately jump into things. He decided to wait until he met a girl who was less forward, which might account for why he ended up with a girl who was half deer. The deer-girl didn't have a wicked bone in her body, but she was so shy that when he took her out with his friends, she wouldn't say a word. She would just sit there looking nervous, whispering that it was time to go soon.

He practically had to move in slow motion around her, and when they kissed, he had to keep his finger on her pulse for fear of giving her a heart attack.

Her panic and lack of social skills didn't bother Grandfather, but her paranoia did. She complained about everyone looking at her funny—talking about her behind her back. She always thought there was someone out to kill her. She would put locks on her front door, and if someone rang the doorbell she would drop the plate she was holding and scream.

Grandfather knew that loving someone is a risky thing that takes a lot of guts, and the deer-girl just didn't seem to have the courage it takes.

Here, my brother interjected, agreeing with Grandfather for dumping her.

"I would've done the same!" my brother cried.

There was a girl who followed him around the schoolyard but was too nervous to say a word. She always wanted to sit next to him quietly, and it drove my brother crazy. Men.

* * *

Several weeks after breaking up with the deer-girl, Grandfather attended an island social dance and it was there that he met a half lion named Leona. She was so much more laid back compared to the other girls he had dated. She slept about sixteen hours a day, and when she was awake, her favourite activity was lying out in the sun. Grandfather would read her poems while they lay together on the beach.

But of course, Grandfather soon began to discover the darker side of dating a lion. Whenever anyone showed any weakness, she said they should be put out of their misery. His friend Paul, who worked in the lab with him, had asthma, and one day when he was using his inhaler, Leona slapped it out of his hand and told him that a man didn't need training wheels to breathe. At the time, Grandfather had found the remark rather witty; but several days later, when a blister on his heel forced him to walk with a limp, he found her lack of sympathy hurtful.

"Why don't you lie down and rest, little baby-man," she said, licking her back molars, and Grandfather limped off as quickly as he could, her cruel laughter echoing behind him.

"Love should make you ten feet tall," he said. "If only in the eyes of the one who loves you."

* * *

Grandfather had really liked the way the lion-girl had stretched out her whole body when she yawned, and she did have a sexy voice that sort of purred when she talked, and so he decided he could get all of that—minus the threat of violence—from someone who was half cat. And so he asked out the little cat-girl he saw drinking a milkshake by herself late one night.

She was definitely a cutie, but one day, while searching for a cigarette lighter, he discovered that her coat pocket was filled with dead sparrows. Later she even gave him one as a birthday present, a red ribbon tied around its crooked little neck. She handed him the gift with a look on her face that Grandfather found adorable, even though it was revolting.

Everyone told him not to get mixed up with a nocturnal animal, but he ignored them, and soon he discovered that she could never stay in bed at night, preferring to amble across the way to an island bar called the Sinking Ship, where she would get drunk and make out with the bouncer.

She eventually told Grandfather that she needed someone who was also nocturnal, and Grandfather acquiesced.

"I discovered that small cats can be every inch as hurtful as big cats," he said, "because when your heart is vulnerable with love, even a fly with a mind to can break it."

* * *

After the cat-girl, the deer-girl and the swan-girl, Grandfather was more than ready to give up on dating altogether. But then one day he met the monkey-girl. On the whole, the island's monkey-people seemed a ridiculous lot. You'd see them at the bar, ranting and raving at one another and then, a minute later, weeping and declaring their undying love. They were so open with all of their feelings that it almost made you embarrassed.

Still, to their credit, they were more at peace with themselves than the other creatures of the island. They didn't have an inferiority complex about their animal side like the other creatures. They didn't seem to want to be human. They didn't like wearing clean clothes or the idea of having to live in a designated hut—or that when they decided to sleep on the beach, they were told to move along.

"She just loved me," Grandfather said. "She didn't care that my socks had holes in them or that I was broke. She laughed at all my stupid jokes and could never stand seeing me sad. It was really beautiful, something I had never had before."

She forgave him for everything. He wrote her a poem filled with spelling mistakes and she didn't care. He loved how she would look through his hair for nits. He had never imagined how intimate that could feel.

Grandfather told us that he knew pretty much instantly that she was the girl for him. And he realized that he wanted to go back home and start a real life with her in Montreal. Of course the monkey-girl was up for anything, and so she agreed to go.

"But . . . she was, you know, part monkey," I said.

"I didn't care," Grandfather said. "She was so pure. I think we humans have evolved into a stinking, unhappy, disagreeable mess. If there really was a Garden of Eden, then I think Adam and Eve must have been a couple of innocent monkeys madly in love."

When they arrived in Montreal, Grandfather taught the monkey-girl all about human society, even giving her the human name Margaret.

"Wasn't that Grandmother's name?" asked my brother, slightly alarmed.

"Shush!" yelled Grandfather. "I'm telling a story!"

Margaret didn't even have the natural sense of shame that full-fledged humans have about being naked. Once, on the island, she had come over to his house on a bicycle, wearing only a pair of underwear, a sweater and a pair of rubber boots. He had found it charming, but he also knew this wouldn't do, and so he showed Margaret how to act like a proper lady. He showed her how to cut her hair into a bob and comb it, how to bathe herself and trim her fingernails, how to put on high-heeled shoes and wear a scratchy wool dress-suit that limited the movement of her legs. He taught her how to type, make omelettes and use a vacuum cleaner.

They had a gay time too, going out to ballrooms and drinking till one in the morning. His mother was a little concerned that Margaret was too much fun, but he knew that she only had eyes for him. Everything made them happy: their little tiny house on Colonial Street, their first rickety car.

"And God rest your Grandmother's soul," he said. "She gave me so many good times, that woman."

"Grandmother—our grandmother—was the monkey-girl?" my brother exclaimed.

"Our grandmother was so not part monkey," I asserted. "She barely got off the couch. Remember once the remote control fell off the arm of the couch and she just left the television on all night?"

"Monkeys get old too, you know. And look at the two of you," Grandfather said. "Obviously part monkey. Do you think it's normal to tear around the house all day like lunatics? You can't sit down in class either. I heard it from one of your teachers. Terrible, really."

Then my brother started acting like a monkey, jumping from the couch to the chesterfield. And Mother came in and sent us to bed.

"Oh, leave them alone," Grandfather told her. "They can't help it. Throw them some bananas, or let them sleep out in the trees. It's cruel to keep those little animals inside. Send them back to the wild!" he cried as we climbed into bed and prepared ourselves for the jungles of our dreams.

THE STORY OF LITTLE O
(A Portrait of the Marquis de Sade as a Young Girl)

She had always been little for her age. That's why her grand-father Joe had started calling her Little O.

* * *

Joe would sit in the big armchair and Little O would climb up on top of him. It was the best place in the house to watch television from and they very much liked to share the spot. They sang along to the commercials. She loved when Joe sang while she was on his tummy. His belly would roll around and rumble and it made her feel as though she were on a life raft and the sea was stirring underneath her.

She liked when he would fill up the measuring cup of warm water and dump it on her head in the bathtub—like he was making a big pot of soup and she was the little dumpling inside of it.

When she would fall down and scrape her knee, Joe would blow on it. He used to give her a glass of milk anytime that she had a nightmare about there being a serial killer under the bed.

Joe was proud of her because she was so cute. He would put her in the grocery cart and all the people would stop him to say how beautiful she was. He loved it when people made a fuss over the baby. He would say she was his daughter. And wasn't she?

Sometimes Little O imagined herself growing inside an egg. It must have been a very big egg, like an ostrich egg. And Joe had come along with a little spoon and tapped the egg and she had come out of it.

* * *

When she was very little, Little O thought that everybody had a Joe the way that she had a Joe. He would answer all of her important questions. There was this deep dark hole in Joe's mind where all the answers to every question were. It was like when the shopkeeper goes to get something from the back, you have no idea how big it is. You can only imagine how enormous it must be to have every shoe size in the world back there.

What does a skeleton eat for dinner, Joe? What does a baby bat do if it is afraid of the dark, Joe? Are there mashed potatoes on the moon, Joe?

These were all things that Joe knew.

* * *

They had a stack of telephone books in the corner of the living room. She used a new one every year to sit on and eat
breakfast. Each was filled with pressed flowers that they had
picked up in the park that year.

* * *

Before long there were ten telephone books in the corner and
Little O still lived with Joe in the ugly little apartment on the
sixth floor of a building with no elevator. Joe had gotten more
and more overweight. It was too hard for him to go up and
down the stairs all by himself, so Little O would have to do
all the errands.

She bought him nine child-sized hamburgers on Mondays,
when they were forty-nine cents at the corner restaurant. They
were each wrapped in silver aluminum paper like tiny gifts.
He was always so happy to get those hamburgers that it would
make Little O want to cry.

Little O would sit next to him on her knees on the couch
and run the comb across his head. He very much liked the
feeling of it across his scalp.

He knew he had saved her. He had fed her with a tiny
spoon, out of tiny jars, even though she wasn't his. He had
changed all of her diapers. And so now she owed him things
and had to take care of him forever. He did not have to worry
about ever being alone again.

* * *

Little O never had any sense of decorum. She brought the garbage down wearing a pair of rubber boots and a really short nightgown. You could see her behind when she bent over. She didn't care and she didn't know why she should.

The mothers in the neighbourhood would have told Joe about how Little O was dressing inappropriately, but they didn't want to talk to him. He had been gruff and argumentative years ago in the grocery store. They could only imagine how crazy he had gotten after spending a year cooped up in that apartment.

What else could you expect from a little girl who had been abandoned by her parents and raised by her welfare-case grandfather? they thought. They hoped she would stay away from their sons when she got older.

* * *

She brought in Joe's welfare stub, which he had to sign every week, to the social worker. The social worker asked Little O if she was happy living with her grandfather, if she wouldn't prefer to live with some other girls her age. The social worker did not say what would happen to Joe, so Little O said that she and Joe were fine. The social worker said that she was sure there was a big apartment in heaven waiting for Little O one day. And that she was such a good girl.

* * *

When she was eleven, Little O sat on Etienne Metivier's couch, wearing a tie that belonged to his father around her neck. It made her feel fancy even though she was wearing a tank top with a number on it and jean shorts. She crossed her legs politely. He went and served her tea from a very elegant cup that his mother kept locked away so that no one except special guests could use it.

"Do you want to maybe go to the swimming pool later, sir?"

"That sounds like a good idea, sir."

"Very well then, sir."

It excited him that they were calling each other sir. He had no idea why. That's why boys liked Little O. She knew things that they would like before they did.

* * *

She went over to Scott LeDuc's house. He said that he had a whole basket filled with kittens under the kitchen table. She knew that he was watching her pet the kittens. He thought there was something so beautiful about the way she did it. When she whispered words to the kittens, it seemed strangely indecent.

"That's a sweet little pussy. That's just a lovely little glass of milk. Oh look at your little wee blinking, twinkly little eyes. Oh what tiny little raspberries for paws. Oh God loves you so much. Aren't you the prettiest thing that God ever did invent in his whole life? I want to keep you in my inside coat pocket for days and days and days. Until you are a little old lady cat. And listen to your mews! I am going to take you to have your mews recorded for a symphony orchestra. And we will tour Europe and drink milk out of teacups and take naps together and eat crème brûlée."

And then she scrambled out from under the kitchen table, shook hands with him and was on her way. He didn't even know what hit him. He sat right down on his ass on the kitchen tiles, no longer able to even look at the kittens. It was troubling to feel so much.

* * *

Little O noticed that boys noticed her. Although she didn't know why they did. She didn't have trouble attracting their attention the way some of the other girls did. When she would sense that a boy had fallen in love with her, there would be a peculiar feeling, a magical sort of lonely feeling. When you realized that someone was in love with you, you got to see yourself from the outside, just for a minute. You could finally have proof that you existed. You could look at yourself as though you were a fabled creature, like a unicorn.

* * *

She looked through Patrice's notebook that was filled with spelling tests. His talent for spelling was legendary in her class. On top of each page was a small star.

She couldn't imagine what it would feel like to have that many gold stars. The notebook was such a marvellous little universe of constellations. You couldn't see the stars in the sky at night in the city. If you wanted to look at some stars, you had to befriend a boy like Patrice.

* * *

She let a boy named Jesse hit her hands with a wooden ruler. Then they went into his kitchen. He put ice cubes in a tube sock and then wrapped it around her hands. He kissed her on the cheek and apologized.

* * *

What did Little O look like? She was pale and had long, dirty-blond hair. She had big cheeks that made her head look too big for her skinny body. She wasn't the prettiest girl in the class, but she would grow up to be. Somehow the boys knew this.

* * *

When she was eleven and a half, Little O found out about a gang of little boys that called themselves the Black Sparrows. The group was made up of seven skinny boys who all happened to be cousins. After school, they met in an apartment building that was made of orange bricks. She crossed the train tracks to go meet them.

They all squeezed together on the chesterfield in the living room as Little O sat on a wooden dining room chair, facing them. She said that she would like to join their gang. As an initiation ritual, she said she would have sex with all of them.

They sat there quietly, not knowing what to say. They were all too embarrassed to say anything. In fact they each secretly wanted to be thinking whatever it was that the others were thinking. It was the sort of thing that they had fantasized about before. But now that it was here before them, it seemed too strange.

Although they had all always found Little O to be very beautiful, they saw flaws in her appearance. They noticed that one of her stockings had slid down into her shoe and that there were permanent yellow stains in the armpits of her T-shirt. They noticed that she had a pimple on her cheek.

It turned six o'clock as they were all sitting there. The mother of two of the boys came into the living room and announced that supper was ready. They asked if it would be all right if they invited their little friend to have dinner with them. The mother looked at Little O and naturally she wanted to say no, but she said, "Fine."

Sitting around the kitchen table, the boys were suddenly happy. They had never felt so comfortable with a girl their age before. They felt the way that you feel after you have slept with someone for the first time and here they are in your kitchen the next morning. Here they are suddenly sharing your life. One of the boys had a sudden urge to put his head on her lap and weep.

When she laughed, she snorted. Now it was as if everything ugly about her was beautiful.

* * *

The sky became pink as the sun set, like someone had poured a packet of pink Kool-Aid into a glass of water.

* * *

She told the boy that he should go and get her a bottle of beer from his fridge. She said that he should take a deep, deep gulp and then kiss her immediately afterwards.

She asked him if he would like to watch her cry. He shrugged. She sat there for a while, looking straight ahead. But she could not make herself cry.

* * *

She would go to do the laundry late at night when there weren't any people there. When she opened the bags they always smelled so bad that everyone in the laundromat would turn to look at her. The owner of the laundromat would sometimes give Little O an extra quarter when she was missing enough change for her load. He told her he had never seen such a good kid who did so much for her grandfather. He told her that she was truly wonderful, as spotless as a clean sheet.

* * *

Little O was getting married in the alley. There were three brothers who lived on the third floor of the building who kept tossing garbage down on their heads—banana peels and stuff like that. All the kids that were attending the wedding turned their faces up to the heavens and yelled at them to stop ruining their fun.

The boy was wearing his Sunday clothes. Little O had a paper doily bobby-pinned to her hair and was wearing a long silky nightgown that went to the ground. She was carrying a bunch of bluebells in her hands, which she had plucked from the train tracks.

Most of the kids were there because they wanted to watch Little O and the boy kiss. Most of the kids were there because they wanted to watch them do something bad. They knew it was bad, but they couldn't figure out how bad it was.

The boy's name was Murray and Little O hated this name. She was chilly in only her nightgown. She felt as if the other children were nothing more than a mad, terrible little mob. They were like the exact sort of people that would turn up to see her execution if this were another time.

Little O wondered whether if in all her past lives she had been humiliated in public this way. It seemed entirely possible. Because the feeling seemed so familiar to her. It was as if she had been born to be humiliated. She wondered if other girls felt the same way.

The minister was a boy named Bertrand. He was wearing a tuxedo jacket from his clown costume from last Halloween. He had long bangs that he wore down over his face. He spent most of the time in public fiddling with his bangs. They were a great burden to him.

He gave a good speech though. Nobody knew the difference between really bad and really good, so they chose instead to think of it as magnificent.

"Here we are. We are together to mention the coming together forever of this man and this woman. Murray Estaban and Little O. They will always be together even when they are sick and they are old. They will have sex. They will be stuck being married by the power invested in God. You, Murray and Little O, may kiss and may the whole city of cities fall on your heads if you try not to be married."

* * *

There was a man who had a heart attack in Little O's building. Since he had no relatives, the landlord put his possessions into boxes and put them out on the street corner. Little O looked through all his things.

There were a lot of pots and pans and a box full of books. There was a big book called *The Joy of Sex*. She held it against her chest and brought it up to her apartment immediately. The couple in the drawings were her new secret best friends. She could look at them making love in ridiculous ways for hours.

She also found a sailor's hat that day that made the mothers think she was maturing too quickly for her age. They wished some sort of authority would take the girl away.

* * *

The mercury in the thermometer went down like the ink in the teacher's red pen as she wrote criticisms all over everyone's homework.

* * *

She was walking home in her underwear and a blue parka with a sheepskin-lined collar. She had lost her skirt in a game of strip poker. Why hadn't she thought to gamble away another article of clothing, like her gloves or her earmuffs?

* * *

She asked Luke if she could watch him pee. But he couldn't go while she was watching.

* * *

When she was twelve, in Grade Seven, she was the only girl who wasn't dressed up for picture day. She had a white button-up shirt with a tie that you pinned on. She had on a pair of jeans with big holes in the knees. Perhaps she was dressed up.

There had to be one child who was a sacrificial lamb, one who all the mothers looked down on in order to raise their own child up on a pedestal. And that was Little O. Mothers loved it whenever their children came home with news about the terrible situations that Little O had gotten into.

They pointed out to their husbands her terrible outfit in the school photo and said they would never let their kid have their picture taken like that.

* * *

Little O went with the grocery cart to return all of Joe's empty Pepsi bottles. Because it put him in a cheery mood, Joe's favourite thing was to drink Pepsi. The store owner handed Little O the change and let her choose a chocolate from the fishbowl on the counter. She always chose the mint one. When she bit in, it was like there was a piece of winter hiding in the middle. The owner felt guilty that that was all he could give her. He had never seen a child who went about her errands so effortlessly. He told his wife that Little O would be a saint in two hundred years. His wife rolled her eyes.

* * *

A group of girls sat on the swings in their skirts. They looked like bells ringing back and forth.

Little O never hung out with other girls. She didn't know what had happened first. Had they started rejecting her or had she decided that they weren't worth her time? There were times when the boys wanted nothing to do with her. There were times when they needed her to leave them alone.

* * *

She went into the secondhand store. She tried on a pile of underwear and some bras in one of the changing cabins. She felt happy. She was all alone with her reflection and she felt as if no one else in the world existed. She knew what the reflection was going to say. It was sweet and kind and said, "I love you."

* * *

She didn't want to go home because Joe was in a foul mood. She wandered around and decided to stop into the pet store. The boy who worked there was the son of the owner. That's why he was able to be there by himself. He sometimes let her sit next to him behind the cash register. It made her feel as if she was his wife.

She imagined him standing in front of the stove, heating up a can of pasta for the two of them to eat. They would laugh about who had the idea of making pasta into the shape of trucks. Their lips would get a pretty orange colour from the toxic tomato sauce.

You could hear the doves cooing in their cages. Little O thought they were making the sounds of babies crying. They made her think of her own future little baby that she would treat so well. She would be so good to her little girl: she would dress her in fancy baby clothes with frills and buy her those hard cookies that are impossible for anyone other than a baby to bite into.

* * *

She gave the boy across the street a haircut. All the tufts of hair fell down around him, like some birds had been shot out of the sky and now were falling and falling. It looked terrible. And later in life, when women were yelling at him that he was a loser, that he wasn't any good, that he didn't do anything for anyone on earth and that he had never come close to making anyone happy, he would close his eyes and remember this haircut.

Because it was when he was having this haircut that he had been able to know for absolute certain what it was like to feel free of doubt.

* * *

Little O refused to be ashamed of the fact that she put her hand under the covers and touched herself. She imagined the security guard at the department store making her go into the backroom and have sex with him for stealing a pair of neon shoelaces.

She would not be one of the cowardly girls who said that it was only men who were dogs, that boys were perverts, that men couldn't be faithful. Because these were wonderful attributes. They belonged to people who would not be judged by their imperfection, who knew that this was merely one small part of their identities.

The ones who weren't afraid of others knowing that they were perverts were the ones who were going to rule the world. Little O would not be chaste.

* * *

Mrs. Thibault came home one afternoon and found Little O tied to the tree in her yard with a skipping rope.

"Will you please untie me?"

She untied Little O and she walked away without looking back. Mrs. Thibault wanted to ask her so many questions. She would have to spend the rest of her life wanting to ask Little O those questions. There were questions that she would never know the answers to.

* * *

Little O brought Joe's awful black cat to the vet. It was always messy-looking and out of sorts, like a kid that had just had a turtleneck pulled off its head. Her arms were covered in scratches and the scrawny cat hissed at everyone. The vet asked Little O why she didn't go ahead and have the crazed animal put down. Little O said that it made Joe happy, and the vet saw that that was the most important thing for her. He gave her the flea medication for free and called her Mademoiselle Teresa.

* * *

Little O told Zachary that if he put money into the photo booth, she would take off all her clothes and let the camera take pictures of her in the nude. You could hear the machine gulp as it swallowed each quarter. He could see half her naked body beneath the curtain as the flash went on and off. He thought that he was going to faint.

* * *

Little O and Jack were doing their homework for art in the library together. He was obsessed with grey pencil crayons. He thought that real artists didn't use bright colours. He showed her how he was colouring in a tree all grey.

Little O agreed with him that it looked much better that way. She would go along with every wrong little idea that a boy would have. She did this because she was encouraging them to follow their dreams, however idiotic those might be. She liked stroking their tiny egos. This is what women were supposed to do. They were supposed to believe in the dreams of their men as if they were God.

Jack suddenly loved Little O madly. It was the first time he was falling for this stupid pleasure.

* * *

Sometimes she wanted to live on a little planet where she was the only girl. On this planet, she would have seven husbands. They would be so demanding that she would have no time whatsoever for herself.

She would have seven beds to sleep in. Very much like Snow White and the seven dwarfs. She would have so many dishes to wash. She loved washing dishes in the evening.

* * *

She liked to read *Tintin* comic books. She imagined Tintin telling her that he loved her passionately. She pictured taking off her clothes on one side of the bed and Tintin taking his off on the other. She and Tintin would be dressed in under-clothes and stand at the sink, brushing their teeth together. She imagined them both looking in the mirror—giggling at finding each other in the reflection together.

* * *

She let Tobias draw all over her arms and legs with a ballpoint pen. He drew everything that he knew how to draw until she was completely covered. He illustrated her with panthers and ninjas. She liked the way it felt. As if he was a doctor with a scalpel slicing through her anaesthetized body.

"There!" he said, when he was done. "Now no one will have you except for me. Now no man will look at you."

* * *

He went into the pantry and gave her a can of No Name diet lime soda even though he knew that he wasn't supposed to give these to his friends. She slurped from it while trying not to get the carbonated bubbles up her nose, making an awful lot of noise with that can.

She told him that he must be a millionaire because he had a chandelier in his living room. His family lived in a four-

and-a-half in a big building and the chandelier came with the apartment. It was small and made out of brass and some of the lightbulbs didn't glow.

He wondered if it was true. Maybe he was rich and he didn't even know it. Everybody was envious of him, but he just hadn't noticed before. Little O told him that she didn't love him for his money though; she loved him absolutely for himself.

The mother thought about how Little O was unsupervised all the time. She knew where her child was at any given time during the day. And there was Little O, sitting in their living room with nobody in the entire world having any idea whatsoever where she was. The world simply couldn't work that way. It would all run amok. It was like a social experiment that was going to lead to bloodshed or total chaos. The mother looked at Little O as though she were Robespierre, with her skinny legs crossed on the couch.

* * *

When asked if she needed anything, Little O would always ask the social worker for something for Joe. He needed a walker to help him get from the couch back to bed. She knew that Little O couldn't help but be anything but selfless. The social worker put together a bag of things for Little O all the same one day. She gave her a pair of used ice skates and an empty notebook with a photograph of a horse on it. Little O smiled and said, "You shouldn't have." The social worker almost began to weep.

* * *

They were selling aluminum balloons that had roses on them. Little O had terrible taste. She always went for that sort of thing.

* * *

Little O was sitting and peeling a hard-boiled egg on the steps of her building. The boy in Apartment 12 came and sat down next to her. She told him that her grandfather was from a little village outside of Poland and that if a little boy and a little girl sat across the table from one another and ate hard-boiled eggs, then they would be married.

* * *

The little children were all coming from a festival in the park. They had butterflies and cat faces painted on. They lived in a completely different world than she did.

* * *

His mother had a huge pitcher of water filled with slices of lemon in the fridge. It weighed about as much as a bathtub at the bottom of the ocean.

They went and looked at the strange and beautiful and mysterious things that his mother kept at the bottom of her underwear drawer. There was a pack of playing cards with naked men wearing construction helmets and firemen hats. There was a lozenge container full of pot. There was a package of specialty condoms.

It was strange that adults all had sex. It was strange how appalled they were about the idea of young people having sex. Why that of all things?

* * *

Joe would never actually be able to go in for a parent–teacher interview and they had no telephone. So Little O photocopied the report card and gave herself all As. The whole night he talked about how she had inherited her smarts from him and that he had raised her right. He had tears in his eyes. Joe put his arms around her. Her face was damp with his tears.

* * *

Little O and Guy were sucking on jawbreakers. Their tongues were changing colours inside their heads.

* * *

She went to the zoo to feed the elephant peanuts. When its trunk gently touched her hand, it always turned her on.

Many of the animals were fed from baby bottles. She thought there was something wrong about that. They couldn't have liked being treated like babies. She didn't think that there was anything worse on earth than being treated like a baby and having food shoved down your throat all the time. It was rubbing the fact that they weren't free in their faces.

One of the zookeepers knew her. He told her that when she was eighteen, she would come to the zoo and he would make love to her. Would she like that? he asked. Yes, she said.

* * *

She went and sat on a stool at the Chinese restaurant that was on the first floor of her building. The stools were covered with red vinyl and little tiny gold stars. The placemats had drawings of fancy goldfish on them. The place was filled with the late-night crowd. She sat there in her pyjamas and watched the television that was above the cash register. The owner always gave her free soup and fortune cookies.

A man came in after a hockey game and lit up a sparkler. He waved it over his head in the restaurant. Everyone laughed. Little O put her hands over her head as if it had just started to rain.

* * *

She wanted to know if she could come over and they would read *Slaughterhouse-Five* together.

* * *

She put a balloon under her T-shirt. Taking his hand and placing it on her belly, she asked him whether or not he could feel the baby kicking.

His mother watched them out the window. Of course she was going to end up being pregnant young, the mother thought. There was no way around it. She did not want her son involved in that. Little O would ruin the future prospects of whichever boy got her pregnant.

The mother couldn't believe that she was having those kinds of thoughts. She blamed Little O also for putting such terrible thoughts into her head. She really hadn't known that she was that type of person until Little O came along into her front yard.

* * *

There was supposedly a little boy who lived in that apartment building who could sing Elton John songs really well.

* * *

He was wearing a pair of penny loafers. There was a penny in one of them. The other one seemed to have disappeared.

* * *

She took all her clothes off and weighed herself on a scale in her bathroom. She liked that she was skinny. She didn't know why she was proud of the fact that she was thin, except that it was the type of thing that girls were supposed to feel accomplished about. The other girls would point out in an admiring way how skinny she was.

* * *

Little O had to put Joe's socks on for him and then take them off. Sometimes Joe was afraid to tell Little O how much he needed her. Because he thought that if he did, she would pack her suitcase with clothes and climb out the window and run away. So he yelled at her out of desperation. The logic of love is often incredibly faulty. Love has a lot of trouble making sense out of anything.

Joe screamed at Little O that she had gotten the groceries all wrong. He told Little O that she never did anything for him. He said that she was a useless little girl and that other girls helped their parents out around the house.

Little O knew that Joe didn't really mean it, but it made her cry all the same. She went down to the stoop to cry all by herself. The tears streamed down both of her cheeks as though her eyes were broken faucets. A neighbour stopped to look at her on his way up the stairs. He had never seen eyes so blue. It was as though he were witnessing a miracle.

* * *

She climbed into the bathtub. The water rose up around her. She pretended that she was the moon making the tide rise.

* * *

She climbed up his fire escape. The cats in the windows raised their eyebrows in surprise as they saw her go.

* * *

They decided to have phone sex. She went down to the lobby and dialed up. He could hear the echo of the lobby as she talked. She stopped for a moment because someone came in. It was Mrs. Foucault from Apartment 7. By the time she was done asking Little O what she was doing there, he had lost his erection.

* * *

He had his plastic wristband from the amusement park on his wrist from eight months before. Holding up the scissors from the kitchen, she said that it was time to let her cut it off. The scissors made the sound of a guillotine's blade descending. He felt completely naked after she snipped.

* * *

The winter wind blew the last orange leaf off the tree just like it was blowing out the flame of a candle.

* * *

Little O and Joe put on paper crowns at Christmastime. She had a yellow one and he had a purple one. They watched the show about Rudolph. She ate her fruitcake out of a soup bowl with a spoon. It had started snowing outside.

* * *

The big red pompom on her knit hat looked like she had an apple balanced up there and she was waiting to be shot by William Tell.

* * *

She didn't know how she felt when a dodge ball hit her hard.

* * *

The man in Apartment 6 used to open his door and look every time she passed. It was that kind of building.

* * *

He had a calculator on his wristwatch that he was wearing over a tattoo of a tiger that was half scratched off. They were sharing an armrest and his wrist was coming awfully close to hers.

* * *

She was reading a paperback book called *Calories*. It gave you the amount of calories that an apple or a piece of pumpkin pie might have. She was tearing through it as if it was an engaging spy novel.

* * *

His mother called him Bird affectionately.

* * *

There were naked girls all over the city. They were in bath-tubs. They had just been made love to. They were in tiny changing rooms with dresses all over the floor around them, like cherry trees that had dropped their blossoms.

* * *

Her smooth white stockings made her look like candy canes whose red stripes had been licked off.

* * *

She rode this ten-speed bicycle that was too big for her. Sometimes she fell over when she was trying to get off it. It had belonged to Joe when he was much younger. He said that it was a top-of-the-line bicycle that Olympic cyclists in France used.

* * *

She was trying to blow bubbles out of a bubble wand with some dish soap. The bubbles kept popping automatically. She had wanted to bring things of wonder into this world.

* * *

When she was thirteen, she put on a pink velvet dress to go to a bar mitzvah. She had a card with a Star of David and fourteen dollars in it.

There was a long table with little boys in suit jackets eating hot dogs. One boy had a burgundy-and-yellow-striped turtleneck under his band jacket. He had a single mom.

There were paper napkins with Hebrew letters written on them. There was a band dressed in black tuxedos that glittered. She hoped that they would play "Billie Jean" by Michael Jackson. That song always made her want to cry, even though she had no idea what it was about.

* * *

She sat on the pee-stained couch at the Salvation Army and read Harlequin novels. Sometimes there were horror novels. She would put a bookmark in the book and put it back on the shelf and hope that no one would buy it.

* * *

She liked paper dolls when they were in nothing but their underwear. She didn't know why you were supposed to put those awkward dresses on them.

* * *

She said that she wished she could meet a man who was as sexy as Felix the Cat.

* * *

She liked when boys wore their grandfathers' hats. It was as if an old man had wished to be young and got his wish.

* * *

The nurse had to show Little O how to help Joe with the oxygen mask. The nurse told Little O that it was a tragedy that she had to live this way. But she didn't do anything about it.

Little O stood under the forty-watt bulb in the lobby. The landlord was too cheap to pay for a one-hundred-watt one. It made the lobby look dim and golden. The nurse reflected that the girl looked like an angel in an oil painting that she had seen in a museum. The nurse couldn't stop herself from kissing Little O on the forehead and said that she was an angel.

* * *

When she started Grade Ten, there was a new boy in her class. They made each other laugh in chemistry lab. They liked all of the same television shows. They both thought it might be kind of interesting to be movie stars when they grew up. They both liked crossword puzzles. They agreed to disagree about music.

She went out with his family to the chicken restaurant. It had a blue neon rooster that blinked on and off in the window. There was wood panelling on the walls and fairy lights along the edges of the ceiling.

They had paper napkins with red flowers on them. They had alcohol wipes that smelled of lemon for you to clean your hands off with when you were done.

There was a jukebox, and the mother gave them a quarter to put in it to choose their song. After dinner there was a scoop of vanilla ice cream floating in the big glass of Coca-Cola, like it was waiting for the *Titanic* to hit it.

Little O didn't feel as if there was anything wrong with her. She wasn't tiny. She wasn't poor. She didn't live in a dirty apartment with a grandfather who made her sad.

The boy and his family had mistaken her for a regular girl. And if she could fool these people, then she could fool the entire world. And then it occurred to her that maybe they weren't mistaken at all. Maybe she just happened to be a very ordinary little girl.

THE SADDEST CHORUS GIRL
IN THE WORLD

Before Forester came into their lives, it had been just the two of them. Violet and her mother lived in the east end in the comfortable squalor of their apartment. There were mauve flowers on the wallpaper, and the arms of the couch had been destroyed by a cat named Charles. The east end was known as a squalid, poverty-stricken area of town, but Violet adored the place. She found odd things beautiful instead of ugly. On her way home from school every day, she passed a liquor store that had a handsome gargoyle of a curly-haired baby above the door. She was in love with him.

It was 1922 and Violet's mother had a job teaching French to some rich English children in Westmount, the very fancy area of town. She was supposed to take the children to the park and point out all sorts of things and tell them what they were in French. This was the lovely idea. But she mostly ran after the children saying, "*Non, non, non.*"

Violet's mother dyed her hair a terrible shade of red. She

had a navy blue coat and her shoes were scuffed. The poorer they were, the fatter Violet's mother became. She would eat a huge piece of cake at the café and then she would feel weak. The doctor told her that she should eat healthier, but she said that really it was her only pleasure.

Her mother was so soft and fat that you always wanted to lean against her as if she was a pillow. She made everybody in the room lazy and sleepy. That's what people liked about her. And she laughed at every joke. She would start laughing sometimes and people had no idea that they had said something clever. Her blue eyes sparkled when she smiled widely and her face seemed so beautiful and full of life for a brief moment that you felt it was a shame she had married so poorly.

Her mother had always drunk a lot. But Violet didn't mind it. Especially when they had lived alone in the little apartment in the east end. Then her mother would lie on the bed with her eyes closed, saying sweet things under her breath. Her words almost sounded like she was talking in her sleep. She would say half a sentence and then she would only mouth the rest of the words.

"My darling pretty little cupcake. Little Valentine sweet wee little anemone of the deep blue ocean," she would say.

No one could come up with compliments like that. They were the prettiest things about Violet's childhood. Before Forester she had always slept in the same bed as her mother.

Violet's mother would have her come and meet her at work whenever she was in trouble with her boss or when she wanted a raise. She knew that Violet could beg without ever saying a word. She knew that Violet was capable of making people feel ashamed. People were afraid of her big brown eyes. She knew that Violet was her winning lottery ticket. She really was an extraordinary child.

They rode the trolley all the way down Sherbrooke Street one afternoon to her mother's work. Violet loved that ride. She stuck her head out the window and she felt so free. That's what everybody in the world wants, isn't it? To feel free? That's what Forester stole from them: their freedom.

Usually after Violet met her mother's employer, they would have a healthy bonus in their pockets. They often went to the museum. There was a painting that the mother liked to look at because she swore that it looked exactly like her when she was young. Violet didn't really believe it. Today, she took her mother's hand. They went to a pretty café by the museum to drink *chocolat chaud* to celebrate. Everything in the restaurant was painted gold. Even the chairs, even the tables, even the hanging lights. There was a vase on the table with a white tulip in it. The bulb of the flower looked like a naked girl sitting on a bed with her arms wrapped around her knees.

Violet was wearing a white shirt with a black tie and a pleated skirt that went down below her knees. While they were seated in the café, Violet took out a book of poetry from her pocket and began to read aloud. Her mother couldn't listen to a single page without starting to nod off. The milk in her mother's coffee looked like a swimmer doing a lazy breaststroke.

That's how Forester found them. Violet saw him first because her mother was asleep. She thought Forester was ugly from the moment she laid eyes on him. His cheeks sagged so much that they looked like jowls, and they were covered with acne scars. He had black hair that was thinning on top, and he put black powder on his scalp to hide the bald spot. He came right up to their table to talk to her mother and her.

"Do you find the service slow at this restaurant? I do believe that the waitress takes my order and then goes in the back and writes a chapter of her memoir before returning."

The waitress seemed to know Forester well and she hooted at his joke. Violet's mother, who was wide-awake and flirtatious and happy now, also doubled up at what Forester had said. He was the type of man that could make women laugh. He had a sparkling wit. It made people forget his appearance and get excited anytime he walked into the room.

He insisted that Violet and her mother order whatever dessert they wanted from the menu. When her mother couldn't decide which one she wanted, Forester insisted that they order all of them. It was clear that money was no object to him. Violet's mother half-believed that they were in a dream as she sampled each of the desserts.

Violet had a chocolate egg covered in pink frosting on a plate in front of her. Forester looked at Violet and the chocolate egg with more desire than she could possibly understand at her age. When Violet bit into the egg, he looked as if he could taste it.

She blushed when their eyes met. Forester couldn't stop looking at Violet. Violet knew that it was love at first sight. She knew that it was because of her that Forester married her mother.

* * *

Of course Forester had an enormous house. He lived in a three-storey stone fortress in Westmount. It was on the hill, and there was a garden with pink hothouse roses that looked like cancan dancers lifting up the fronts of their skirts. There were birds on the wallpaper in the living room. Violet wished that she could scream at the top of her lungs and startle all the birds so that they would fly away.

Forester thought Violet was unbearably lovely. He had needed her to belong to him in some way. If it couldn't be as a lover, because she was only thirteen, then at least she could be his daughter. Once he met her, he could never not have her in his life.

At first, Forester tried everything to be nice to Violet. He gave her the prettiest room in the house. She left her clothes all over the floor and wouldn't let the maid in. He hired an artist to paint her portrait, although she refused to smile. He enrolled her in Miss Laymore's Finishing School for Girls, although she was largely a truant.

Violet flinched whenever Forester came into a room. She blushed when they made eye contact. He thought that she always looked at him with disgust. He found it insulting. Why couldn't he simply go to the breakfast table and sit down and spread some jam on a piece of toast without being looked at with utter contempt?

It was ridiculous because he had climbed so high up in the world that surely he was now above the girl and her mother. They were penniless. He was a wealthy man with many, many friends. In fact, his friends had warned him about getting involved with the pair of them. You cannot help drowning people, he was told, because they will only drag you down with them.

Violet knew that Forester always thought that they were supposed to thank him for having rescued them. But Violet didn't feel that they had needed to be rescued.

When he complained to her mother, the woman would weep and weep and say that she had no power over the girl whatsoever and it wasn't her fault. One night there was a huge row because her mother asked her if she would put on a little dance number the way she used to in the little apartment in the east end. How stupid her mother was! Of course she wouldn't dance in front of Forester.

Forester picked up an armchair and threw it at the wall. Violet just stared at him.

Violet wasn't the only subject that Forester and her mother fought about. They were always fighting. He berated her for hours when they returned from going out on the town. He complained that she embarrassed him, that she came across as ignorant, that she told off-colour jokes and that she ate like a pig, that she was too friendly with the waiters and she came across as a slut.

He said her English was awful. He said that he couldn't believe that he had ended up with a woman like her. He said that he was certain that all his friends could tell only by looking at her that she had a history. He said that they must be shocked, because surely everyone expected him to end up with a girl from Westmount with a similar background as him. Surely everyone expected him to end up with a girl with class.

Her mother mostly countered his accusations by sobbing. Every now and then her mother would let out a greater cry. As if this was some sort of defence. As if this was the only way that she knew of fighting back—by being weaker. And begging for pity.

"I know I'm a cow and a bore, but can't you please forgive me? Can't we somehow get along? Please don't yell at me anymore."

Violet was not allowed to come out of her room while they were fighting. Violet sat in her room, listening to his awful insults coming through the wallpaper.

* * *

Violet became prettier and prettier. At seventeen she had developed an elegant body. She had lovely new breasts that slung down in her dresses, and her legs were so long that she was always folding them in intricate ways so that people wouldn't trip on them. One afternoon, Forester walked into the kitchen and found Violet sitting at the table, reading a book. She had on a little squashed black velvet hat with an enormous ostrich feather sticking up from the front of it and a long black coat that went down to her feet. The cat leapt up on the table. Violet put the book down and held up a tiny ribbon and dangled it in front of the kitten's face, making it dance about. He could not believe that she was more adorable than even a kitten.

He didn't know why it bothered him. He didn't know why he wanted to reach across the table and slap her face. He was more and more outraged with her for reasons that he couldn't put his finger on. He didn't even know how far his thoughts about her would go, because he always stopped them. That infuriated him too: worrying about what was in his own head. And then he blamed her for this too. If she had made more of an effort to act like his daughter, then he would have thought about her more naturally as though she were his child and not a beautiful stranger.

Her mother would beg and beg and beg Forester to give her more money to buy Violet pretty clothes. The mother didn't insist on any other sort of frivolity and was considerably less expensive than his previous wife had been, so he gave in once in a while. He would give her money that should have been enough for at least three or four dresses, but then they would spend it all on a single pink hat that turned up in the front. Of course it was a splendid hat. He had trouble looking at Violet when she wore that hat.

All these ridiculously splendid hats that he had paid for. Did she say thank you to him every time she left the house looking so pretty?

He knew that all the other girls would probably hate her because of those outfits. What was the matter with her mother? She was unhealthily obsessed with everyone finding her daughter attractive. She didn't trouble her daughter to learn any other skill. She didn't suggest she read or go to school or even have any manners or bloody well go and get some exercise.

It seemed to Forester as if Violet did nothing except day-dream. The way that he remembered it, she only seemed to want to go out for walks when it was raining. Quite possibly so that she could catch a cold or some snivels so that she would have an excuse to lie in bed and nap in the middle of the day. She was able to stay in her room for hours and hours at a time because she liked to read. She had little piles of books all over her room. After she read them, she laid each one down as though it were a brick in a wall that she was building.

* * *

Forester was screaming at the maid one day for breaking a vase. The young girl sat in a corner of the staircase later, crying. Violet looked at her and thought she and her mother also had a job. He was their boss too. They were expected to earn their keep like the servants. The maids had to scrub the floors, and she had to adore him. Violet had to be sure not to appreciate anything that Forester gave her. As long as she refused to get one shard of pleasure from anything in this world, she didn't owe him any love.

After her mother had a heart attack in the bathtub one evening and was buried in a fancy cemetery on the mountain, Forester kicked Violet out. He didn't want to have anything to do with her. He was glad to have his revenge. He let her take the clothes. He didn't want to have any reminder of Violet hanging around. Anyway, she would certainly see how far her pretty clothes would take her now. She would probably end up selling them to pay her rent.

Forester knew that Violet could easily get a rich man to fall in love with her and take care of her. But he also knew that Violet had terrible taste in men. She couldn't stand him, after all. She would be attracted to her own idiotic kind, back in the east end. What a fool, he thought, someone who wants to move down in the world.

And suddenly, watching her go, Forester was filled with a terrible longing for her. She was the great love of his life, and it had been an unrequited one.

* * *

Violet took the trolley to the east end. She had hardly ever gone down to this part of town since she and her mother had left it. There was no reason to. You didn't come to this neighbourhood unless you lived here. Forester hated this part of town and could never forgive Violet's mother for being from the east end.

The streets were narrow and were still cobbled. The buildings were tall and had black soot stains on them. A woman who looked impossibly tired passed Violet. Her mushroom hat was down over her eyes and her coat was old. Her four children followed after her, holding one another's hands. They all had short, stringy blond hair like milkweed pods that had just split open. The whole family looked messy and malnourished.

Violet was shocked at how squalid it all was. For a minute she saw it through Forester's eyes. But this quickly went away.

She went to stay at the Eiffel Tower Hotel. It was a skinny grey stone building with stone roses framing the big wooden door. The carpet running up the stairs had red and yellow flowers on it. The concierge seemed a little surprised to see such a refined-looking eighteen-year-old girl checking into her establishment. She looked Violet up and down. Violet had on a top hat with a blue veil and a pretty white collar around her neck.

It's because of my clothes, Violet thought. I am dressed like a very rich woman. Perhaps she thinks that I was kicked out by my lover. Perhaps she thinks that I am the type of girl that entertains men until they tire of me.

She felt more at home in this hotel room than she had during all the years she had spent at Forester's house. The hotel seemed so familiar. It was because she somehow knew that she would be spending the rest of her life inside these hotels. She also intuited that more concierges would judge her. She would come to learn that if you ever enter a hotel and find a concierge that does not judge you, then you know that you have died and that you are in God's Hotel.

The wallpaper in her room made her sad. But at Forester's house, the wallpaper had also made her sad.

* * *

She got a taste for travelling from reading books. She had no idea how a girl was supposed to go anyplace in this world if she didn't have a cent to her name. As she walked downtown, she saw the posters that were advertising different acts coming to Montreal from all sorts of foreign places. They travelled all over the world and they had roots nowhere.

Violet went to see a friend of her stepfather's named Mr. Bertrand a week later. Bertrand had come over to their house for dinner several times. Each time he hadn't been able to keep his eyes off her. This was a strange basis for believing that you could go to someone for help, but it was all she had. She went to the office where he worked as a barrister on St. Jacques Street. The secretary supposed that she had to let the girl in.

Bertrand was surprised to see her.

"I have been thinking that I might like to go on the stage," Violet said. "But I need some money for dancing and singing lessons, you see."

Bertrand looked her over. She had a brown derby hat with a little rim and a giant brown and purple ribbon tied up in a great bow on the side. Her brown jacket matched it perfectly. She looked like a beautiful lost schoolgirl. Women would probably want to be cruel to her. But why shouldn't they be? What right did she have to go about acting like it was criminal not to do something for her? What right did she have to sit there asking to be saved? Perhaps she had practised having that woebegone face since she was a child. And now her entire life was going to be shaped by that expression.

"Can I at least hear you? Will you sing for me?" Bertrand asked.

Violet sang with a bit of hesitation in her voice—the way that we sound after we have been crying for a spell and are no longer sad, but our body, for some reason, does not want to give up crying yet. He couldn't even quite make out the words as she sang. She sang as if she was doing something that was completely humiliating. She sang as if she was standing there naked.

Maybe men in the audience would like that, Bertrand thought. Some of the men definitely would, anyway. They would look at her and they would feel as if they were degrading her. As if they were talking her into doing something that she didn't want to do.

He was suddenly afraid that someone would walk in and see him having this girl sing and dance in his office. And what would they think about him offering her advice? They would think that he must frequent nightclubs. They would change their opinion about him and he would never, ever be able to make them change it back.

He gave her some money to take singing lessons, feeling that he had played a part, although he wasn't at all sure why he had to play a part at all. He didn't think she would spend the money on singing lessons. He thought she would just use the money to survive a little longer.

* * *

But despite this prediction, Violet did spend the money on singing lessons. She auditioned for an American touring company when it was putting on a show in Montreal a month later. The director didn't know quite what to think of her either, but he thought she was beautiful enough to take a chance on. He told her to pack her bags and that she could be a member of the chorus line. Getting an opportunity because of her looks gave Violet the feeling that she had begged for it. But what were her options? She put her fancy clothes back into a suitcase. The motley company travelled on a train from one little town to another.

The girls stood in a row with their identical blue dresses and headbands with silver buttons on them. They tapped their feet and blew kisses at the audience. The sound of the taps hitting the floor sounded like a knife being sharpened.

They sang a song about being flowers. Or something so stupid that Violet thought it was practically criminal. She wondered if wondering this while she was dancing affected her performance. Women were all made to be idiots one way or another, there was no way around it. In each town, the seats were filled with people who dressed and talked like Forester.

There was a popular act in which the chorus girls dressed up like sailors. They wore white top hats and bathing suits with small white sequins. Cardboard clouds dropped from the ceiling and a huge fan blew their curls about wildly. There was a big metal drum that someone pounded when they needed thunder. A girl named Rose would roller-skate around the stage with sparklers in her hands, representing lightning. She always had burn marks on her wrists.

Violet didn't care what anybody said: nobody sang in the rain. They were each given an umbrella to hold over their heads. What bad luck! she thought. What bad luck!

A girl named Lily got a starring role. They dressed her up like a peacock, literally. She had all these tall peacock feathers sticking out of her ass and a little tuft of black feathers on her forehead. She sang a number about being vain and about how all the boys were wild about her.

Lily had only been doing the act for a week and men were crazy about it. Here was a woman who was telling the truth about her sex, they thought. Finally a woman was admitting that she was vain and stupid and mean. Women got what they had coming. They deserved to be beaten if the beef bouillon wasn't ready when their husband walked through the door.

Petunia dressed up as a black cat and did a ballet number on pointe shoes. Violet liked her. Petunia always fell asleep as soon as the train started moving. She would fall right to sleep with her head on Violet's shoulder. And she would wake up with her curls all over the place, looking like she'd come from toppling down a hill. It reminded Violet of her mother.

Petunia told Violet that she liked to be beaten by a man she was seeing. Everyone else thought that Petunia was so pathetic to stay with such a brute. But Violet didn't find her so at all. Once when Petunia came back from visiting the man, she took off her clothes so that Violet could look at the red welts all over her body. How extraordinary, Violet thought. To have a beau who was so honest about his hatred of you that he would just go ahead and pound you senseless.

There was a girl named Iris who liked to sit and complain about everything. She thought that she had the best singing voice in the whole company.

She said that the director kept her in the chorus because he was terrified of her. Because she would be better equipped to run this company than he was. So he had to keep her down.

Iris wore a black velvet jacket and a little black top hat perched at the side of her head. She looked regal, but not in the way that women tended to look noble—all otherworldly and painfully aloof. She was carefree and arrogant and bold—she was noble the way that a man was.

However, Violet preferred the company of the girls who were as terrified as she was. She and Petunia shared a room together in the hotel. It was a tiny room with blue striped wallpaper and a sad little chair in the corner with roses on it. There was a framed drawing of a nightingale over the washstand.

The moonlight lit up Petunia's body. It made her look like she was made out of smoke. They fell asleep with their arms wrapped around each other: the prettiest girls in the world.

* * *

Violet was well liked by the other girls. With her big, dark eyes, she would take in every word they said. The girls had been taught that other girls weren't important and that real life only happened when you were with a man. What was the point of talking to another make-believe person like themselves? But Violet was sad when the girls fell in love. She thought that each of them was in full bloom, and when a man plucked them, they would start their decline.

There were men in the audience who had come specifically to look for girls. They had wallets that were fat with money. They drove big cars and ordered tremendous meals for themselves. Were you to be chosen by one of these ostentatious fellows, you would have a marvellous life. You would take on their last name. Your new life would begin the moment that they married you. You could forget all about the grungy little childhood that you had come from. That was really the point of all that dancing. When they were up on stage under the spotlight, everyone in the room was able to stare and stare and stare at them.

The girls, on the other hand, because of the glare from the footlights, were not at all able to see anyone in the audience. Everyone in the audience was a complete mystery. Nonetheless, Violet knew the faces of all the men in the dark. Each one of them was Forester looking at her, wanting to own her.

There were some other really very pretty girls who didn't have a whole lot of talent but who had such big smiles and radiated such happiness that their joy in itself was a spectacle. Violet felt so much disdain for the men in the audience that it reflected in her dancing.

* * *

Violet liked to read on the train. And she liked to look out the window at all the trees and the strange houses in the middle of nowhere and the animals in the backyards. The cows and horses looked like little toys that she could reach out for, pluck from the earth and stick in her purse. She had signed up for the chorus line in order to be independent. She had a vague notion of what she wanted, which always seemed to be slightly beyond her reach. She spent all her time with her head in the clouds, trying to figure out just what that might be. She felt lazy and restless because there was something that she was meant to be doing that she just wasn't doing. The piles of books she always had with her sometimes aided in distracting her and holding her attention.

The other girls taught her to drink gin and that helped too. She thought that she became an alcoholic the very first time she had a drink.

When she drank, her mood was like a firecracker that lit everything up, and when it passed, she knew that the whole world would seem darker than it was before. She would be utterly miserable when that mood passed. She kissed one of the girls on the lips. She threw her arms up in the air. She could tell that girls fell in love with her as much as men did.

She ought to have known about drinking, shouldn't she? She didn't blame it for her mother's poor health. She didn't believe it could kill you. She thought it was only a fairy tale that you could drink yourself to death.

Violet tried to think of other ways that she could kill herself. A dancer in the company named Daisy told her that chorus girls all thought about killing themselves. She shouldn't pay any attention to those thoughts when she had them. She shouldn't go around telling anybody that she was feeling suicidal, because nobody felt sorry for chorus girls. They were pretty—what more could they possibly want?

But the more she drank, the sloppier she was in the chorus line. Her dance steps were off only by seconds sometimes, but the chorus was so synchronized that any tiny uncoordinated move made the whole production seem shabby. Suddenly, instead of looking like perfect and happy angels, because of Violet's mistakes they all seemed to be flawed. They seemed mortal. You could see that they had personalities and that they were anxious and desperate and tired.

The director grabbed Violet by the wrist and pulled her out of the line one day and took her aside. He asked her what on earth was wrong with her smile.

"Are you deliberately trying to be the saddest chorus girl in the world?" he asked.

Violet stood there in her see-through minidress and her sequin-covered high-heeled shoes, not knowing what to say. She hated herself for wanting to cry. Sometimes she thought that that was all she was going to amount to: a puddle of tears.

* * *

At times there was nothing Violet dreaded so much as the future. Why on earth did she take this job? It was ridiculous. What would she do afterwards, once she retired and her reputation was ruined?

There were two ways to leave the chorus line. If you had dignity, then you would get engaged to a man. You would give your notice. There would be a little farewell party for you backstage. Each of the girls would give you a flower or some other incredibly cheap, incredibly beautiful parting gift. You would all drink some wine and then you would disappear with all your things stuffed into your cardboard suitcase, like a big shot.

Or you could leave after being called into the office and told behind a closed door that your time with the company was over. Here is your last cheque. Please don't sit on the stairs outside the office and weep. Try to control the sort of look that you're going to have on your face as you leave this place.

The second was the way that Violet assumed she would leave. She had always had so much pride—but still she sought out humiliation. She would be a chorus girl until they wouldn't let her be a chorus girl anymore. Until they kicked her out, like Forester had done.

* * *

In every city where they played for more than three nights, Violet would fall in love with a different man. She belonged to a certain strange subspecies of man. She was attracted to men who were still children. She liked men who didn't make a fuss when you didn't clean up or when you were too drunk to wake up. She admired others who were half-asleep and living in a dream world, just like her.

There were certain men who lasted longer than others. There was Alexander, a dashing fellow who played the piano and toured with the troupe. She never knew when Alexander was going to show up. That's what she liked about him. He would climb up the fire escape to her hotel room in New York and knock on the window. He would have to be very quiet because she didn't want the concierge of the hotel or the director of the company to know that she had a man come spend the night. Although they probably guessed it, she wanted to keep them guessing.

She was so happy when he would creep in through the window and come into her bed. Their happiness was so rich because they knew it could never last. It had all the same effects on the body as suffering. They lay in bed after making love, completely stunned, as if they had been dealt some terrible, terrible news. Their love was like a death in the family.

"I like the way you break my heart every night around nine p.m.," she told Alexander while they were in bed one night. "You are the most dependable man I have ever met."

"Violet, you're too crazy for any man."

Alexander was looking for a rich woman. He was sick of poverty. He told Violet one day that he had gotten an heiress pregnant and that he was going to marry her. She closed her eyes so that she didn't have to see him walking out the door.

Violet's mother had liked ugly, mean men. There was nothing that she could have done about it either. Life is too short for us to fix our flaws. By the time we realize what fools we have been, we are, unfortunately, already dead.

But Violet realized that her taste for handsome, feckless men would end up giving her as much trouble as her mother's tastes had given her. The handsome men she dated were terrifying. They were so light that any wind might blow them away in another direction. They could disappear over a weekend. At least the ugly, mean men Violet's mother had dated had been able to put a roof over their heads. At least they had been able to take them out to restaurants and buy them enormous pieces of steak and great glasses of wine.

Maybe it was because of Forester that she was attracted to shiftless men. She blamed Forester for this too: for sticking her with his opposite.

* * *

The other chorus girls said that it was a pity she didn't sing well. It meant that you were expendable, that your position in the line was vulnerable, and that you didn't have a future. It was 1929, Violet was twenty and she was beginning to feel old.

Then the troupe was going back up to Montreal. She didn't like the idea of it because of the possibility of seeing Forester and his friends, but she did long to see home again.

The winter wind knew that Violet was coming back. The sky was holding its breath, and when it saw Violet step out of the train station, it finally exhaled and beautiful snowflakes began to fall. Children all over the city were noticing the gigantic snowflakes that were stuck on their mittens. They had been specially designed to impress Violet. The winter wanted Violet back.

She went for a walk in the east end. The gargoyles wanted to crawl right down off the buildings and put their arms around her. She was the only one who had loved them and who had thought they were beautiful. She was the only one who had chosen this neighbourhood over Westmount.

She walked into a small tavern with a blue door that she and her mother used to go to. She sat down on a chair at a table in the corner, but before she had even managed to settle in, a person had sat down beside her. It was a young man with fair hair who held her hand and kissed it and introduced himself as Pierrot.

The other chorus girls said that Violet fell in love for stupid reasons. This was true. She fell in love with Pierrot because he whistled when he got dressed in the morning. He had the intelligence and mannerisms of a very polite eleven-year-old boy. They went for a walk in the park and he walked on the cement border around the pond. He started swaying uncontrollably, as though he were about to lose his balance and fall in. Violet stood with her arms out as if to catch him, laughing and yelling.

Pierrot was broke and came to stay with Violet in her hotel room and ate her food. The other girls in the chorus were shocked by this. Violet said she didn't mind at all. He kept telling her that he was going to come into loads of money, but she couldn't imagine how. He said that he was waiting for his partner to come to town so they could make a venture together that was guaranteed to make him flush.

She just thought that Pierrot was a big talker. She liked men who made plans that they never followed through on. This might seem like a trait that was impossible to admire, but Violet liked it. It was as if he were a little boy who was making plans to be a knight and an ambassador.

"Let's try to keep secrets from one another for as long as possible," she told him one night. "That way, things will always be romantic."

"Of course, my wonderful girl."

But then one night she came home and Pierrot told her

his venture had been successful. They went out and ate steak and potatoes at a fancy restaurant. He was able to pay the rent for that month. She stopped working as a chorus girl. All the pretty girls stood in a row as Violet bid them goodbye at the train station. She kissed Marigold, Tulip, Magnolia, Pansy, Daffodil, Petunia, Rose and Lily adieu. And then she stayed in Montreal for good.

For a month or so, things went really well for Violet and Pierrot. He bought her some pearls. Every time she wore those pearls, it started to rain. One night Pierrot was arrested and a detective came to see her and said that the pearls were stolen. So she gave them back.

She went to see Pierrot in prison on Sundays. It was a three-hour ride and it was an expensive ticket. They had cut Pierrot's blond hair short and it made him look older. He had a lovely last name: Bazil. She might like to have a name like that for her own. She hated having her father's ugly last name. He was the one who had started this dying business in her family.

"Will you write to me every day?" he asked.

It was the only promise to a man that she ever kept, but she found that she didn't do it out of obligation. She liked writing these sad and joyful letters that were filled with lies. She had a strange, funny sort of inkling that it was the one thing she was good at. She felt that she had an ease with writing that she didn't have with tap dancing or singing or trying to twirl a baton. When she would sign her name at the bottom, she would have the feeling that it was the only thing she knew how to complete.

Was a piece of paper with a daydream transcribed on it any more concrete than the daydream itself?

What would she do with Pierrot once he got out of prison? He would have no money. Does it feel better to have someone with you in a lifeboat when you are cast away at sea?

What would she do now? It was the end of the 1920s, and the Depression had hit. The company would never let her back in the chorus line. Perhaps she would end up working in a strip club with pink sequined butterflies on her nipples. What did it matter? And what on earth would happen to her when she was too old for even that? Well, that would have to end up being a good thing. It would! She was a prisoner to her youth. When she finally wasn't young anymore, she wouldn't be dependent on it. She would be forced to find her own way in the world.

But in any case, Forester still hadn't won. She would continue to hate Forester until her very last day on earth. That was the one thing she knew about herself. That was the one thing she would remain true to.

HEAVEN

Grandfather claimed to have been dead a few seconds once, when he was nine. The story went that he'd been so cold in his house that he froze to death in the middle of the night. Lucky for him, his mother had been boiling water for tea and porridge early in the morning and had come in to wake him when she did. Seeing that he was blue, and that his hair was frozen and sticking straight up, she put him in the bathtub and covered him with tea and hot water and she yelled for all his brothers and sisters to come and rub his fingers and his toes. And finally, he came back to life.

"Impossible!" my brother would scream when my grandfather told his tale.

"It's not impossible at all," Grandfather would counter. "You get perfectly preserved when you're frozen. They defrost cavemen all the time. Even after five thousand years. The scientists buy them a fashionable suit, take them out for a steak dinner, and they're as good as new."

My brother and I believed that my grandfather, as he

often did, had mistaken something he'd seen in a Hollywood comedy for real life.

Just the same, the time he had died was far and away one of Grandfather's best stories.

* * *

Grandfather had no idea what actual heaven was like because he had never gotten that far. He just knew about the train ride there. You see, according to him, when you died, you ended up on the platform of a huge railway station. There were thousands of cars, such an impossibly long line of them that you couldn't even see the last one. He said you don't realize how many people die in a single morning until you're dead and standing in a crowd among them. He said the crush of people was worse than Coney Island on the Fourth of July. The conductor had to make many stops at many platforms so there wouldn't be a stampede.

He said the year was 1942, so a lot of the adults showed up in terrible shape. Especially the soldiers, who were missing limbs and drinking from metal flasks. A soldier in a wheelchair was softly asking an angel if there was any way he could get his legs back, and the angel told him it wouldn't be a problem once he got to heaven. Then he safety-pinned a little blue card to the soldier's jacket that read "URGENT." Quite a few people had these cards pinned to them, and despite all their infirmities, Grandfather said, they were the happiest-looking people he had ever seen.

* * *

The angels sorted through everyone, rushing about and chain-smoking cigarettes—for as it turned out, in heaven, smoking was good for you. They gave all the children first-class tickets that allowed them to ride in the cars at the front of the train. There were hordes of children too, Grandfather said, as children died all the time back then. They were all dressed in the tuxedos and little white gowns that their mothers had dressed them in before laying them on the living room table and weeping over them. They held the flowers placed in their hands when they were laid to rest, and their hair was combed neatly to the side. Grandfather met a child who had drowned who kept making sudden panicky swimming motions before realizing that the struggle was over. There was another child who had died in a fire who kept coughing up smoke. But other than that, they were an entirely well-groomed bunch, and they filed onto the train in a well-behaved manner.

Animals got to go to heaven, too. There were cows and chickens and pigs everywhere. They were put into the same cars as the children, to cheer the children up. All these wheezing geriatric cats were there and an elephant that was being led by an angel.

The angels yelled at the kids, "Move along, move along. Nothing to see here." The elephant received its own compartment, as did a giant squid. There were compartments that were huge aquariums filled with fish that had passed away, and as Grandfather walked along the platform, he could see them swim by through the train windows.

One little boy with two black eyes was leading a swan around by a belt that he'd looped around the bird's neck. There was an ostrich speaking Russian to another little boy in black boots, who kept responding, "*Da, da, da,*" while nodding his little head, for in the afterlife, animals and humans can talk to one another.

There was a lone cheetah that came and sat in the same compartment as Grandfather, and the cheetah spoke in Polish and Grandfather realized he could speak Polish too. It seemed you could speak any language you wanted after you died and were on your way to heaven.

The cheetah had been to heaven just last month when he had died of dehydration in Kenya, but then he had been resuscitated by a sudden rainstorm, only to be trampled to death by a pack of stampeding wildebeests a few weeks later. He already knew what heaven was all about and so was offering tips.

As the train began to move, the cheetah told Grandfather that heaven would be fine if not for the angels.

"They're a brash bunch—so full of themselves," said the cheetah. "And no people skills at all." He said it was best to completely ignore them.

All over the tracks were feathers that had been shed from the wings of the angels who ran the operation. They pulled out business cards that said things like "Ezekiel, angel extraordinaire, right arm of the Lord's wrath."

"It's useless making conversation with them," said the cheetah. "Angels have too many anecdotes and never let you get a word in edgewise."

Later, Grandfather watched two angels discuss the Battle of Bosworth, and what a jerk Richard III had been.

"A mediocre monarch at best," said one angel, "and at night, under the blankets, a big fat blubbering crybaby." And in response, the other angel laughed.

* * *

Some of the angels who carried trumpets opted to ride on top of the train. Grandfather said you never really heard the trumpet until you heard an angel playing one. All through his life, Grandfather collected records of horn players, always trying to find that wondrous sound again. There was a recording of a Hungarian Gypsy trumpet player that came the closest, and Grandfather would play the scratchy record over and over with his eyes closed.

One of the clipboard-toting angels climbed into Grandfather's car at one of the stations and offered him a cigarette. That's where he claimed to have picked up smoking. He handed Grandfather his file, which covered his good and bad deeds. But, said Grandfather, it was virtually impossible to decipher the texts that angels wrote. It was like reading footnotes. They were overeducated because they had been alive so long, and their written assessments of people looked like equations that were too complicated to follow. As a result, all of your good deeds became almost indistinguishable from your bad deeds. And in the end, it didn't matter, because everybody got to go to heaven anyway. God loved and wanted everyone. For Him, you were as innocent as the day you were born. Grandfather was certain of this because at each stop, murderers stood on the platforms weeping as they confessed their crimes out loud. Some of them felt so guilty that they didn't even want to get on board to go to heaven. But the angels patted their backs and whispered things in their ears that only made them cry more. And eventually, they got on board.

All that we'd learned about the rules of good and evil was finished with. Grandfather said that, as it turned out, our souls were bigger than all of our deeds, and after life was over, it was finally freed from all that we'd ever done.

* * *

At the next station, Grandfather saw that there was an angel on the platform that all the other angels crowded over by the window to look at. They whispered that it was Lucifer. He was wearing a top hat and had blond hair down his shoulders and in his coat pocket was a book by Nietzsche. Lucifer called out loudly that he was glad he wasn't aboard that crowded train.

Lucifer walked up to Grandfather's car as it sat by the platform and took a marble out of his pocket. He held it up for Grandfather and the other children to see. There was a tiny trout swimming around in it. The children gasped in amazement and Lucifer winked and put it back in his pocket. He took off his top hat and shook it, causing a hundred doves to fly out, and all the children applauded.

An angel shrugged. "If you think he's impressive, wait

until you meet God. Lucifer's fun to hang out with for a while, but you get tired of all that hocus-pocus stuff."

And Grandfather believed it, too, because as they rode along, nearing their destination, even more wondrous things began to occur.

Grandfather opened a book that was lying on the seat beside him and he found he could read. This despite never being able to keep up in school. Grandfather never got a single word right on spelling tests. He had started skipping school and he had come to believe that he would always be an idiot, but here he was, reading. It was such a beautiful feeling that he put his hand up to his mouth and laughed out loud.

As the train moved farther along, the doll that the girl next to him was holding began to speak back. The doll asked for a little something to eat and an angel offered her a cookie. Another girl reached into her pocket and pulled out a red mitten that had been lost for months. Her grandmother had made such a big deal about her losing it, too. And another little boy, who had always been afraid of the dark, began to emanate light.

Outside the windows it started snowing and one of the children put his hand out the window and declared the snow to be as warm as bathtub water.

"Which one of you silly children wished for this bit of nonsense?" yelled an angel through a bullhorn as he watched the snow accumulate on the tracks. "You must wait until heaven before you start making your wishes. All that you're doing now is making a big mess and delaying the schedule."

The cheetah addressed the presence of the miracle by explaining to Grandfather that creation was easier in heaven, as you could have whatever your heart fancied. On earth, God had made sure that no one would have that power but Him. But in heaven, the angels were always pitching their preposterous ideas—new creatures that would give humans a run for their money. For instance, one angel, he'd heard, had recently proposed a tiger that was five times the regular size and came with opposable thumbs.

"Get out of my office!" God had yelled at that angel.

Suddenly, Grandfather saw that outside the window of the train, the snow had been replaced with balloons—thousands of red, blue, yellow, green and orange balloons descending slowly from out of the sky.

"One more wish," cried the angel through his megaphone, "and so help me God, I'll turn this train right around!"

* * *

Then as the train began its departure from the final station, a hobo carrying a small bundle in his arms came running along the platform. The hobo jumped onto Grandfather's car at the very last minute and squeezed in between Grandfather and the cheetah. He placed the bundle he was carrying gently on his lap and pulled back the blankets to reveal a tiny baby's face. It was smiling peacefully even though its cheeks were blue. The baby couldn't have been more than a few minutes old.

As soon as they were settled in and the train began to

move, the hobo and the baby continued a conversation they seemed to have been in the middle of. The hobo was asking the baby what it was like to be in the womb.

"You don't remember?" said the baby. "How could you forget such a thing?"

Everyone in the car got quiet, because they too wanted to hear what it had been like in the womb.

But how could the baby explain it to them? How could he, having only lived a few minutes in the world, compare it to anything on earth? But the funny thing about the train was that not only could you speak any language, you suddenly knew the exact words to explain things, too.

There were always the right words. All you had to do was close your eyes and they would come to you. The baby closed his eyes and read the hobo's mind and described what it was like to be in the womb in a way that the hobo would best understand.

Grandfather said he read the hobo's mind as it read the baby's mind, and what he read was this: "It's a warm feeling like when Maria put her hand on your leg and then left it there the whole assembly. And how nobody knew it was there. It is like the first time you drank a bottle of warm beer on the beach and everything made you laugh. And you rode back to the city in your uncle's car and you were squashed in the backseat with five cousins. And everyone was squeezed in so tight in the car that when someone laughed, you all jostled. In the womb, you hear people talking and their voices sound like someone you're in love with talking in their sleep."

Grandfather said that in that moment, everyone realized that the baby was not only describing the womb, but was also somehow describing heaven.

Everyone understood it in their own way, and for Grandfather it would be like the time a lady from his church made him a whole box of candied apples to take home. And how he hurried home with them, thinking about his brothers' and sisters' faces, how they'd look when he opened the box and showed them that there were enough for everyone.

All the passengers were waving their handkerchiefs as they neared the gates of heaven when suddenly Grandfather was back in the world, alive, his mother and siblings pouring cups of Earl Grey tea onto his face.

"And it's a good thing for you too," Grandfather told us, "because otherwise, you'd never have been born."

"But that story's really hard to believe," my brother said, and I nodded my head in agreement.

"That's exactly what the cheetah said happened to him!" shouted Grandfather. "He wasted his breath trying to explain what went on above to the other cheetahs, but no one believed him." Grandfather then shrugged his shoulders, leaned back in his armchair and left it at that.

THE DREAMLIFE OF TOASTERS

In the year 2089, due to unprecedented advances in the field of bioengineering, androids were invented and introduced into the general population. From all outward appearance, they seemed to be exactly like people. But although their cognitive skills were similar to those of humans, they were unable to experience the same feelings and sensations. Most emotions were deemed unnecessary for their specific function in the world, so rather than possessing the regular gamut of human emotions, they were instead endowed with an innate amazement at mathematical problems and repetitive actions. For this reason, to them, working in factories, laboratories and engineering plants was most enjoyable, and because of their contributions, the human workday was reduced from eight hours to two.

Androids were made with better eyesight than humans so that they could work on the tiniest computer parts. A side effect of this provision was that when they looked up into the sky at night, they were able to perceive thousands more stars, thousands more configurations and astral phenomena than the average human eye could ever discern. And so when they walked at night, they could not help but look up into the sky and marvel. In fact, this became the easiest way to tell an android from the general human population. Androids were the ones on the street with their briefcases dangling at their sides, staring up at the stars in wonder. For this reason, androids were not given driving licences. It led to too many accidents, this ability to be struck by perfect things.

* * *

In the summer of 2112 a female android named 4F6 stopped on her way home from the pharmaceutical factory and stood looking up at the stars above. As she looked, visions flashed before her. She imagined the stars were a group of ancient coal miners with lamps on their hats, being lowered by elevator into a deep dark hole.

Imagining in this way was not typical of robots; but 4F6 had known she was different from other androids for a long time. Once, at rush hour four years ago, she had been shoved to the subway tracks by accident, and as she hit the rail, an electrical current surged through her. Since that time, her electrical currencies had always been too high.

She had already experienced some peculiar side effects from her accident. She was able to turn on lightbulbs solely by looking at them. And unlike other androids, she was able to tell what was funny. She was forever explaining jokes to the androids she worked with, but they couldn't understand at all. To them jokes were merely equations with slightly incorrect answers.

As she was standing there, peacefully looking up at the stars, she realized that another android in a tweed suit was standing right beside her, also looking up at the night sky.

Naturally, they introduced themselves. Androids were always very cordial and polite as it greatly increased workplace efficiency. 4F6 liked BX19 immediately. She liked his brown eyes and his pale skin. He told her that he worked transcribing trials at the courthouse. He began to repeat verbatim one of the cases he had sat in on that day. A man was on trial for murdering his ex-wife's new boyfriend. He had strangled him with his bare hands and now showed no remorse. Then he told her the story of a man who had robbed a convenience store and only got away with fifteen dollars and had subsequently been sentenced to fifteen years in prison.

4F6 was moved by these stories. She had never had anyone say such things to her. The only kind of talk she heard was from the androids at the pharmaceutical factory, who only spoke of formulae and the table of elements. All this talk of murder and love, to her, was like poetry.

Somewhere within 4F6's circuitry there stirred a desire to reach out and touch BX19. Androids often mimicked human behaviour out of curiosity. They had, of course, tried kissing and lovemaking, and certain androids claimed they had felt something, but it was the general consensus that they were unable to feel anything at all while engaging in such human activity. 4F6, herself, had never been kissed before, but now, for the first time, she wanted to be.

"Please kiss me," she said.

BX19 leaned over and did as he was told. He was being polite, but when his lips touched her lips, 4F6's heart felt like it had dunked into her stomach. When that happens with humans, it is merely a sensation, but with an android, every emotion has a definite mechanical reaction. Tiny wires and bolts fell from inside her chest and into her stomach. 4F6 felt the metal parts moving around in her belly. But later that night, lying in bed, the discomfort she was feeling in her stomach was the furthest thing from her mind. She replayed the kiss over and over, until her short-term memory projector snapped off as she drifted into sleep.

* * *

The next morning as 4F6 was gaining consciousness as she lay in bed staring at the ceiling, she felt something fall between her legs. She pulled off her blankets and rummaged through the sheets, searching for the errant part. Suddenly her hand touched something cold and metallic. She pushed away the blankets and there, wrapped in her bedding, was a tiny stick-like figure. 4F6 was horrified.

Its skeleton was made of wires and tiny screws and bolts. It had a tiny spring for a spine, and small frayed, spliced wires grew out of its head like hair. It had tightly wound wire for a neck, and where a heart would go there was a tiny valve that looked as if it could be cranked. The little thing started to move its arms in the air over itself. It was obviously some sort of android, but it didn't look human the way other androids did. No skin had been grafted onto it.

The little thing looked at 4F6 through the holes in the minuscule bolts he had for eyes. There was an awful darkness and limitlessness to those eyes.

She realized that it was a baby, her baby, conceived from her kiss. The gestation period for the tiny robot had only been a day. She had never heard of robots making robots—perhaps on a factory assembly line, but never without being told to. Never in a bed, and never as the result of a spontaneous kiss. 4F6 knew that something horribly wrong had happened.

Although androids didn't really know what it meant beyond the softer skin and crooked teeth, they somehow wished to be human. They considered themselves inferior and tongue-tied around people. Whenever they saw a human, they couldn't help but think, He invented me. Humans did not know what their origins had been. They believed in God and searched for the meaning of life in the Bible. Androids, on the other hand, had no Bible. The closest thing they had to a Bible was the original grant application that requested funding for robotics research. Every android had a copy of this proposal. It was a bestseller among androids. It said that the applicants of that grant would like to create a robot capable of operating all of man's other inventions, thus reducing the workday. There was never any debate about the origins of existence or the meaning of life among androids.

But now this baby robot had been created by some unknown force, independent of man. 4F6 knew that this would not be taken lightly.

She knew that if the scientists found out about the baby, there would be a mass android recall. They would tamper with their insides, making sure that no other android would be capable of experiencing love as 4F6 had, because it was love that had created the little spring man, she was sure. They would take away androids' ability to be amazed by stars, too, for good measure, and 4F6 didn't want to be without those parts. Without those things she would only be an appliance—a machine.

She wrapped the tiny robot up in a sock and put him in her briefcase. She called work to say that she would be a little late that day because she was going to stop at the Android Servicing Unit to be recharged; but instead, she took the bus all the way to the edge of town.

When the bus reached the end of the line, she walked down an empty street, and as she walked she convinced herself that what she was about to do was necessary for the safety of androids everywhere. It was not an easy task, this convincing. 4F6 was programmed to know when to yell and when to whisper, when to fuel up and when to rest; but in this matter, she was not at all certain what she knew at all. Had anyone been watching her, they would have seen a woman walking along haltingly, as though looking for a street address she was not certain existed.

She had been to the dump before. She had enjoyed estimating how many pieces of debris were contained within each pile, but she was not interested in that today. She had no desire for calculating. She took the baby robot out of her briefcase and threw it over the fence onto a heap of garbage.

That's where it belongs, she thought. It was junk, a broken, incomplete thing.

She repeated this idea to herself over and over as she waited for the bus, boarded it, and returned to work.

Several years earlier she had had her temperature regulator exchanged. In the moments when she lay on the metal gurney, her chest plate opened, the old part removed and the new part not yet inserted, she had really felt fine and complete. The little wire thing that had fallen from her was not even half the size of the temperature regulator, yet back at the factory assembly line, as she stood making calculations on her clipboard, she had the sensation of being empty. As much as she considered it, it did not make any sense to her. Yet there it was.

* * *

At the dump, there were seagulls circling above and crying out as though in pain. The tiny robot, lying on his back, wished that one of the birds would swoop down and pick him up in its claws, because he wanted so badly to be held; but the seagulls seemed interested in everything in the dump except him.

As it started to get dark, the little robot began to feel more and more alone. He stood up on his feet, which looked like tiny salad forks, and stumbled over the garbage. He passed a used shoe, piles of books and tin cans, and green metal chairs and couches with cushions covered in coffee stains. Then, among all of it, he saw something that comforted him: a toaster, lying all by itself. The robot hurried over and wrapped his arms around it, circling its electrical cord around his body. He lay there, entwined with the toaster, and in this way, he tried to assure himself that, somehow, he was loved.

When the stars came out, so numerous and fantastic, the little robot was so struck by the utter mystery of being alone that he forgot, at least for those moments, how painful it was.

As he gazed up at the stars, he was struck by quizzical thoughts, thoughts that, could he articulate them, might take the form of such words as *Why am I here? How big is the universe? Why am I me and not someone else?*

Although androids all over the world were coming up with an infinite complexity of answers, the little robot was the first to ask a question.

MESSAGES IN BOTTLES

There was once a boy and a girl who were twins. They lived in Montreal. Their mother was a famous cellist. She composed a tune so complex that no one could play it except for her. Their father was a famous physician. He had invented several unsuccessful treatments for polio. But unsuccessful treatments were all the rage back then.

They were serious children, as the children of eminent people so often are. They practised sitting utterly still, in case they ever needed to have their portrait painted. They were able to walk all the way to the park with ten library books on their heads. They were able to use big words that they themselves didn't know the meaning of. When they sat down to eat, there would be eighteen different forks and they used each one correctly. At ten years old, they worried about death. They never made small talk.

The twins both did very well in their classes at school, and their jackets were covered with little pins for punctuality and attendance, as though they were war heroes. If the children weren't geniuses, then at least they comported themselves as if they were.

In addition to their reserved disposition, the twins were known for their beauty. They had black hair and pale skin, which had the effect of making them both look uncannily like Snow White. People who manufactured cracker boxes were always trying to get them to pose for them.

One day in 1913, the twins' parents were invited to attend the World's Fair. Their parents made the children pack their very best clothes and they boarded the Stromberg ocean liner on the dock in Old Montreal on a cloudless afternoon. The circular windows were in a long row on the side of the ship as though a child had tried to multiply a million times two on a blank sheet of paper.

It was a famous ocean liner. Back then ocean liners were like movie stars. No one ever thought that this particular ship would sink, because so many famous things had happened aboard it. A Bulgarian prince had committed adultery in one of the cabins with a young girl. A French philosopher had composed a text so difficult that no one had even been able to get through the title.

The shipwreck made headlines all over the world. It turned out that the lifeboats had holes in them from termites and they simply sank. Down went all the tea sets and half-written novels and brand-new suits to a watery grave. It was a terrible tragedy.

It was reported that there were no survivors. The twins, however, were saved from the wreckage by climbing onto their mother's cello. The cello made such a mournful noise as it rode over the waves that a whale fell in love with it.

After three long days at sea, they were washed up onto the shore of a deserted island.

For the first night all the twins could do was sit on the beach and feel homesick. They missed going to the zoo. They missed a cat named Clyde. They missed their mother and father. They even missed their classmates and going to school.

The twins had been taught to never sulk and to always be industrious. The next day they began collecting oysters. They opened each one up and peeked inside. By the end of the day their pockets were filled with pearls. They strung the pearls into a long necklace that resembled a diagram of the moon's phases. They traded it with a pelican for some fish to eat.

The next morning an old turtle stopped by the island. He was brilliant because he was two hundred years old, and he was able to give the twins lessons in philosophy and morality. He came by every morning and in that way, the twins didn't fall behind on any of their schooling.

Sometimes sea creatures tried to seduce the little girl. She was much too dignified to encourage any of them. The octopus would sneak up onto the beach and place his tentacles around her neck. It felt like she was being kissed by twenty lips at once. It made her feel so strange that she blushed and told him to please return to the bottom of the sea.

The clamshells opened and closed like the eyes of an ingenue blinking slowly at them. As if they were flirting with the children.

Sometimes swans would show up, having heard from birds that the girl was unbearably lovely. The swans were used to being the prettiest creatures on the sea and they, therefore, would go out of their way to the island in order to convince themselves that she wasn't all that. The girl fell in love with a terribly handsome male swan, but he mocked her affections when she confessed them. With its little Zorro mask, the swan turned his head up to the sky and laughed, which sounded like a bicycle horn being squeezed. She wept at his insensitive response.

The girl wondered if they spent their whole lives on the island, whether she would have to marry a walrus. They were respectable and dependable. They wouldn't cheat on you. But it would be a loveless life. Some of the swans told her that it took seven years to learn to love a walrus. After that, though, everything was okay. More or less.

The twins saw so many sunrises and sunsets. They watched them as if they were at the theatre. Sometimes they found them so silly that they wept. Sometimes they found them so sad and powerful that they wept too. The sky dressed itself up in a new, fabulous outfit each night before heading off to a nightclub.

One day a current passed by that was filled with the tea that had fallen off a cargo ship en route from Sri Lanka. The twins dipped their teacups into the water and had a tea party. They stayed up all night, alert from the caffeine.

They cast a net in the water that night and pulled in a load of starfish and empty bottles. Lazy pirates, who had no consideration for polluting the sea, would finish their bottles of Coca-Cola and beer and then toss the bottles overboard.

The girl sat by moonlight and wrote letters on the backs of musical scores that were inside the cello case, in order to stick them inside the bottles. She began filling the bottles with letters every night and then tossing them into the sea to be found.

She would sometimes write descriptions of their adventures. She wrote down observations they had made about marine life, and facts about never-before-seen creatures. She also included long descriptions of loneliness and isolation, knowing that these would be valued by the new science of psychology. Like every writer, she felt absolutely sure that her readers were out there. Every night she implored them not to forget about her brother and her on the island.

The boy also wrote letters. He used ink from a murdered octopus and the quill of a pelican to write them. His were chastising letters, remonstrating that people had not found and rescued him and his sister. He sometimes called his readers terrible names.

The boy's personality was coming undone very quickly. He was getting wild. He was killing more fish than he needed to eat, and he wore a necklace of shark teeth. He stung himself with jellyfish every night because he liked the paralysis and numbness. He practically glowed because he had electrocuted himself so often. He harnessed the electricity from a jellyfish in order to light up blowfish and use them as patio lanterns.

Some nights there were terrible storms out at sea that

would frighten the twins with their violence. The following morning all sorts of things would have washed up on shore from the different shipwrecks.

One day a telephone washed up on the beach. The twins were ecstatic. The girl called home, but there was, of course, no answer. She called a friend from school named Antoine, and they talked for three hours. She called the police station in Montreal. The officer on the other end of the line told her that he couldn't possibly imagine where this island might be. Therefore, he couldn't send his men out to rescue them.

They used the phone for a month, but then the line was cut, since there was no way for them to pay the bill.

One day a queen-sized bed with a golden frame washed up on shore. The twins decided to climb onto the bed and sail off on it, hoping to encounter another ship.

The bed was at sea for a number of days. One day they passed a swan with a monkey playing a banjo on its back. The twins stood on the edge of the bed with their hands clasped together in supplication and implored the monkey and the swan to help them. But the swan and the monkey did not even deign to turn their heads as they continued on their way.

The full moon was laughing at the twins as they sailed on their bed across the Atlantic Ocean.

After their sixth day at sea, the twins awoke to the sound of an ocean liner blowing its horn at them. They scrambled from underneath the covers. They changed out of their pyjamas and made the bed as quickly as possible. Then they stood up on the mattress and held their arms up in prayer, begging the mariners to take them aboard. Naturally, they were granted voyage on the *Moby Dick*, which was on its way to Europe.

It didn't take long for the crew of the *Moby Dick* to realize who the young castaways were. The captain telegrammed ahead to say that he had rescued the famous young authors of *Les messages dans les bouteilles*.

The bottles filled with the twins' letters had washed up on the shores of little resort towns outside of Brighton. Whenever a new message was found, it was printed in the leading Paris and London newspapers. A collection of the messages had been published as a book and received almost universal acclaim. The critics said that longing and loneliness had never been so heartbreakingly captured and in so pure and simple a form.

Their book had become a bestseller. It was translated into thirty-six languages and was awarded the Prix Goncourt. Lovers gave each other copies for Christmas. An old lady had her favourite of the messages carved as an epitaph on her tombstone and there was one embossed on a plaque in front of the library. Even children loved the stories and their mothers would read them the letters as bedtime tales.

Children would weep in their beds at night because they wanted so, so much to rescue the twins. There were funds collected to help the search at sea for the mysterious tiny island that the twins were stranded on.

Upon arriving in Europe, the twins discovered, much to their surprise, their widespread renown. A huge crowd of people had gathered to witness the arrival. Many people had taken their own children out of school that day. Every single person stood on their tippy-toes in anticipation.

The crowd was carrying gifts for the twins: new clothes, expensive toys, piles of books, notebooks and pens. They were given, altogether, eighty-nine puppies. They were given a pretty house to stay in.

Their publishers were eager for them to go on speaking tours. But they felt like just not saying anything at all for the next few years.

Now that they were in Paris, the twins didn't write anymore. On the island, they wrote because they thought it would rescue them. They wrote their letters to prove somehow that they existed. Their letters had a theme. They knew what was wrong with their lives and how it could be fixed. As there was nothing missing from their lives now, why should they write?

The twins settled in Paris, taking up residence in a little house on the rue de Cherbourg. The boy filled his bedroom with his eighty-nine puppies. He was rumoured to own 345 pairs of shoes, all very fancy, with ruffles and buckles. Some had bows on them that were like Kleenex half-pulled out of boxes. And yet, even with all these shoes, he found himself leaving his room less and less.

The boy would get love letters from little girls. The perfume from all the love letters was so overpowering one day that it made him faint. Wearing a hat and sunglasses, he went for walks down the street, but he would invariably be recognized. He had a different girlfriend every night. Each one sillier than the next. Each one wanting simply to say that she had dated the famous co-author of *Les messages dans les bouteilles.*

The boy found that he was angry with everyone and preferred drinking champagne at home by himself. He would sit on the side of the bed and try to untie his shoelaces, but finding it impossible, would fall back and pass out for days. The mattress rocked back and forth beneath him as though it were being carried along by waves.

With her impeccable breeding and manners, the girl was a hit in Paris and the city was enchanted by her. A song inspired by her was sung in all the taverns, and there was a dessert named after her. Everyone wondered what she was thinking. Once someone took a photograph of her sitting by herself on a bench and it was in the newspaper the next day with the heading, "What is she thinking?" By walking down the street and sighing, little girls tried to emulate her. Smiling went out of fashion.

She could never keep her hair up, for the wind would take it down immediately, pulling out the pins and tossing her hat in the pond. Everyone said that the wind had developed a funny sort of thing for her. She was known for only wearing white, which contrasted so beautifully with her black hair. Her nude portrait was kept in the basement of the Louvre because there had been a riot when it was displayed.

The girl was so beautiful that everyone who met her fell in love with her. She got marriage proposals all the time even though she was only twelve years old. All sorts of men courted her, but the papers hoped that she might be smitten with a lord. The men with the most terrific moustaches in all of Europe would come to see her. She rejected them all. One aristocrat showed up to tea completely naked, wearing a line called the Emperor's New Clothes, which was the height of fashion.

She was at a zoo when a polar bear escaped. The polar bear walked right up to her and reared up, looking like the tip of an iceberg. It took her hand in its paw and kissed it. The polar bear then proceeded to saunter off and kill three guards, and all the while her heartbeat did not quicken. She would go to the park to look at swans. The swans would remind her of the swan that had rejected her out in the middle of the ocean. Nothing matched that feeling of rejection.

The matter of how to make the pretty castaways happy became a question that was asked all over Europe.

The king of Siam sent a dollhouse that had little mice dressed in tuxedos and dresses running around in it. The emperor of Russia sent some highly trained clowns from Moscow. Thirteen of them fit into a car that was the size of a shoe box. But the twins sat in the audience and did not even so much as crack a smile.

And nobody could understand why they weren't happy. They were famous and surrounded by strangers who were madly in love with them. Wasn't that what everybody deep down really, really wanted?

On the island the twins would sit and imagine being rescued. They imagined every mundane daily task, except to them it seemed miraculous. They thought about how unbearably lovely it would be to skip to the store and buy a carton of chocolate milk. They thought that happiness was on another shore, calling for them. When they arrived, they were shocked that they weren't delighted. Having grown accustomed to imaginary couches and birthday cakes, they couldn't be satisfied by things that were real. On the island they had felt their hearts fill up with hope, like sails filling with wind. All that desire had made their hearts enormous. Their longing for happiness was happiness itself.

One night the twins crawled out a window. They hurried down the winding back alleys and went down to the river. The puppies followed them all the way to the riverbank. They bought a tiny ship. They left all the maps on the shore so that they would be sure to get lost.

As the ship pulled away, all the dogs began to moan and howl and bark. They sounded like a choir of baritones. The noise was so loud that it woke people up throughout the city. People got out of their beds wearing their striped pyjamas and their hair in curlers. Realizing what was happening, they hurried down to the river in their bare feet and slippers.

By the time the crowd had gathered, it was too late, the twins had already set sail. They cried for the twins to come back. The twins merely waved a little. Their faces, so pale and unhappy, were like two small moons. The people stood silently on the banks, watching the twins getting swallowed up by the distance.

And then one day about six months later, a group of bottles, travelling together like a school of salmon, washed up on the shore of Brighton beach. The twins were back on a desert island, trapped, and were writing again. There was rejoicing.

And over the course of the next decades, there were to be many wondrous epistles from the twins, who had settled into their strange identities as artists and had found their places apart and yet part of the world.

STING LIKE A BEE

1.

Ferdinand was a little boy with black hair who lived on St. Philippe Street in Little Burgundy, a neighbourhood in Montreal. His family lived in a tiny white bungalow that had been in the family for two generations. It had a cast iron fence out front that had been painted light blue. There was a pot of flowers on each step on the front stoop, one of which had a little Quebec flag stuck inside it. There was a little errant rosebush growing next to a gas pipe in the ground, and its lone flower blew in the wind like a child with a sweater stuck over its head. Theirs was the only bungalow on the block. There was a brick building to the left of it, painted bright red, and one to the right that was painted blue. His family was proud because they owned their own property and didn't have to rent like nearly every other family in the neighbourhood.

Ferdinand was the youngest child of this noble family. He grew his hair long over his ears and his eyes. He was so skinny that his shoes always looked five sizes too big. When he took his shirt off at the swimming pool, everyone was amazed that anybody could be so skinny. It was strange that he in particular was so skinny, because his four older brothers were such strapping teenagers. When they walked down the street, people got out of their way. They were always in fights and some sort of trouble.

But not Ferdinand. He always wanted to be around his mother. He wanted to ride in the baby part of the grocery cart, even though he was nine years old. He would make himself all weepy at night, telling his mother how he was never going to move out when he grew up.

Ferdinand was a sensitive little boy. He didn't want to eat his shelled peanuts because he said that they were so cute and that they looked like little babies wrapped up in blankets and he didn't want to disturb them. He pushed a water balloon around in an umbrella stroller for an entire afternoon. He even told the balloon to settle down or it wouldn't get to watch TV when they got home.

Ferdinand wanted to be left alone to daydream. He lay in his sleeping bag, all zipped up, for an hour, trying to imagine exactly what it would feel like to be swallowed by a whale. He sat in the big cardboard box that the television came in, with his head protruding from a hole. He wanted to take the opportunity to spend one single afternoon being a turtle.

Ferdinand's most favourite thing, however, was to lie in the sun. He lay like that in the public park, near the statue of a mad French-Canadian general. There were always people with suitcases looking for empty cans and bottles that they could return to the store. They circled around Ferdinand, who paid them no mind. He liked feeling like the sun was melting him, that he was turning into liquid and spreading all over the ground.

His father worried about what on earth would become of Ferdinand, because he had never seen such a lazy child. Ferdinand fell asleep watching television in the evening while squashed on the couch between his brothers, with a chocolate sundae on his lap. He wanted Velcro shoes because he didn't like tying his shoelaces.

Ferdinand's father also noticed that Ferdinand showed no disposition toward being an athlete. Everyone in the family boxed. He himself had been an amateur in his day. His other sons all boxed and won prizes and trophies in all sorts of tournaments. Ferdinand's father ironed the patches that his boys won onto their sweaters. One of the boys was eventually going to be a champion boxer, he was sure. The father fantasized about the day that he would be photographed for the newspaper with his arm around one of his sons.

Ferdinand's father adored having a big family of boys and he liked how masculine his older sons were. They always had pretty girlfriends sitting on the porch with them. He could never remember which girl belonged to which boy. He liked how rambunctious they were, even though they got out of control sometimes.

He had no idea what to make of Ferdinand. Once he came home from work and Ferdinand was on the porch, sitting on a chair with his legs spread and playing an imaginary cello. His eyes were closed and he was violently twisting his head around, as if in a fit of rapture.

Another time, when he went to take a leak in the bathroom, Ferdinand was in the bathtub. He had a big pompadour of suds stacked on top of his head. "Please, call me Prince Antoine," Ferdinand said in a Parisian accent while batting his eyelashes.

Ferdinand's father felt full of dread. Maybe there was nothing wrong. Maybe he was just imagining things, but he didn't remember imagining things with any of his older boys. He had had no sneaking suspicion about anything with the others.

He had named Ferdinand after his grandfather who was built like a bull and was never affected by the cold. But he sometimes thought they had brought the wrong kid home from the hospital. His real youngest kid was out there winning every boxing match he entered, while Ferdinand liked to take the boxing trophies down from the shelves and play with them like they were Barbie dolls. Still, the father enrolled Ferdinand in a boxing program. He decided to let him do whatever the hell he liked as long as he agreed to join the gym when he was thirteen years old. It was a family tradition.

Ferdinand would never in a million years have signed up for it on his own. He didn't complain though. He was aware that he was not acting the way that his father wanted, and since he wasn't willing to give his poetic way of life up, the least he could do was to go to box once a week. It couldn't be that bad.

Ferdinand walked down the street to the gym, carrying his duffel bag with a drawing of a bull on its side. He limped as he walked, supporting the weight of the bag on his right leg. His silver mesh shorts seemed to be almost as big as pants.

A twenty-year-old drug addict wearing an acrylic vest and jean shorts and moon boots called out to Ferdinand for change. Little Burgundy had always been a lower-class neighbourhood. The houses were all cheaply built and there were no fancy stores or fancy restaurants. There was a religious store that sold statues of Jesus and saints. People liked to buy them and load up their front yards with them. All the saints crowded into the little yards like commuters on a bus on their way to work.

There are certain parts of the world where certain things come from. Oranges grow in Florida; olives grow in Italy. It was the same thing with people. Lots of writers grew in New York City. And, for reasons that weren't always entirely obvious, boxers grew in Quebec.

The gym was in a redbrick building with an enormous door. The entrance was covered with framed photographs of boxers no one had ever heard of. The smell of sweat hit Ferdinand as soon as he opened the door. The squeak of sneakers was oddly almost deafening. They sounded like someone writing curse words with a magic marker. The sounds all had echoes. This was what it felt like to be a fish when someone was tapping the sides of the aquarium, Ferdinand thought.

Ferdinand walked down the hall and into the huge gym. It was filled with lots of older boys who were constantly moving. They danced around on their toes, jumping back and forth, their feet looking like flies hitting a windowpane as they tried to figure a way out.

After they warmed up, the boys peeled off their oversized sweatshirts. Underneath they had on only tight undershirts or no shirts at all. A lot of the boys started training when they were only eleven years old. By the time they were nineteen, they didn't have an ounce of fat on their bodies.

Jules Pieton had a lilac tattooed on the back of his neck. Marcel Girard had a tattoo of a group of violets going down his biceps. Paul Miron had a tattoo of a black-eyed Susan between his shoulder blades and you could see it when he took off his sweatshirt for a fight. Claude Archambault had a tattoo of a rose on the back of his skull, right where a bald spot was going to appear in twenty years. Martin LeBlanc had a tattoo of an iris on his right pectoral muscle. He had been raised by his English grandmother, who was named Iris. Phillipe LaMonde had an entire lower tricep covered with red poppies.

Ferdinand found that he didn't want to fight at all. He only wanted to look at the pretty tattoos on the other boys. The lilacs and the tiger lilies and the roses . . . all the roses. He wished he could go up and smell them.

2.

The old man's dog was sixteen and a half years old and had arthritis and was deaf. They walked slowly down the street together, taking twenty minutes to get around the block.

The old man had spent his whole life in this neighbourhood. When he was younger and met girls in the big dance
halls downtown, he wouldn't tell them that he lived in Little
Burgundy. It had always been working class and poor. And it
was literally downhill and on the other side of the tracks. A
girl would look for a boy from Westmount or Outremont if
she had any sense, not a boy from this part of town.

Still, you would see some very pretty women who lived
around here. They were mostly the young single moms who
wore miniskirts and high heels and rabbit-skin fur coats.
They would carry home bags of groceries from the food bank,
smiling whenever drivers honked at them. They would save a
little bit of money from their welfare cheques to buy a tube
of lipstick. They were still dreaming the same dream that the
little kids were dreaming, which was that they were going to
grow up and get out of this neighbourhood. They still hadn't
accepted that they were moms now and that their future was
already here. They paid the old man no mind even though he
stopped to stare at them. He had cataracts in his eyes as if he
were looking up at the full moon.

In truth, when he stopped to look at the women, he really
was pausing just to take a break from the long walk. When
he and the dog would get to the foot of the stairs, they would
stand there trying to muster up the courage to climb them.

The dog was a golden retriever and everything in the
apartment was covered in its long white hairs. The curtains
and the chesterfields, his clothes and hats, all the floors, even
the dishes were plastered with white dog hair too. The old
man had stopped waging war against the dog hair though,

because you had to choose your battles in life. Then, one sad morning, his dog passed away in its sleep.

The old man was lonelier than he had ever been that week. He made several trips to the supermarket, buying only one thing at a time so that he would have an excuse to come back again. He dressed like many of the old people in this neighbourhood. He had on an old suit jacket that had survived from the 1950s. It looked as though he had made the pinstripes on his jacket with a ruler and a piece of soap. He also sported a checkered tweed hat, matched with a pair of bright green jogging pants that he had got from the Salvation Army.

"Do you think I'm sweet enough to buy some of these sweets?" he said to the cashier, trying to be funny.

She smiled weakly. She looked bored out of her mind and he knew that she was looking forward to him walking away.

On the way back to the apartment he tried to talk to the neighbourhood children. They were all over the place. They were dressed in faded Cookie Monster T-shirts or heavy metal T-shirts that had shrunk in the laundry. They had little broken arms and scabs on their knees. Their chronic lack of supervision led to them doing things like falling off roofs on a regular basis.

They would grow up to be criminals: the unacknowledged drug dealers and burglars of the world.

A future car thief hurried by with a tiny Matchbox Porsche in his hand. The old man tried to ask him about his car, but the child continued on. He saw a skinny boy with long hair who was carrying a duffel bag that looked bigger than him. For a second he thought that the boy was wearing sunglasses, but then realized that he had two black eyes. He stopped to wave at the boy, who responded with a sad smile and a tiny little wave but kept going. It was a shame, he thought, that children were not allowed to talk to strangers anymore. He would like to pass on his wisdom about old TV shows that had gone off the air, and the price of hot dogs before the war. He could tell them about scandals that had ruined the careers of politicians in the 1950s.

A bus zoomed by, coming so close to the sidewalk that it seemed to grab hold of the old man's jacket. One day he would get dizzy and he would teeter over and fall into the street and be run over by a bus, he thought. He imagined everyone gathering around to look at him in the middle of the street, crushed and dignified.

He knew not to talk to any of the men, because anything could set them off. You would see groups of them yelling at each other and flashing knives. They were at an age when they enjoyed endangering their lives, but the old man was careful with his life. As though it were an egg balanced in a spoon in a children's race.

In the coming days, he found that he couldn't deal with the loss of the dog. It made him feel terrible to wake up in the middle of the night and go for a pee and not trip over his buddy. It made the hallway seem to go on for miles and miles. Even though the apartment was tiny, it was amazing how much emptiness fit into it.

Finally he thought that getting another dog would be the only thing that would cure him of the loneliness. He called his daughter, asking her to get him a new dog. He said that he was miserable without one. She didn't seem very concerned, probably because she wasn't listening.

The old man had been too strict with his children when they were younger. Now they resented him. He knew this, but he could not go back into the past and change the way he had been. He was even alone on Christmas Day. Each year, he sat in front of the one channel that he got, waiting for the Charlie Brown special to come on. "It's starting!" he would call out and then he would realize that no one was there.

In this world, there was no one, other than dogs, who could love him now. Putting aside his preconceptions, he talked to all the aggressive-looking young men about getting a new dog. Those guys had a way of making just about anything happen. One of the old man's neighbours, a twenty-year-old guy who wore a shiny silver tracksuit, said he had a cousin who wanted to unload some Rottweiler puppies.

"They usually go for eight hundred dollars. But it so happens that he's worried that the girl he broke up with is going to tell the police he had a puppy mill. So I can get you a dog for two hundred."

At first the old man was completely taken aback by the price and couldn't speak. That's the way he got when he was faced with almost any amount these days. He still couldn't get over the fact that things weren't five cents and a dime anymore. Still, he surprised himself when he went into his old Chinese tea box, where he hid all his money, and took out two hundred dollars. The money in the tea box was for a rainy day, and there had been a storm cloud following him around for a month. The tea tin rattled like a Gypsy's tambourine as he was off for a new adventure.

He named the dog Ferdinand after a man who had sat next to him in a cubicle at work. They had worked together for twenty-four years. It was the only job that he'd ever had and he had felt so lucky to get it too. His father had been a construction worker, so for him there was something so elite and classy about working in an office. He and Ferdinand had been friends, eating lunch and talking about politics in the park together. It seemed strange to remember that he had had a friend once.

Ferdinand the dog grew bigger and bigger each day. But he also grew gentler. Mothers would move their babies away from him even though the old man would swear over and over again that the dog wasn't violent. If Ferdinand pulled, he would be able to knock the old man over and drag him down the street. But he never pulled. A grey striped cat, looking like a skinny British aristocrat in a topcoat, gave Ferdinand his sourest, most conceited look. But Ferdinand didn't growl or make any aggressive motion. He followed the cat's drama as though it were a late-night foreign film on television, having nothing to do with him really.

That year the old man found himself getting older and more tired than ever before. He couldn't hear anything at all.

He found it too difficult to go to the corner store to get groceries. He would settle on eating out of an old peanut butter jar for dinner. He didn't change his clothes. The old man went to get his mail wearing a sweater vest and his underwear.

He came down to make conversation with the mailman but he wasn't sure he was making any sense.

"Do you know that my father built the funeral home around the corner? No kidding. Of course he did. He painted it too. It wasn't there since the beginning of time, you know? Don't you believe me? Yes or no, man? Yes or no?"

He couldn't walk the dog much anymore. Sometimes he wasn't able to take the dog out on time and it would pee on the floor. The neighbours called the health inspector because of the smell. The old man answered the door in a dirty sweater and his jogging pants and with his white hair looking greasy. The inspector was surprised to see a giant dog that looked the picture of health, standing behind the man. He didn't seem to be the right sort of dog for a man his age at all. He had expected a blind Shih Tzu or a toy poodle with Alzheimer's.

To appease the health inspector, the old man looked for a dog walker. The dog was so gentle that he was able to pay the four-year-old boy who lived next door a dollar to walk it around the block. Four-year-olds were always good if you were looking to hire someone under the table. The little boy strolled in nothing but his slippers and jean shorts next to the dog, making it look like a giant from some place like the bowels of hell. He ran into his cousin—a troublemaker—on the corner. The older boy had a handkerchief tied on his head and was wearing a terry cloth baby-blue tracksuit. He was always on the lookout for dogs for fights that he organized in secret spots for interested gamblers. He had a gold eyetooth that you could see as he smiled at Ferdinand.

"Not this dog," the little boy said. "He's a good dog."

The old man would simply open the door and let the dog spend the day in the small back courtyard of the building. There were flies and bees everywhere from the garbage in the alley. Ferdinand liked to lie and watch the little patterns that they made, even though they were too complicated for him to understand. The flies were like mathematicians at Harvard standing on ladders and drawing wild equations on enormous chalkboards.

One day Ferdinand was sitting in the yard, but he was restless now because he was hungry. The old man had no sense of time passing by anymore and Ferdinand hadn't had anything to eat in almost two days. When a tenant from the third floor dropped a garbage bag out the window into the lawn, the dog started to root through it immediately, smelling a hot dog somewhere in the great darkness of the sack.

When the bee stung Ferdinand, he was suddenly filled with a terrible pain that flooded through his skull. He tore around the yard, trying to make the pain go away, terrified that it would happen again. Who could be so angry with him? He had always minded his own business and now someone was trying to kill him. He didn't know where the invisible villain had come from, so he didn't know in which direction he should flee. He was like the old man when the bank teller asked him too many questions instead of just cashing his cheque. He smashed his head against the fence.

Coming down the alleyway, the little boy's cousin and his friends could hear Ferdinand barking and growling before they even saw him. The alley was filled with garbage and old

furniture that people had thrown out. The young men spotted a pile of vinyl kitchen chairs with giant green hothouse
flowers exploding on them. They pulled the chairs over to the
fence so that they could get a look at this dog.

The men stood perched on the chairs, wild and hyper-
active and excited, their eyes opening wider when they saw
Ferdinand. All they saw was a dog shaking his face wildly
like a fist. Its muscles heaved like lava coming down a mountain. They could see all its enormous teeth and black gums
and they could smell its angry breath. The men looked at one
another happily, thinking that fortunes were about to change
on their block. The little boy's cousin opened the door of the
fence slowly, whispering for the dog to chill out and that no
one was going to hurt him.

3.

All the women in Isabelle Ferdinand's family were loud. Her
father had left when she and her sister were both still in diapers. Her aunts were always over, because there were no men
to toss them out or put them in their place. They would fight
with the kitchen windows open, and everyone in the neighbourhood could hear their business. They didn't care. They
put the TV out on the sidewalk and ate their dinner with their
plates on their laps, screaming at the game show.

Even their style was loud. Her mother wore high-heeled
slippers and tight jeans that had patterns of roses on them.
Her sister would walk to the store to buy a carton of milk
wearing a striped bikini. Her sister was attracted to all the

boys, especially the ones that made a lot of noise. When a car of boys slowed down next to her on the sidewalk, she leaned in the window and wiggled her butt back and forth as she talked to them, like a bumblebee getting nectar out of a flower. She and her mom liked talking to everyone, popping into different doors, pollinating the neighbourhood with fantastic gossip.

Isabelle, on the other hand, didn't like to draw attention to herself. Even when she was in grade school, the teachers would write on her report cards that she didn't play well with other children. The kids asked her if she wanted to play Red Rover or soccer or baseball and she would say no, no, no, no. She was always by herself in the corner, flipping through picture books.

Now she was in high school and her name was at the top of the honour roll list when you entered the school. She didn't really have any friends though. Now that they were teenagers, it was like the other girls carried around bullhorns that they held up to their mouths when they laughed. She liked to go straight home after school and go to her room and read books until the sun went down. They lay scattered about the room, open to hold their places, like drawings of seagulls by little kids.

One of her aunts drove them to a wedding on a Saturday. When she was there, relatives she barely knew kept asking her whether or not she had a boyfriend yet. That's what they wanted to talk about all the time. They used to be interested in her marks and all the awards for academic excellence that she had won. Now the bigger news was that one of her older cousins was engaged to a millionaire who owned a spaghetti restaurant franchise. They were all worried that Isabelle would be unlucky in love, like her mom.

There were things about herself that Isabelle knew should be evolving. She was fourteen and she still had a school bag with Kermit the Frog on it. In the winter, she wore big moon boots and a Canadiens toque with her curly and frizzy hair sticking out from underneath it. She figured that she would have to make a concerted effort to change. Things just weren't happening naturally, the way they were for everybody else.

The next Saturday, as she was walking home, her path was blocked by ambulance workers pulling a stretcher across the sidewalk to the truck. The body was covered, but she knew it must be the old man with the big-assed dog. She crossed herself as she wondered what had happened to the dog and about how life is short. When she got home, she went straight into her sister Corinna's room.

"I'm going to a house party," Isabelle said. "This girl in my class said that I should not be a ninny, and come. I think I need a makeover, though."

Corinna jumped up and down on her bed, clapping her hands. She handed Isabelle a T-shirt with a print of a unicorn on it and one of her jean skirts that she had cut ludicrously short. Her sister fixed Isabelle's hair up with dozens of little butterfly clips and she put the reddest lipstick in the world on her. Her mouth was the colour of Superman's cape when he was standing in his ballet shoes, about to jump off the roof of a building.

Corinna said attitude was also important when it came to boys.

"You should crawl on your hands and knees across the bed. Men get crazy when you go at them like an animal."

Most boys liked it a little rough, she assured Isabelle.

"You should try to slur when you talk too. Guys are like crazy about that speech impediment thing."

The way that a cheetah would go after a gazelle with a broken leg, boys would go after stupid girls.

Her mother was playing cards in the kitchen with two of her sisters. They all made such a fuss when they saw Isabelle.

Isabelle's stomach was fluttery, and she felt like she had to pee the whole way over to the party. The yellow reflective lights on the pedals of the bicycles passing by looked like the eyes of wolves catching the light. She passed a store that gave massages and had all its windows painted silver. There was a jewellery store that sold huge hoop earrings and rings that had giant gold lion heads on them. The moon looked like the Day-Glo face of a wristwatch. Everything had Saturday fever!

It was near the first of the month, when people got their welfare cheques, so they were out. She saw some men that looked familiar from the neighbourhood, but they had a wildness about them now, as if they had been infected, like pet dogs who had got rabies. They all turned to stare at her in her party outfit, as if they were wondering if she wanted in on their secret. Did she want to join them and be a vampire and live forever?

There was a little boy, carrying a paper bag with milk in it, stuck outside his house because he had forgotten his secret knock. A piece of newspaper flitted by in the breeze like Mikhail Baryshnikov in the frenzied finale of a ballet.

The party was on the third floor of an old triplex. There was a big gargoyle of a demon on top of the building, looking down. Most of the gargoyles had committed suicide, falling to the ground like the rest of the old masonry on the buildings. When they leapt, they would hit the pavement like an asteroid and you would feel the ground shake while in your bed.

She went up the steep staircase that led to the top apartment, where all the windows were lit up. It was like someone had propped a ladder up to the moon and had told her to go ahead and ascend. People had locked their bicycles to the outside of the staircase, like they were magnets stuck to a fridge. There was a familiar little piece of paper next to the doorbell, saying it didn't work. There was a sign like that on everyone's doorbell. There was one at her apartment and it made her feel at ease.

When she walked through the front door of the girl's apartment, the sound system was making so much noise that Isabelle couldn't hear herself think. Everyone was dancing while they held their plastic cups of beer over their heads. The kids had formed a tight circle around the carpet, watching a boy dance. He was rolling his fists around each other as if he was rolling up a ball of yarn. He swapped spots with another boy who put one hand on his heart and the other in the air and jumped up and down. A different boy pushed his way in and kept tucking his hands into his armpits, leaning his torso back and strutting in a circle like a rooster at a cockfight. Then he dropped to the floor and moved his hands around like he was trying to put together a puzzle at record speed.

The girls gathered in clusters, like horses worried about a storm. Their long skinny legs looked impossibly vulnerable.

She saw Luc, a boy from a grade higher, coming toward her. He had on a bolero jacket. He was legendary. He'd become quite the player since he had had his braces taken off. No girl was able to resist him, and a huge number had lost their virginity to him. He liked girls that were hard to get because he needed a challenge.

She was glad when Luc took her hand and led her down the hallway, away from the party. He opened a door and led her into a bedroom. Isabelle knew that if she let Luc go all the way, when they came out of the room, everyone would be happy and congratulate her. Everyone would want to hear about it in school the next day. She would finally have a subject of conversation that they were all interested in. They would applaud her, go nuts, and sit with her at the cafeteria table. They were like a coliseum full of people waiting for her to take off all her clothes.

He gave her a sip from a bottle of beer and it made her feel warm and glowing, like there was a spotlight on her. Like she could open her mouth and a song would come out and everyone would be entranced by her. She laughed. The laughter sounded strange. It didn't sound like herself laughing at all. It was like she was listening to her own voice on a tape recorder.

"Come on, sweetie," Luc said. "You're so pretty. I can't keep my eyes off of you. You're like the best-looking girl in the room. And you're so smart too. I just want to hold you.

I was watching you when you were giving a science report and I thought, That's the kind of girl that I would want to wrap my arms around. You're the kind of girl that a guy gets serious about."

Each compliment was like a spear right in the heart that was meant to take her down. So that she would be lying on the bed, waiting to be slain.

Luc pulled Isabelle's shirt off over her head. As it was coming off, she felt as if she was going through a dark tunnel. There she was with a tiny white training bra with a blue bow in the middle, sitting on a bed at a party. He was able to see all the birthmarks and moles on her belly. No one but her family had ever seen those before.

She had nothing to say to him. This boy didn't know a thing about her. She was going to make love to somebody who didn't even know her. He might get her pregnant and then not return the baby's calls for the rest of his life. She would end up getting the cheque like her mother and trying to make the best of it. She didn't like the way his hands felt on her. She turned her face away when he tried to kiss her. Her body went stiff when he tried to put his hands around her hips.

"Aww come on, Isabelle," Luc whispered. "Don't be a frigid bitch, okay?"

All she could think about was home. Her mother was probably singing along with the radio while turning the pages of a magazine with her ridiculously long fingernails. She made her face all crazy with longing when she sang Céline Dion. The scratch of his zipper sounded like the arm of a record player suddenly being jerked off.

Isabelle opened her mouth and yelled a rather preposterous and loud "No!"

She had learned to project her voice like that from her family. It was like her whole family and all the different generations of loud people were helping her assert what she needed to say. The only thing that they were blessed with was lip, but they didn't know how and when to use their gift.

"Get the hell off of me, would ya!" she shouted. "You think I'm going to put out for a bum like you. Let me out of this shithole, pleeeze!"

And so Isabelle Ferdinand changed her mind. Isabelle still wanted to be a kid and to be loved the way that a kid who has a future is loved. She put her shirt back on quickly, causing butterfly barrettes to fly every which way, and stood up and left the room. She went down the hallway and pushed through the crowd of wild teenagers to get to the front door. She hurried down from the moon and got back to earth.

Sneaking down the hallway of her apartment, she passed her mother in the kitchen, humming along to the radio. She walked really quietly because she didn't want to attract anyone's attention. She flopped onto her own bed. The quilt was covered in flowers and smelled like her childhood. She wanted to bury herself in the ground, like a mustard seed, until she was ready to grow up wild and enormous.

The next day she was at the library in her bell-bottom corduroys and a sweater with a rose on it, reading paperback novels. And wherever she is now, she is probably still doing her own thing.

THE STORY OF A ROSEBUSH

My parents sent my brother and me to spend the weekend with our grandparents on the south side of Montreal, which they did once in a while so that they didn't have to go themselves. My mother especially couldn't be around Grandmother. We always told her that she should make an exception for Grandmother. She had lived through the war and had lost her entire family when she was little. Look at all the things the poor lady had been through. Cut her some slack, for crying out loud. But all Mother knew was that she couldn't stand the old woman.

Grandmother was sitting in the kitchen in her wheelchair when we arrived. She raised her small hand and gestured for us to eat whatever we wanted of her leftover scrambled eggs. "*Allez, allez,*" she said. "Don't be shy. The guilty are never shy. The innocent are shy and it gets them nowhere."

We pulled our chairs up close to hear her. Grandmother had a soft voice, as if she had been eating powdered dough-nuts all day long. And like a cassette that had been repeatedly played, her voice got harder and harder to hear as she got older. I was complimented for my Parisian accent all the time, which I'd picked up from her. Grandmother said she couldn't understand the French in her neighbourhood. I think she just used it as an excuse not to make small talk.

There was a can of pea soup balanced on her lap. Grandfather yelled out from the bathroom for us to make her lift it. About six months before, Grandmother had had to have bypass surgery because she was having trouble breathing when she walked. She didn't want to go and we all had to beg her. We told her how much nicer her walks to the Salvation Army around the corner would be. However, due to complications during her operation, she became paralyzed from the waist down, and she couldn't walk anymore at all. She kept shaking her head at us when we came to visit her at the hospital, bewildered that she had ever listened to such idiots.

After she came home from the hospital, a physiotherapist told her that she should lift a can of pea soup above her head to get her strength back. As was our custom, my brother and I stood next to her wheelchair and yelled and screamed at her to raise the can way up, but she couldn't be bothered. Instead she decided to eat marshmallows without her dentures in, looking as though she was trying to squash her face into a permanent frown. She told us we were welcome to lift the can up and down ourselves if we wanted.

She lit up a cigarette. She was always setting the blanket on her lap on fire. She even somehow managed to get cigarette burns on my underwear. She had been smoking for so many years that she could suck half the cigarette in one inhalation. Right then, she exhaled a white cat that stretched its limbs and descended from her mouth and curled up under the table lamp.

She asked us to pass her two cold spoons that were in the fridge, to hold under her eyes to help prevent dark circles.

Grandfather came into the kitchen after being in the bathroom the whole time. We asked him if he needed anything at the store. He said yes, and that we should bring Grandmother and the dog along for the walk. As was their habit, Grandfather helped her put on makeup before she went out. He put on loads of blue-green eyeshadow over her eyes and she looked like a clown, but she liked it that way. He stuck some random bobby pins in her hair too. Her hair was so fine that you could see the scalp through it, which gave the hair the effect of looking pink. She put on this enormous pair of sunglasses that might make a person question her sanity. She had seen a documentary about Jim Jones and decided to get herself a pair, that being the only thing she took away from that horrific tale.

She wore a Star of David around her neck even though she claimed that she wasn't Jewish. She said she only did it because she would get bargains at the butcher.

My brother and I put a ski jacket on over her housedress, pulling her arms through the sleeves as if she was a little kid. She never wore shoes, only a pair of black slippers with embroidered roses. They both fell off while we were running across the street at a yellow light and pushing her like mad. The German shepherd picked one up and carried it to the other side of the street.

Not yet accustomed to the wheelchair, my brother and I were always getting into situations with it. Like that day we tied the German shepherd to her wheelchair and it had pulled her halfway down the block by the time we got out of the store. She accused us of treating her no differently than a dog. We piled the groceries on her lap, which she wasn't too crazy about either. She lit up a cigarette and smoked indignantly.

Grandfather still thought she was so beautiful. He was afraid that she was going to fall in love with a war veteran who was also in a wheelchair. He wore a fez and a burgundy suit and sat next to a fishbowl outside the Salvation Army. When we saw him, we followed Grandfather's instructions, which were to just keep pushing if he was outside the store, even when he waved hello.

And Grandfather had a point, because even though she was a slob and had to live among us bozos, Grandmother was entirely elegant. Occasionally she would let out some pithy little remark in order to remind everyone that they would never have her pedigree. When we passed the playground, she said, "When I was a child, children recited poetry and suffered existential angst. What on earth are those ninnies preoccupied with?"

* * *

Mother claimed that when she was little, Grandmother had ignored her and treated her as if she too were rather dull and a ninny. She said that Grandmother had spent much of Mother's childhood in bed with the lights off. She didn't think anything that was happening in the household was of any interest.

We didn't mind Grandmother in the way that our mother did. She didn't depress us. She was almost kind of funny. She was different from anybody else we knew. She had this incredible story. It was the most incredible thing about her. Actually, it was so incredible that it was probably the most incredible thing about us too.

Our grandparents had both been born into happy families in French cities, one in Montreal and one in Paris. They had both drawn pictures in chalk on the street outside their buildings. They had both gone to elementary school. They had both worn little black berets on their heads at one point or another. They had both listened to the war being announced on the radio. But once France was occupied, nothing about their stories was similar at all. Even though he was only seventeen, Grandfather got himself a fake birth certificate and enlisted in the army. He headed off to fight in Europe, determined that his fate was over there, despite his parents' protests. He said that he knew in his heart that the love of his life was on the other side of the ocean and needed him.

This weekend, like the others, my brother and I tried to coax the story out of her. If she had had a few beers, she would tell it. We waited patiently, until she was drunk enough. During that time, Grandfather tried, as usual, to tell her story for her, patching together things he'd seen in television documentaries about occupied France, things he'd seen himself when he was a soldier in the Canadian army, and some things that he just plain made up. Grandfather said that at the beginning of the occupation in Paris, you ran into newly broke aristocrats everywhere. They would be lying on the side of the road, reading books of poetry. They carried around suitcases filled with violins and tea sets. The children held cages with canaries in them while yelling at their poodles to behave. They would sit sighing and discussing philosophy on the benches.

You had to donate your clothes to the war effort so that they could make parachutes out of them. The Germans were all masturbating when a parachute that was made out of girls' underwear came out of the sky.

The Germans took away some of the statues. They thought it was fine to have a certain amount of statues, but they said the French had gone too far. There were statues of saints no one had heard of and poets who were long, long out of print.

The Germans took away all the French people's guns, so they had to hunt with traps. There were always children stuck in the traps, hanging from trees in the morning and needing to be cut down. It was like the morning dew. If you had a teenage girl who didn't come home at night, you could rest assured that she was curled up out of trouble in a net, tucked up warmly in her peacoat and beret.

When there were four empty beer bottles on the end table around the lamp, like spies meeting beneath a streetlight on a corner, Grandmother suddenly shook her head.

"*Ce n'est pas ça de tout!*" she said.

* * *

Although she had been born in Paris, Grandmother's parents were from Poland. People said they were Jewish, but Grandmother swore it was a lie. Her mother had died from an illness when she was very young and her father looked after her all on his own. He was a philosophy professor and they lived in a huge apartment filled with books and sunlight. They had a cleaning woman in once a week who sometimes brought her daughter, Marie, along. The two girls became best friends.

It was well known that Marie was a wicked little girl. Marie used to take her finger and write curse words in the air. She would pull the tail feathers off the peacock at the zoo. She taunted cats. But she and Grandmother would walk down the street with their books balanced on their heads and their tongues stuck out, trying not to laugh. Grandmother thought she was so alive.

On the morning of June 16, 1941, Grandmother and her father were arrested. There had been rumours of a roundup, but Grandmother's father had, despite his extensive philosophical training, a tragic proclivity to err on the side of goodness. The pounding on the door was like the banging of a gavel. Grandmother put on a white dress and a black coat, packed some things in a suitcase and followed her father. He held on to her hand too tightly, and they climbed onto a bus with strangers. When the officers looked at their papers, seeing that Grandmother had been born in Paris, they decided to release her. Such was the terrifying power of whim during wartime. She stood all alone with her white dress blowing around her like a white flag trying to surrender. She wandered, frightened, without a family, and then decided to find Marie. When she arrived at the door she swore that her father would give them all the money he had when he was freed, and they let her in. She looked around, needing to see her best friend.

Fifteen-year-old Grandmother sat on Marie's couch and looked bewildered that night. She was still wearing her coat over her white dress and her hair was sort of messy. She gazed around the strange apartment, so different from her own. The wallpaper had brown and orange flowers on it and was coming apart near the ceiling. There were fingerprints all over everything. Everything was old. The couches were all lumpy and the covers were threadbare. Clothes that had been worn too many times were hanging from a line in the kitchen.

That night the family was in an uproar. They were in the middle of a fight when Grandmother came by. The fight would continue for the whole time Grandmother was there and for the rest of their lives, actually. Grandmother was shocked by the way that Marie's mother talked. She would hurl all sorts of invectives at her boys. "Stop talking right this second, Buddy, or I will come over there and smash all the teeth out of your mouth."

Grandmother had had no idea that people could talk that way to one another and then fall asleep and wake up in the morning as if nothing had happened. It was so dirty and dark. It didn't even seem like those types of words belonged in the house. It was like discovering a rat in the kitchen.

All the children in the family had been raised on these harsh words. You could tell that at first glance. They all had nasty looks about them. It was hard to even tell what their appearances were actually like because their bitter expressions got in the way.

Grandmother had been raised differently. It had never occurred to her that there was a possibility that she might not be loved. This made her a trusting, sleepy little girl for the first years of her life. She was good at the things that a little girl is supposed to be good at, which are not necessarily things that are great in themselves. And they were useless during a war.

Marie was always hungry for any sort of affection. She was like a stray dog in that way. Grandmother got too much affection. She was like a fat, declawed house cat with a little bell around its neck in that way.

Marie let her sleep in her bed and let her tell the authorities that she was her cousin. If it was known that she was a Jew, she would have to wear a yellow Star of David, be banned from movies, cafés and parks, be denied a radio and be subjected to curfews. She would never be allowed to have any fun at all. And you never knew when she'd be sent off herself.

Marie noticed that songs on the radio always sounded better now that Grandmother was around. She liked lying in the dark and whispering aloud a question like, "Do you think that we only started existing when we came into this world or since the beginning of time?" And hearing a voice whisper back, "Only since we were born."

They could pass as cousins too. They both had dark hair and blue eyes. Only Grandmother was a million times prettier.

Grandmother had enormous eyes. She said that they were never like that before the war. When she was separated from her father, she got a shocked expression on her face that she couldn't get rid of. That's why she was beautiful. She had eyes that looked like those of a frightened animal.

The girls went to the same school now. Because it was wartime, all the boys fell in love more easily. All the boys liked Grandmother more than Marie. They passed her notes in class. Each note, in boy's handwriting, said more or less the same thing: "You are the one." Marie hated Grandmother with a passion because of this. As they were walking home from school one drizzly day, two boys passed, riding together on a single bicycle. They laughingly professed their love for Grandmother, blowing kisses that came at her like moths to a lightbulb.

Marie stopped and turned viciously toward her friend. She reached out both her arms and shoved Grandmother hard in the chest. Grandmother toppled off the sidewalk and fell into a puddle on the cobblestone street. Her skirt was covered in mud and her knees were both bleeding. She held her hands in front of her and saw that the palms of both were red from being skinned. Grandmother looked up at Marie and Marie looked down at Grandmother.

Marie was the type of girl that cannot tear herself away from the people she abhors. Grandmother had a streak in her that made her fall in love with those who treated her badly.

And thus their feelings for one another intertwined like the branches of two unattended rosebushes in a garden.

* * *

Marie now sometimes ignored Grandmother in the playground at school, telling the other girls to turn away from her too. Or she would walk ahead of Grandmother on the way home, quickening her pace any time she almost caught up. She complained while changing into her nightgown about not having her own room anymore. She told Grandmother not to talk for the rest of the evening, so that she could pretend she wasn't there. Grandmother tried not to breathe a word. Marie yelled at Grandmother to make herself smaller in the bed. And the two girls grew closer and closer.

* * *

As the war went on, Marie's feelings toward Grandmother spread quickly to the rest of the family. They deliberately forgot to set her a place at the kitchen table. She started to feel anemic because she hadn't had any meat in ages. When she was feeling faint, she would hallucinate. She chased a little white kitten down the street. When she finally caught up to it, it was only a white paper bag being blown by the wind.

She decided it was too much effort to escape their grasps, so she started sleeping with Marie's brothers. She slept with them in the bathroom and in a toolshed down the street.

She said sex happened much faster back then. It happened

so fast that you were barely aware you were having it. You never got naked. You only moved away whatever parts of your clothing absolutely had to be moved. She didn't know that you took your shoes off for sex. She didn't even know there was a way to have sex without her stockings still on and her underwear around her ankles.

Her foster mother told her that it wouldn't hurt to indicate to the baker that she might be willing to sleep with him. She set Grandmother up on dates with men she met on the street. She told Grandmother that she should be very, very friendly with the butcher.

She waited in queues for their rations. They always made her go, but she didn't really mind. She liked that there was something useful that she could do. She would bring home the meagre groceries, knowing that there wasn't much in the bag that would be hers.

One day the German officers set up a canteen on the street. They called out that they were offering free bowls of soup to anyone who wanted some. Grandmother had been hysterical with hunger for the past couple of days. She had twitches, as though she were a telegraph receiver that was being sent messages. She walked up to the canteen and put her hands out. The officer winked at her and gave her a bowl of soup, and she ate it ravenously.

When the neighbours saw Grandmother sitting on the curb, eating her little bowl of soup with her legs crossed, they sent their children out too. For some reason, because she had gone first, she took the brunt of the shame. They could hate her for it afterwards. She was like shame personified.

Grandmother sensed this, but she didn't care all of a sudden. She held the bowl up in the air when it was empty. She kissed the side of it.

* * *

Grandmother and Marie liked to sit around and discuss the atrocities of the German officers. For instance, the Germans bought all the gloves in the shops in Paris and they mailed them to their sweethearts and wives in Berlin. Grandmother and Marie would insult the German girls. They thought they had really fat legs and had faces like men. They made up all kinds of things about German girls. Of course, they hadn't a clue what they might possibly look like, except that they were wearing gloves that rightfully belonged to Parisian girls.

One day, while they were talking about their stolen gloves, Marie picked up a stone and threw it at a cat. The surprised animal moved back as suddenly as though it were a child grabbed by the scruff of its neck by a schoolmaster. Marie yelled out that she was miserable because she was poor and ugly and no man would ever buy her anything like gloves. She held up her hands for Grandmother to see. The tip of each finger was pink because of the cold. Grandmother thought that if Marie was made happy, then her heart would thaw and she would be kinder to her.

That was when Grandmother decided to find a way to get Marie a pair of gloves and many other things. It was also the hunger that lived in her belly like a small animal. It gave her the determination to do anything. She shrugged off her notions of what was intolerable and unimaginable and got on with the business of surviving.

* * *

Grandmother approached some German officers who were standing outside a post office two days later. She asked where she could get a pair of black gloves. One of them whispered the way into her ear. She followed him back to a hotel that German officers had taken over to live in and use as head-quarters. He led her up a flight of stairs, down a hall, past numerous doors and into a large apartment. She was so nervous with the officer that he gave her a glass of champagne to make her calm down. It made her laugh, and she laughed so hard that she started to cry.

He made her sing him the alphabet. He wept because he thought it was so lovely. She mostly knew the words to nursery rhymes and the songs that she had been forced to learn at school. She sang him a song about cleaning off the top of your desk.

He made her take a bath because she smelled so bad. He had a French maid, who scrubbed Grandmother under her arms with a rag and washed her hair. The maid brushed her hair and combed it over to the side. He gave her a pair of lace underwear with little bows along the elastics to put on. The comforter on the bed was covered in a pattern of roses.

When they were done, the officer gave her a pair of black gloves. He also gave her a mark, which was supposed to be some crazy amount of money now. And he gave her a fancy pastry, the likes of which had not been seen in Paris since the occupation began. She couldn't wait to eat it in private. She peeled off the paper, which rattled like a tiny fire, and ate it as she was walking home.

She was whistling a German tune that the officer had put on the record player. She couldn't help it. It bothered everyone that she whistled that song. But once she had been made love to while listening to that song, so how could it not be stuck in her head?

She said that he made her take off her shoe and sucked on her toe. She said he sat on a chair, pulled his pants down and started masturbating. She got embarrassed and turned to the wall. He begged her to turn around and just look at him once.

But afterwards, she sat happily watching Marie pull the gloves on and off. Marie threw her black hands around Grandmother's neck in gratitude.

* * *

With most of the soldiers, it went pretty quickly because they didn't speak any French. She was made love to by one soldier while standing on her head. She got down on her hands and knees and pretended to be a dog for another. One fair-haired and gentle-looking soldier tied her wrists to the bedpost. A fat soldier wanted her to give him a hickey on his neck while he banged his knee and laughed uproariously.

One, who was a teacher in Berlin, made her pretend that she was back in school, practising her handwriting. When she made a mistake, he bent her over his knee and gave her a spanking.

One wanted her to cry. He made her sit quietly, naked on the side of the mattress. He had found that if you let a girl sit without any clothes on for long enough, then she would always start to feel melancholic and begin to weep. And then, when Grandmother did inevitably start to cry, he kissed her face madly. He said there was nothing that he loved more than kisses that tasted like salty tears. He had gotten a taste for it while he was on the Eastern Front.

Afterwards, she would always stuff a pastry into her mouth before heading home. She wasn't letting herself be starved to death anymore. But she felt more guilty about eating those cakes all by herself than she possibly could about sleeping with the German soldiers. She didn't feel anything about that at all. She knew that it wouldn't matter when the war was over. The important thing was to survive. And then somehow—in a way that you couldn't rationally grasp—all this would be gone. Like when you wake up from a nightmare and everything goes back to exactly the way that it was before.

When a soldier with black eyes picked her up and began fucking her against the wall, she tried to convince herself that it wasn't actually happening. There was a yellow lampshade with little crystals hanging from it on the table next to them. The crystals were knocking against each other violently. And if this act didn't really exist, then what was making the lampshade shake like that? It must be an army coming, or an earthquake. The act of the soldier making love to Grandmother was as violent as all the German tanks rolling into Paris.

She never went to dinner with the officers or hung around longer, because she wanted to get back to Marie. She would dress so quickly that she would get tangled up, trip on her stockings and bang her chin on the floor. Each time, she would get more and more desperate to get back to Marie.

*   *   *

It was Grandmother who started it. Everything that she had known before the war had been taken away from her. There was no way that she could deal with that. She couldn't just sit there and be overcome with loss. She had to make Marie her whole world. She became fixated on Marie.

Sometimes the things that Marie did filled her with so much wonder that she would feel herself trembling. She watched Marie's fingers lacing up her shoes and she thought it was so exquisite.

The way Marie would shake her curls out after pulling on a tight turtleneck was so wonderful too. She would try and do it herself in exactly the same way, so that she could feel what it was like to be Marie. She was the only person in the whole world that got to watch Marie sitting on the side of her bed in her underpants. And see Marie's bare feet at the end of their bed.

She liked the way that there always seemed to be dirt under Marie's fingernails. She liked the way that there were hairs around Marie's nipples. She would lie closer and closer to Marie as they were sleeping. She marvelled over Marie the way that a mother marvels over a newborn baby.

When she was asleep, Marie would swat at Grandmother with her little hand in the air as if to wave off a fly. And she would murmur from somewhere deep in a dream for Grandmother to get the hell away from her.

Grandmother knew that she was getting on Marie's nerves. She knew that she was so adoring of Marie that there was nothing that the girl could do but despise her. But the more Marie abhorred her, the more madly she tried to somehow possess her. Isn't that the way that love works?

One night she put her hand on Marie's belly. She knew that Marie was still awake. She knew that Marie wanted to push her hand off, but she also knew that for some reason, Marie could not. Her hand had put a magic spell on Marie.

She put her hand down Marie's underwear. Marie was helpless. Marie was desperate for her to do what she was about to do. She put her finger on Marie's sweet cunt and began to rub. When Marie moaned, everything in the world was filled with sweetness. When it was over, Marie rolled over, still pretending she was asleep.

The next night she kissed between Marie's legs. One officer had given Grandmother a bottle of champagne. He had six cases of it. She and Marie burst it open in their room with the lights off. It was warm and the suds poured all over their knees.

* * *

There was a light layer of snow all over Paris, as though it had been dusted like a bundt cake. Grandmother's coat left her chilly. It was threadbare and had gone to seed and the lining had long since been torn. She had always hated the cold so much. Her father would laugh and say that she needed more meat on her bones. She took the money that she had made and went to see a dressmaker that an officer had told her about. She wanted to get herself a coat that fit her and kept her warm and made her feel like a human being again.

She looked at the reflection of her body in the dressmaker's full-length oval mirror that had the ghostly effect of making her look as though she were lying at the bottom of a tiny boat adrift on a river. She felt a little bit good about herself when she noticed how much she looked like an adult. She was able to buy herself a coat. She had a little bit of independence and power in the world now.

She knew that her foster mother wouldn't say anything about her coat. She had started to give money that she made to Marie's mother and nobody could say anything to her after that. They left Grandmother in peace. Actually, Marie's mother wondered why she even wanted to stay in that crappy little apartment. After all, she could get her own little place with wallpaper with birds on the wall and a big brass bed by the window.

And Marie was not jealous, because Grandmother had bought an identical coat for her. Whatever she bought for herself, Grandmother also bought for Marie. They had matching black high heels with buckles across them. They had matching blue dresses with a circle of little white buttons shaped like roses around the neckline.

Marie's feelings for Grandmother changed from moment

to moment. She would feel so incredibly good about herself when Grandmother was around. She would feel like a million bucks. She knew that it was Grandmother who had made her feel so cocky and bold and full of herself. Her mother didn't really care for her, her father knew nothing about her, and her brothers were little better than thugs. They would never be able to see the things in her that Grandmother saw.

She loved her new things. No one in her life had ever bought her anything special or given her any gifts. But as much as she loved these pretty things, she loved revenge more. What would make her feel the most good about herself would be to see Grandmother destroyed.

* * *

When they were standing next to each other, Grandmother and Marie would always be touching. They always walked down the street with their arms linked. But one chilly afternoon, when Grandmother tried to take her hand, Marie jerked it angrily away. Then when they were in the secrecy of the stairwell up to the apartment, Grandmother tried to kiss Marie. Marie gave her a violent little shove.

"Why do you want to kiss me?" Marie asked. "You spend all day kissing people. You must be exhausted."

"Why would you say something like that?" Grandmother demanded, helplessly.

"Anyways, I can't afford it. I know that it's very expensive to kiss you. I guess that I have no choice but to find somebody who kisses for free."

"You're not going to get a boyfriend, are you? You're not going to let anybody touch you?" Grandmother asked. She was seized by panic.

"Are you nuts? How can you ask me something like that? You let men stick their things in you? And you don't want me to even hold hands with a boy?"

"It's not the same."

"You think I'm wicked and that I have no feelings at all. You think that it doesn't bother me that you sleep with those men. You think that I have a rock for a heart."

"Do you want me to stop? I will."

"What, so then you can mooch off my family again and go around acting like you're afraid of your own shadow? No, thanks."

She stormed ahead of Grandmother into the apartment. Grandmother sat down on a step and started to weep in frustration, and her sobs echoed so loudly in the stairwell that it was as though she were a monster. Coming down the stairs, the neighbours stepped nervously around her as though her crying might be contagious. It was so difficult to love Marie. If only she could make Marie happy, then all her problems would go away. Not even the war or the winter would matter.

Grandmother knew that Marie had feelings for her. But she also knew that Marie was ashamed. After they made love one night, Marie sat up in bed and glared at Grandmother angrily.

"This is what you do, isn't it? You seduce people. You imagine that I'm going to continue doing this filthy thing with you for the rest of your life. Well, you're wrong. This is disgusting. I can't wait for the liberation."

* * *

Marie knew that any mention of the end of the occupation bothered Grandmother. She would bring it up every time they were together. Marie said that, once the Germans were out, they were going to serve cake to everyone and give out medals for valorous deeds. She said that there would be fireworks. People would throw their boots into the sea. She said that there would be black jazz players on the roof who would play all night. Marie was even practising some English words in order to make a speech to thank the American soldiers for helping to liberate her country.

For some reason, Grandmother was never included in any of these plans. It was somehow implicit that she wasn't going to be a part of the festivities. Moreover, Marie seemed to imply that Grandmother would be punished for what she had been up to with German soldiers. Marie informed Grandmother that they would give twelve-page reports on what each citizen had been up to during the war. All the other children would go back to being children, but she didn't know if she would be allowed to. Where was she going to live? Who would look after her? She had such a bad reputation that nobody would marry her.

Once the war was over, everyone could stop pretending certain things. You could stop pretending that people who hadn't come home were coming home. Her father wasn't coming back. She would be homeless. Marie was her only home now. And so time passed.

* * *

When the occupation was over, a new sort of terror immediately began. They had to take their aggression out on someone and the Germans were leaving. They couldn't just go back to ordinary life. They were like a cat that had climbed up on a table and had lapped up a glass of whiskey and was now so drunk that it was taunting dogs. They looked for collaborators to prove that they were not collaborators. They ferreted out the weak to prove that they were strong. They wanted to be good, so they acted in an evil way.

People were going crazy when Charles de Gaulle took over as president. As a form of celebration, people threw tomatoes and rocks at Grandmother as she walked down the street. They called her a whore for having slept with Germans. Her head was shorn, because she had been cornered by a group of men who shaved her hair off. A girl who had fallen in love with a German soldier and had been living with him was tied up and forced to walk down the street naked while three-year-olds screamed at her, calling her a whore.

It was Marie who had turned Grandmother in. As she walked down the street, she held her head high. She didn't care. Her heart was already broken. They could not touch her.

* * *

A year later, Grandfather was still dressed in his Canadian uniform, celebrating the end of the war in the streets of Paris, when he chanced upon her. Grandfather had spent the whole war hoping most of all to stay alive, but also, when he had a moment to daydream, hoping that he might get a chance to see Paris. And here it was, in its wonderful glory. The buildings were so elegant and the cast iron balconies grew on the sides of them like beautiful climbing vines that covered the whole city. Who would imagine that a boy from Saint-Henri in Montreal would find himself here, in the city of culture and refinement?

When he saw Grandmother leaning against a stone wall, it was love at first sight. She was eighteen years old. She had a black top hat perched at an angle on her head. Her hair had grown out since it had been so brutally cut, and it now curled around her earlobes. She was so pretty in her black dress and high-heeled shoes. She had a brand-new coat slung over a suitcase that she was carrying in one hand. She was smoking a cigarette with her other and she was the only person in the huge mob who wasn't smiling. He knew right away that she was a displaced aristocrat. She had ridden out of Paris when it was first occupied in a car with a pile of birdcages, a poodle and three maids. She was the type of girl who could write poems in cursive with a piece of chalk. She knew magical things about forks. There were probably philosophical texts that had been dedicated to her. She was exactly the type of girl that she was before the war. He took her away from France when she asked him to.

* * *

And when she was done with her story that day, she held up a hand mirror in front of her that had a painting of a rose on the back of it.

"I wonder what Marie would think of me now," she said. "She wouldn't be so angry with me. She wouldn't be jealous of me now. I wonder if her hair is still so dark. It was so pretty. A lot of people didn't think that she was pretty, but I really thought she was so lovely."

Grandmother could get lost looking in a mirror and wondering out loud to herself about what Marie was up to, for hours sometimes.

"She must have gotten old just like me. Of course, she would have had to. How strange? We were the same age, you know. She was three days older than me. We both named our cats Napoleon Bonaparte."

Grandmother was always wondering what on earth had ever happened to the magnificent Marie. After all these years, she still longed to have Marie whispering questions to her in the dark.

"The way that air smells like snow reminds me of Marie. I can't imagine why."

She sighed, and we knew that for a moment she had forgotten about my brother and me. This was what had enraged our mother so much when she was young.

You might assume that our grandparents had an unhappy marriage. But Grandfather never seemed to mind coming second place to Marie or that he could never live up to the events that had happened in Grandmother's past. Grandfather felt that he had pulled a fast one on the world by marrying someone so classy and refined. Naturally she was harder to please than the wives of his friends, but that was because she had much more sophisticated tastes.

Just as Grandmother was finished telling her story and had put down her hand mirror, Grandfather jumped up and hurried across the room to turn on the radio that was in their big wooden stereo. There was a radio show that he liked that played old-timey records. He was doing some sort of dance move where he snapped his fingers and bent over and took little tiny steps backwards. My brother and I found his dance routines hysterical. Grandmother looked at him for a moment as if he were completely insane. And then she couldn't help but start laughing out loud. She laughed just like a child.

BARTÓK FOR CHILDREN

Once upon a time there was a young Quebec soldier in occupied France. The Germans couldn't differentiate between a Québécois and a Parisian accent, and so French-Canadian soldiers made perfect spies. This unfortunate Canadian soldier, however, had been turned in by an angry Parisian girlfriend and was shot fifteen times in the chest by a German soldier. He lay on the ground in the woods, looking up at the sky, waiting to die.

The branches of the trees were all laughing at him. It was winter and the snowflakes were falling from the sky slowly. They were enormous, as though old women had crocheted them for a church sale. Looking at them, the soldier didn't think that death would be so bad after all. All he had to do was close his eyes for good this time, but he kept opening them to get one more peek at the world around him and because he wanted to be human for one more second.

His life wasn't flashing before his eyes at all. In fact, he couldn't really recall anything about who he was. Or perhaps he couldn't be bothered to remember anything. He just wanted to have these last moments to himself. He felt as if he was on the verge of figuring something out, as if some greater meaning was about to be revealed to him, but then it wasn't.

Two faces appeared above him. They were the round faces of two little girls. They had on black peacoats and red mittens. One had a pale face with blond curls tumbling onto it. The other had short black hair and thin bow lips.

"*Bonjour, bonjour*," they said.

Their words turned into small puffs of smoke in front of their faces. They took him by the shoulders and shook him. Their dogs were hopping all over his legs and licking his cheeks. He felt them lifting his body onto a little cart. They were scolding their dogs and calling them all manner of beasts.

The soldier closed his eyes. It was all over for him. The bumpy road turned into the soft waves of the sea. He was sailing away, away, away to some place.

* * *

As the girls drew up to the doctor's house, one of them opened the lapels of the soldier's jacket and put her ear against his chest. When she raised her head, her ear and cheek were covered in his blood, but she hadn't heard any heartbeat. They brought him to the doctor, who quickly pronounced the man dead. He told them to bring the man to the mortician's, as he himself was in the middle of a meal. The girls decided to bring him to the Toymaker's house instead. He could fix any toy and bring all sorts of broken things back to life. Their cheeks were the loveliest pink known to humanity due to the effort that they had taken in pulling the soldier all the way to the Toymaker's house, which was all the way out of town.

The Toymaker had always been shy. He had thought that he would overcome it as he grew older, but this had not been the case. He walked through the village with his head down, trying not to make eye contact with anyone. He felt wretched when he was anywhere but his toy shop.

His workshop was where all his friends were. He was busy all the time, bringing things to life. He made dolls with porcelain faces that would speak if you pulled the little chain on their backs.

The dolls had red, glistening lips. They looked as if they were dying to say something but had been warned not to say another word by their teachers. Their eyes were so shiny that at times it seemed as if they were welling up with tears. Their cheeks were rosy, as if they had come in from skating moments before. And their hair was so curly that it always seemed to be shaking, as if they had just taken the pins out and now it was tumbling down and they were laughing.

The Toymaker looked in the mirror and couldn't help but notice the contrast between himself and the dolls. He was so old that great bags had formed under his eyes and his nose was bulbous and covered in spider veins, but inside he had always felt like a boy. The voice that spoke to him in his head was that of a boy. He dressed the same way that he had when he was ten years old, always wearing a vest with red buttons. He made toys that were exactly to his liking, which turned out to be the same tastes of the children who came into his shop. His refusal to grow up was what made him so good at his craft.

The Toymaker was also able to make little clockwork figures. He made monkeys in tailcoats and white bow ties—like waiters at fancy restaurants—that would bang their cymbals together. What a strange occupation for a ten-inch monkey. He would laugh and laugh while looking at them. There was a bear that waddled back and forth with a suitcase in each hand as if he were on his way to catch a train. There was a goose that held a trumpet to its mouth and played a lovely tune.

As much as people found his toys wonderful, no one loved them quite as much as the Toymaker did. He thought they were all so, so enchanting. They broke his heart. But what he could not do was get a doll to love him. Every time he created something that was beautiful, he was struck by a feeling of terrible loneliness.

Before the war, the Toymaker charged top price for his dolls. It was only the very richest of children that were able to afford them. His dolls were renowned and were shipped to rich families in other cities throughout Europe. The children would pull off the huge ribbon from the box and then they would gasp at what was inside. Now there were no orders for expensive dolls from the families in Paris or any other big city.

But he had a soft spot for all children. The children from the village would knock on his back door. They would be weeping and holding up their dolls that needed emergency treatment. They brought him teddy bears that looked like they had dropsy. They looked like little piles of cold porridge.

Some had lost their ears, having been viciously mauled by cats. They were anemic and hungry. There were dolls whose eyes had fallen out and others whose fingers had broken right off.

He had an illegal doll hospital. The Toymaker would pull out the rows of tiny screwdrivers and tweezers. They were so small that he might as well be operating on insects, giving a beetle bypass surgery. He would put on special glasses with magnifying lenses. The children would cry out in surprise when they saw his enormous eyes. He would take his tray of ceramic hands out of the oven, and his bottles of glass eyes that looked out at him from the cabinets, and make all the dolls come back to life. He would lay the dolls on the operating table and he would mend their broken crowns.

One little boy arrived once with a notebook and asked the Toymaker if he would do his math problems with him. His father used to help him, but now he had gone off to fight and was in a prison somewhere. They sat together under the table lamp—the golden glow of the dim bulb—doing his homework together.

But the children always went home at the end of the day. They didn't really belong to him. That's why children wanted and loved dolls. They wanted to have something to keep with them always. They wanted to give something a name. The Toymaker wanted that too.

The Toymaker had a black cat named Cleo that hopped around the house. Its slick fur looked as though it were made out of the same material as a magician's top hat. But that wasn't the same!

* * *

The Toymaker yelled at the girls to bring the soldier in. He couldn't believe it. If he fixed this young man, maybe he could keep him. This might be his chance to have a real boy!

He worked through the night, sewing all the soldier's wounds with invisible thread. He mended his broken leg with tiny screws and plaster. He ran wires through his arms and his legs and then put an electrical box at the bottom of his head. He bestowed on him a clockwork heart. Ever so carefully, he placed a small speaker behind his vocal cords. Finally, he filled the soldier with oil. Then he took a step back and hoped the soldier would come to life, but he didn't.

The children came by every day to see if the soldier was up and about and might want to come and play with them. The little girls yelled into his ears, but the soldier heard nothing. They propped up his head and poured chocolate milk into his lips, but he never swallowed. They held flowers up to his nose to try to get him to inhale. They shoved Cleo's kittens up to his face because they thought no one, not even the dead, could resist a kitten. But the soldier did.

One of the little girls was in charge of brushing his hair with a little brush made from the ivory of a dead elephant's tusk that she had inherited from a grandmother. She swore solemnly that she did not have lice. She brushed his hair for hours and hours. What a lovely pouf of hair the soldier had when she was done. His hair was never going to get out of place ever again and all the girls were going to go bananas about it.

They brought in a little boy who was in the Children's Orchestra to perform for the poor Canadian soldier. He played a Bartók tune that he had learned in school. Even though they knew that they were supposed to be sombre, all the little girls began tapping their feet to the tune. One little girl put her index fingers in the air and started waving them back and forth. The tune was so delightful and bouncy that the soldier's heart could not resist beating along to it. And when the soldier opened his eyes, all the little girls applauded. There were tears in the Toymaker's eyes.

* * *

The soldier had no memory of anything that had happened to him before he was shot and left for dead in the forest. He asked all the questions that everyone had been intending to ask him when he awoke. The Toymaker detected his accent right away and was determined to keep him hidden away from the Germans for the length of this interminable war, at least!

Because he was convalescing and couldn't remember a thing, the soldier found that he was often very, very sad. When the Toymaker told him that yes, they were still at war, the soldier was horrified, and he asked him what in the world was the point of any of it. Why should he get out of bed?

"We just have to try and be good," the Toymaker said. "We can't make ourselves happy. That is a foolhardy enterprise. The only thing we can do is make other people happy."

For some reason the Toymaker's words ruffled the soldier. They sounded like advice of some sort. He had an inkling that he had been lectured to before and he hadn't much liked it. He had never liked being anybody's son, he surmised. Why did you have to come into this world beholden to anyone? He didn't actually owe the Toymaker anything, did he? He hadn't asked to be operated on.

The Toymaker handed him a little matchbox. The soldier opened it to find a cricket inside that started to play a sorrowful tune, using its wee legs like a fiddle. It made him feel so deeply all of a sudden that he was almost sick to his stomach. He was worried for a second that the Toymaker had actually put him together incorrectly and that there was something coming loose in his chest. He closed the matchbox quickly.

* * *

When he was able to get out of bed and stand, the Toymaker bundled the soldier up, wrapping a huge scarf around his neck. The soldier argued that he didn't need that many layers of clothes, but the Toymaker insisted. He helped the soldier to walk again for the first time in the garden. His legs were weak from having been in bed for so long. He stepped on the brambles of frozen rosebushes, and the ground crunched under his feet as he walked across it, as though he were walking on and breaking bones.

The Toymaker put out his arms and yelled, "Come to me. Come to me."

The Toymaker had sewn together a colourful ball. They tossed it back and forth so that the soldier could get his

reflexes back. Whenever the soldier would reach out to catch
the ball, he could feel his insides moving mechanically, and
he could sense oil being released from his clockwork heart
and into his veins. At first it was alarming and he would drop
the ball with a shudder. But he soon began to get used to the
feeling of tiny cogs and bolts and springs moving around, in
the same way that one ignores one's heartbeat.

* * *

German officers had been going around to all the houses in
the village, looking for a spy who had been wounded but
whose body hadn't been recovered. The children went home
every evening and they told their parents nothing whatsoever
about the spy they had found in the woods. In that day and
age it wasn't at all the custom to ask children what they were
thinking. So they were able to sit, unassuming, at the other
side of the table, with all the wonders of the world locked
away in their brains. They didn't want the soldier to be put
in prison or hanged. He could stay with the Toymaker in the
woods forever.

The soldier grew restless in the little house very soon.
He grew tired of all the little girls reading him stories out
of their fat books. He had had enough of them telling him
the long and drawn-out histories of teddy bears and handing him tiny cups that they said were filled with coffee but
had nothing at all inside of them. There were things that he
needed to talk about—that he couldn't talk about with little
girls or with an old man who claimed to be his father.

The soldier began to feel the urge to be alone for at least a few moments. Everywhere he looked there always seemed to be little girls. They would cuddle up into his armpit while he was taking a nap. They were underneath the kitchen table and he couldn't move his legs without kicking one. While he was on the toilet, they would come into the bathroom and try to sit on his lap. They would be stomping around the house in his boots and his jacket. There would be three or four of them sitting in the bathtub, pouring cups of water onto one another's head, whenever he wanted to bathe himself.

Although the soldier wanted to be treated like an adult, he seemed so young to the Toymaker. The soldier still had such rosy cheeks and seemed so incredibly foolish. The Toymaker wanted to be a father to the soldier and tried everything to bond with him.

The Toymaker had been working on manufacturing a toy clown that blew up a rubber balloon. He sat across the table from the soldier and set it in front of him.

"Look at this. It will make you laugh so hard! I'm going to write on the box that if this toy doesn't make you laugh, you can get a full refund."

The tiny clown blew and blew until the red balloon was full and round. The soldier only stared at it, unimpressed.

"Oh!" the Toymaker said. "It didn't make you laugh."

"You might want to take off that guarantee, buddy. Especially now we're in the middle of a war. There's not a lot of laughing going on."

"I want you to feel at home here," the Toymaker said, wanting to get to the point. "I think of you as my own flesh and blood. Really. You're the boy that I always imagined having. You're so handsome and so smart. You dress yourself so well."

"Geez," said the soldier. "Do you get like this with everyone?"

The soldier had no intention of spending the rest of his days there. The thought of it made him crazy. But he didn't think there was any point in hurting the old man's feelings, so he didn't bother to tell him so.

"Do you have anything to read?" the soldier asked.

"Yes," said the Toymaker, happy to be useful. He hurried into his living room and brought back a big book of fairy tales.

"Do you prefer to read by yourself, or do you prefer to be read to?" the Toymaker asked. "There's a story in here that my own mother used to read to me when I was little. It is about a goose that always has to protect her goslings from a very fancy wolf who has developed a taste for such birds."

"Are you mad? A tale about a goose? What kind of insight can a goose have? Do you have any of that existentialism that's supposed to be all the rage in Paris?"

The next day, the Toymaker left the house. He knocked on the door of a lawyer who lived in town. The lawyer was surprised to see the Toymaker at his door, and was even more surprised when he asked if he could borrow some books from his library.

When the soldier went to bed that night, there was a copy of a book by Albert Camus on his nightstand, next to a glass of milk and a small plate of cookies.

The soldier felt that on some level he should be touched.

He knew that the Toymaker was doing everything to make things special, but he didn't want to feel indebted. The soldier wanted to pay his own way in this world so that he could act exactly as he wanted. He resented that the Toymaker was expecting things from him.

He had a compulsion to open the matchbox as he sometimes did when he was reflecting on things. He could never bear more than a minute or two though, as the music of the cricket always made him feel kind of sad, even though there was nothing for him to be upset about. And this wasn't necessarily a bad thing. He actually quite liked it. It made him think that there was some part of him that he knew nothing about and that was going to very much surprise him one day. Nobody really wants to know themselves completely, especially not when they are young. What's the fun in that? He didn't mention the book at all when the Toymaker peeked in later that night. This time too he closed the matchbox soon after opening it.

The Toymaker sat by himself on a little chair in the kitchen. He had to admit that he was disappointed because he'd thought that he and the boy would do all sorts of things together. He had pictured them looking for mushrooms together in the forest. He had imagined them on a beach, looking for pretty seashells. But he also had to admit that he wasn't as lonely anymore. It was as if any company was better than no company.

* * *

The boys in the village kept begging to try on the soldier's topcoat. They wanted to play with his radio. The soldier found two of them in his room one afternoon, pretending to electrocute another little boy seated on a chair, demanding he give up the names of Resistance fighters. The soldier yelled at the boys to get lost and chased them right out the door. He sat on the bed, wondering about his aborted mission in France and where he was actually supposed to be.

"You can be a role model to those boys," the Toymaker said. "They look up to you. Why don't you go out and play some football with them? I bet you could take on all of them by yourself."

The soldier didn't say anything, but he slammed his bedroom door shut in the Toymaker's face. All the paintings in the house fell off the walls. The Toymaker thought that this was what being a real parent was like. It was not all wine and roses. You had to try to make your child feel loved and wanted and worthy over and over again, no matter what they did. If he kept at it, he could teach the soldier to be loving and kind.

"They know your face," whispered the Toymaker on the other side of the door. "Your days as a spy are over. You can't go out there, but you can be happy here."

But as much as he tried to be a parent, the soldier refused to be a son to him.

* * *

One of the neighbouring farmers delivered food to the Toymaker's house every week. The soldier always found the culinary selections unsatisfying.

"Don't you have any way to get wine and meat, for God's sake?" the soldier asked.

"You have to go into the Big Town to get them. It's too far a walk for me."

"Well, why didn't you say so? I'll go for you."

The soldier got dressed in a long grey coat and a beret and scowled with feigned disgust. He stood in the living room for the Toymaker and the children to admire his new look as an indignant Frenchman. Although he couldn't remember anything about his past, he had a feeling that his having been shot had had something to do with a woman and not his subterfuge skills.

"You will be found and killed," the Toymaker exclaimed.

"Oh come on, no German in the world can tell that I'm not from France. I just have to scoff at the trees and the rocks and existence as I walk—that's the hard part. I'm going into town now. I'm going to be somebody's Cousin Loïc, okay? If I get shot, it's not the biggest deal in the world is it? A passing mechanic'll surely be kind enough to put me back together. I'll have exhaust fumes coming out of my ass when I run. Or maybe an electrician will find me, and when I wake up in the morning my head will glow like a lightbulb."

All the children laughed uncontrollably at this joke, holding their bellies, which were getting cramps from being doubled over, and crossing their legs so that they didn't pee themselves. But the Toymaker didn't even smile. On the contrary, he was very serious and worried. He interpreted the soldier's lack of sensitivity as being due to immaturity. He was no more than a silly little boy—and silly little boys lost their way in the woods.

But the soldier managed to get to the Big Town after a two-hour walk without incident. On the black market he bought a bottle of wine, a long row of sausages, some bread and a bag of coffee. He walked through the woods, whistling a Bartók tune, looking forward to eating some proper food.

On his way back, he spotted a striking young woman coming toward him. There also happened to be a big tomcat following her down the path. She was tall and had red hair that was coming out from beneath a white fur hat. She wore a black fitted coat that went down almost to her ankles. What a fox! the soldier thought.

"That's a pretty coat," the soldier said.

"I found it in an abandoned house. I knew that no one was going to come back for it. It's so warm. Do you want to buy it?"

"No thanks. That's a giant cat you have there. It looks as if the two of you have had some really good times together."

"He's the only one I can trust in this world. You can't trust people anymore. It's the people that are the animals."

The soldier paused, not knowing what to say for a moment. This girl had an odd way of making small talk.

"Do you want some food?"

"Please," she said, her voice cracking.

She ate a piece of sausage ravenously. She went through all his food, shoving chunks of bread into her mouth. When he was about to object and say that there were others who wanted the food, she hurriedly put three sausages in one of her pockets and the bag of coffee into the other. Then she put her hands up to his face.

"Kiss me. I so want to be kissed right now. I don't care if it's good or proper. I just want to feel alive. I need to be reminded that I'm alive and that I'm not in the grave."

The soldier forgot about anything else that was happening in the world. The girl's cheeks tasted like tears, but oh my lord, how she kissed. It was a bit of a disappointment when she took off her coat. She looked so skinny, her ribs were poking out and her arms were covered in bruises. But the woman had eyes that looked at him in a way that none of the little girls ever could. She was having dirty thoughts. That's what he had felt was missing in him in the quaint little house in the woods. The Toymaker and the little girls knew nothing about getting naked and the secret things that adults liked to do when they couldn't sleep. Nobody had read to him from *The Complete Marquis de Sade* to try to revive him.

"Let's find a place to drink this, shall we?" she said, taking his bottle of wine and waving it.

He looked down at the cat. Maybe he was imagining it, but the cat seemed to have a smirk on its face. The smell of coffee whiffed around him. Oh Lord, how long it had been since he had had a cup of coffee. How long it had been since he had had a naked girl sitting on his face. He suddenly remembered who he was. He was a man. He slid his hand inside the woman's dress and onto her right breast and grabbed it hard. And the woman moaned.

Everything inside his clockwork body began pumping away madly. He didn't even care if his heart exploded and burst into a million little screws and bolts. That was what it felt like it was going to do any moment, and if it did, it would be worth it. She put her mouth on his dick and he turned his head up toward the sky and laughed and laughed. He felt alive.

He knew that he had to get out of that house in the woods—after he had taken her from behind and she had cried out so loudly that it had startled birds in the neighbouring village.

As soon as the soldier was spent, the girl quickly put her clothes back on. The girl picked up the cat and held it tightly, as if it was all that was valuable in the world and she was suddenly terrified of losing it. She barely even said goodbye as she hurried away. The soldier found himself aching when he saw her go. He loved the sensation of it. For the first time since the Toymaker had brought him back to life, he felt fulfilled by an emotion. He wanted to ache like that again and again. He was impressed that the girl had made love to him and then got up and just left. While he watched her disappear into the woods, he decided that he was going to walk away from the Toymaker. It was what adults did.

He felt in his pocket to make sure the matchbox was still there. He couldn't leave the cricket behind as it was a present. The Toymaker had gone through so much trouble to fix up all his parts and build him a new metallic heart. The least he could do would be to accept the gift that he had given him. He was undoubtedly an asshole, but when he felt the matchbox in his pocket, he thought for a brief second that he might have a conscience after all.

Although he was taking the cricket with him, he didn't dare take it out of its matchbox and let it play its bittersweet violin as he walked down the road. The wee violin tune might fill his head with all sorts of emotions that he didn't want to have. Those were the sorts of emotions that ended up keeping you in one place. They would make you feel guilt and a sense of responsibility. Those emotions were like cages.

* * *

The soldier made it out of France. A pretty peasant woman showed him a way out after he made love to her in a haystack. He found his way to the secret rendezvous spot set up by the Canadians to escort Resistance fighters and prisoners back to England. He was whisked across the water in the dead of night. Upon his return, nobody could believe that he was still alive. A doctor looked at the stitches on his torso and whistled at the handiwork. He put a stethoscope against the soldier's chest and said he'd never heard such a regular heartbeat in all his life. He gave the soldier a clean bill of health.

As a reward for his daring spy ventures, he was given a desk job in England for the remainder of the war. He went out dancing every night with the other soldiers, trying to meet local girls. He was happy there. He found that the girls in London sounded like they had lollipops in their mouths when they spoke. They had adorable little beer bellies from being out drinking all night. The girls in England found everything funny. The commanding officer had to tell the soldiers not to tell the English girls so many jokes, because one of them laughed so hard that she had an asthma attack and died.

When he would get back to base every night, he always had the craziest stories about making love to women. He really outdid all the other soldiers.

He made love to a girl under the bandstand. When the drums were banging, it made all his nerves tremble. He made love to a girl a minute after New Year's and there was still confetti in her hair. He made love to a girl in a bathroom while she held both their beer mugs, trying not to let them spill.

He made love to a girl who was six months pregnant and said that the father of the child was missing in action. He put his head against her belly and felt the baby kick. He liked anything new. He liked anything unusual. He went to pick up a girl who wasn't there and he ended up having her mother on the kitchen table. When they were done, she lectured him about keeping her daughter out too late.

Some of the girls would make love to him for a pair of nylon stockings. Some of them, he didn't even know why on earth they were making love to him. They clearly didn't like it. There was something about him that made him irresistible. Maybe it was because he didn't have a soul. Or perhaps it was because he didn't have a conscience. Women go crazy for a man with no conscience.

He never came close to falling in love with anybody. Instead, he went around having trysts, looking for encounters that would make all the cogs and wheels in his heart begin to spin wildly. He could feel all sorts of little bolts sliding into different compartments and prongs going into different levers. And tiny little pistons started going up and down, and oil would be released over all of his hinges and he felt he moved so smooth and well.

One night he was in an alleyway with a short girl with blond corkscrew curls falling down her round face. She was getting on his nerves because she wouldn't put out. He naturally sometimes liked the hard-to-get types, but he had just had enough of them for one week. And she bore an uncanny resemblance to the dolls in the Toymaker's shop, which he found disconcerting.

"Where do you see us ten years from now?" she asked.

"How in the world would I know something like that? What do you take me for? A fortune teller? Am I carrying around a crystal ball?"

What sort of lie did this silly girl want to hear? the soldier wondered. What idiotic fable would she take her clothes off for? She wanted to hear about having a family, of course. If there was anything more ridiculous to the soldier than romantic love, it was undoubtedly this idea that you were supposed to have a family. He felt like lying to her if only to mock her values.

"Well, come to think of it, I see myself living in a really big house."

When he said this, she undid her top button and jutted her chest out toward him. The girl's bust was really large and the dress had to, undoubtedly, be pulled together to be buttoned up. The idea of all those buttons coming undone encouraged the soldier to continue his fantastical lie.

"I see myself reading a newspaper in the mornings. And I want to be a father, because I want to know what that feels like. Because I had such a special relationship with my own dad, you know?"

The girl released another button from its tiny hole.

"That's the most important thing to me: having a close-knit family. I only ever wanted to have one girlfriend, because I know that the task of keeping one girl happy is a big enough job for a fellow like me."

Every time a lie caused a button to jump free, his dick grew more erect. He didn't think that he had ever had such a hard-on as the one he had for this curly-haired girl. He pushed her up against the wall and she let him have his way with her as she closed her eyes and fantasized about laughing children climbing into their bed in the mornings.

Later that night in his room, the soldier felt empty. Each affair left him with more assured proof that he didn't have anything like a soul inside of him, and as though life were insignificant and meaningless. But that night, pretending for a moment that he did care about the idea of a full life had left him with such a sense of the grand futility of everything that he felt as though he were about to be swallowed up by nothingness. That night he decided that he had to go back to France and work as a spy again. He still couldn't remember his former life, but he wondered if this sort of feeling wasn't what had sent him over to France as a spy the first time.

A few days later, as he was packing a small bag with only necessary items, he noticed the matchbox with the cricket in it. He opened it and the cricket started playing the most depressing and creepy Bartók tune. It gave him an unholy feeling and made the hair stand up on his neck. He closed the box quickly.

Honestly, he didn't understand that cricket at all and he wasn't sure that he ever would. He didn't even know how the cricket got it into its head to play in such a strange way. What in the world was music like that for? You couldn't dance to it and it certainly wouldn't put any babies to sleep.

Nonetheless, he stuck the cricket inside his pocket. The cricket had been with him this long and was the closest thing he had to a past. And, in any case, he wasn't quite sure that it was a wise decision to go and leave this little cricket playing its mournful, melancholic tunes on windowsills. Someone was bound to take a shoe and clobber it.

* * *

It was especially risky for this soldier to return, as he had already been found out and the German soldiers would be looking out for him, but he had insisted on returning to finish his work as a spy. He knew that he was doing a deep good, but he didn't even know if he was doing it for the right reasons. Everyone admired his bravery. But was he doing it because he wanted to engage in a profoundly moral action, or was he doing it because he hated himself and wanted to put himself in danger in order to feel alive? That feeling of having a gun up to your heart, about to pull the trigger—at least that would make his damn heart beat faster.

They tossed him out of the plane, his parachute burst above him like a single piece of popcorn in the night and down he went onto occupied soil. He didn't look for the Toymaker, but no one could fault him for that as he was so busy being a hero. He and the other Canadian spies worked hard delivering information and maps to the Resistance fighters, ferreting Allied soldiers out of France and onto boats to England. One night he was hurrying down a road on a bicycle, trying to get to the coast of Brittany. It was the quickest way to get to the coast and he was rather enjoying it, inhaling enormous gulps of air while riding the bicycle over the gravelly ground, when he was stopped by German officers waiting for him at a bend in the path. When they found the radio in his bicycle basket, he knew that he was done for.

* * *

The soldier was in a bedroom. The torturers had secured bolts and locks on the door and had hammered planks of wood over the windows. He was wearing his navy blue cable sweater over a shirt, loose-fitting pants, a coat with a fur lining and boots that went to his knees. He was attached to a chain that had been secured to the metal framework of the bed.

Everything valuable had been dragged out of the room. There were no clothes in the dressers, no books on the shelves. He noticed that there was a small teddy bear in the corner, grasping the leg of the armoire and looking at him. Whether it had chosen to stay behind or had been left there, he could not say. It had probably once been a child's bedroom.

There was no way to escape now. There was nothing he could say or do that would change his fate. He was already a dead man, really.

Since part of his body was mechanical, he was able to withstand pain better than most people, but not that much more. They had broken the fingers of his right hand but those of his left were still working perfectly well. He used them to pull his matchbox out of the breast pocket of his shirt. He opened the matchbox slowly, in order that the cricket might be released. He had given the cricket a leaf to eat a few days before, but he really hadn't thought about it since then. The cricket climbed out in fine form, scurried up the arm of the tin soldier and perched on his shoulder. The cricket was as close as possible to the soldier's ear so that he would best be able to hear what it had to say.

It told him his life story, including all the sad things about his terrible childhood in Canada that he had forced himself to forget. Instead of reminiscing about all the very good times that he had had, the soldier let himself remember his own tragedy. He thought about how his dad would come home and beat his mother in the kitchen and how he would hide in the closet. He remembered how his father had kicked him out of the house when he was sixteen years old. He reminisced about how he'd lived on the streets and in boys' homes for two years before the war happened and how he'd enlisted in order to have a square meal and some new boots. It struck him deeply that nobody had cared when he went off. These were his last moments on earth probably, and he decided that he would allow himself to feel grief. He wanted to feel upset, full of regret and consumed by sorrow. These were the wonderful things in life. These were the emotions that were more like works of art than anything else. That's why we had music in this world, to make us feel such complicated things.

The soldier wondered who would actually notice that he was gone. Who would accidentally put a plate out for him months and months after his death? The soldier tried to recall each of the girls he had been with while in England. He imagined them in their kitchens, at their kitchen tables, eating their clam chowder, their corned beef, their cornbread, their Spam, their pickled eggs, their meat loaf, their ratatouille. But he knew that they were probably not really thinking about him.

The only person who was worried about him was the Toymaker. He was probably painting the feathers of a beautiful bird in his workshop. But perhaps he had stopped painting altogether and now lay in bed, sick with worry over what had happened to his dear soldier boy on that walk that he had never come back from. The soldier thought of that Toymaker, who had nobody but a feisty black cat and a bunch of fickle children hanging around. The Toymaker, who had never known the love of a woman and had only ever wanted a boy of his own.

But he could not think of the Toymaker now. He didn't know the names of his fellow spies or members of the Resistance that he had been working with. They had all been careful about that, so that in the event that one of them got captured, they would have nothing to reveal. Even when he had made love to French girls, he had always warned them not to tell him their names.

He did know the name of the Toymaker, however. The children repeated it about a hundred times a day. He hoped and prayed that he could keep it to himself and not give it to his torturers. It wasn't as though confessing would set you free. Once you had given up your names, they would shoot you in the woods and leave you there, if you were very lucky. Or they would put you in a concentration camp where you would stand in line for death.

The door burst open and two men came for him, unlocking his chains and dragging him off the bed. He couldn't help but fight to get away from them, and he squirmed from their grasp onto the ground. One man kicked him in the stomach, which knocked the fight out of him momentarily. The other man pulled him by the scruff of his neck down the narrow hallway.

He grabbed at the wall with his left hand, but all that he managed to snatch was a bit of the wallpaper with blue roses on it that came off like the page of a book. They pulled him into the clean white bathroom, where another man waited.

The white tiles were slippery. They pulled off his coat and his sweater and flung them aside. The bathtub was filled with water and when they plunged him into it, the freezing temperature shocked his body and his back arched and his legs jolted so violently he thought he might break them. It froze him all the way to the bone as they forced him under the water. He grasped wildly, struggling for some way to come up for air, but there was nothing that his limbs could do for him now. His universe had shrunk down to the size of a bathtub and there was no way out of it. They pulled him out for a second and then shoved him back under.

He had never felt so trapped. Every time he went underneath the water he felt sure that he would drown. He had no idea what it would feel like when he couldn't breathe anymore or how much death would hurt. There was a terror of the unknown all around him. That same feeling was being experienced all over Europe. There was a little boy who had crawled under his kitchen table during an air raid who felt it. It was in the heart of a little girl who had been separated from her parents and was now stuck on a crowded train. There was a boy touching a bullet hole, terrified because he didn't feel a thing. There were ninety children all feeling it at once on board the SS *City of Benares* passenger ship, which had just been struck by a torpedo. And they all kissed their dolls and teddy bears and told them not to worry and wished them Godspeed.

The soldier inhaled and the water finally came in, burning his lungs. They pulled him out and flung him onto the floor, where he lay, coughing and vomiting water. He was shaking so hard from the cold that he couldn't speak. No part of his body was still and his teeth were chattering against each other. The intricate wires in his brain began short-circuiting, the sparks taking the form of a thousand neurotic thoughts all at once and causing an unbearable pressure in his head. His stomach flooded with motor oil, making him nauseous. And his heart was beating so fast that all the bolts and springs began to explode out of their proper spots, like tiny mortar shells being flung about his insides. He wanted everything to work properly in his body, he never wanted excitement again, he wanted this to end.

It was just a matter of time before he gave them what they wanted, wasn't it? Resisting torture is a myth: everyone confesses in the end. There is no way not to. We are humans and we are built to be capable of betraying everyone in the end. Our pain makes us vulnerable. We can all be got to. We can all be turned upside down like a purse and have all our contents shaken right out of us.

The soldier reminded himself again that he was different. He wasn't quite a real boy. He was callous and insensitive and his heart was hard. Those qualities would come to his aid now. If his heart was mechanical—if his parts were all replaceable—then he should be capable of withstanding torture. Let myself break, he thought. I can be put back together.

He went back under three times. On the third time, he came out, sputtering for air and vacillating as the spark plugs in his spine began to blow one by one. And he spoke the Toymaker's name aloud. Or it was more like the Toymaker's name escaped out of him. The secret was afraid of drowning and so it came out of his mouth in order to belong to someone else.

When he heard the Toymaker's name come from his lips, the soldier knew, to his own surprise, that he was a human being. Nothing remarkable could be expected from him.

This time when they pushed him back under the water,

he inhaled and there was suddenly a strange calm that entered his lungs and flooded through his body. He felt the hands of the torturer let go their grip on him. It was as though they were strings that had just been cut. He felt himself sinking down to the bottom of the bathtub, free of all restraint. The bathtub seemed to have depths that he was hitherto completely unaware of. He had kept his eyes squeezed shut until that moment. Now he opened them to discover that there was water all around him. It wasn't the cold clear water of the bathtub, but the messy, strange green-blue of the ocean. It was filled with all sorts of life.

The fish went by like leaves being blown off trees. There were large sea turtles that looked like pyjamas hanging off a laundry line and waving in the wind. A school of shimmering fish passed by, as if someone had tossed a whole handful of change into the water.

He could not say how long he had been under the water, as time seemed to be irrelevant now somehow. His shirt had been torn open while he was being tortured. For some reason he thought to button it up and as he did, the soldier noticed that all the scars and seams that the Toymaker had made while operating on his chest had completely disappeared. You would never know that he had been operated on, or that he had been built and repaired in any way.

He felt the presence beneath him. It was a cold feeling, although it didn't involve a drop in temperature. It was more like the sensation of darkness. He felt the dark shadow growing beneath him. It was so silent and he wondered how anything so enormous could also be so quiet. He thought that he should get to the surface again, so that he could escape whatever was beneath him.

As soon as he broke through the surface of the water, the jaws of the whale also exploded open around him. They then closed around the soldier, swallowing him and bringing him back down into the depths. Deeper and deeper and deeper.

There he was in the great belly of the whale. He thought that it would all be darkness, but to his surprise, there was a light that was glowing. He didn't know what to make of it. He followed it as he climbed over the half-digested creatures. The thin bones of fishes crunched under his feet as the frozen rose brambles had once, as though he was learning to walk again.

There, in the centre of the stomach, was a small table with a candle burning on it. There was a tiny pot that was filled with krill that were jumping up and down in it. The Toymaker was seated at the table, holding a fork and looking into the wide pot. It seemed as though the Toymaker was going to eat the fish while they were still alive.

"Papa," said the soldier.

The Toymaker looked up and cried out, as if his deepest wish had just been answered.

A CHRISTMAS CAROL

Grandfather announced that when he was little, before the war, Christmas was his very favourite day of the year. We couldn't begin to imagine how strange and magical the Christmas he turned seven was, he said as he poured himself another glass of eggnog. My brother and I sat down at the kitchen table, eagerly awaiting the ridiculous things Grandfather would have to say about that particular Christmas. We were undoubtedly about to hear some story about a reindeer with a Russian accent and a drinking problem throwing up on his lawn. That's because Grandfather's stories were always so over the top. According to him, you see, the world before the war was a very different place.

Grandfather used to say that when he was little, potatoes actually had tiny little eyes that would open up and look at you. You could hear seashells laughing and talking to one another on the seashore. When you were at the beach, it sounded like you were in the audience at a circus when the lights went off and the show was about to begin.

At the zoo, there was a lion that knew how to say a few words. You had to yell and scream and beg in order to get it to say them. Crowds of kids would shake the bars and curse until finally the lion would roll over and say, "Go away." Everyone would applaud.

It was harder to tell the difference between when you were asleep and when you were awake. Children would sit and slap each other in the face, trying to wake one another out of a dream when things weren't going right.

When Grandfather was little, there were always people trapped in air balloons. You would stand on ladders, and when they passed overhead, you would offer them sandwiches.

Girls would fall so madly in love back then, it would almost kill them. They would hold on to three umbrellas and jump out the window after their mother locked them in at night. It was very common for pretty girls to have broken ankles.

He said that sailors had tattoos of beautiful women that would literally dance on their arms and pucker their lips for a kiss. That's why almost no one got tattoos back when Grandfather was little. They were harder to live with and sometimes they started to nag.

There were so many babies back then that you couldn't remember where they came from. His mother came home with a parcel wrapped in pink paper. She was sure that it was a little piece of ham that she had bought, but when she unwrapped it, lo and behold, it was a baby.

Grandfather said that when he was little, before the war, he was always hungry. He said that he and his mother would regularly go without eating for five or six days straight and his eyelashes would freeze shut from the cold.

"But the minute I woke up that Christmas morning, I knew something truly out of the ordinary was about to happen," Grandfather said, pouring himself yet another glass of eggnog.

On the Christmas morning that he turned seven, Grandfather continued, his mother dressed him up in a new sweater and said, for five minutes straight, how beautiful and handsome he was. She couldn't stop kissing him, as if it was a curse.

Later in the day, his uncles and aunts, whom he hadn't seen all year, came toppling through the door, wearing fancy outfits and drinking and being merry. They kissed him all over the face with their boozy, boozy breath. They sang songs and knocked over some plates and broke a couple of cups. Cousin after cousin kept showing up, until there were maybe thirteen cousins in the house.

Then his older brothers started arriving with their girl-friends. The girlfriends laughed and sang and drank too much, trying to show off what a good time they were. Grandfather had never seen such pretty girls as the ones his brothers brought home that Christmas Day, with their red lipstick and perfect curls and fancy party dresses. And they all toasted one another and life while sitting on his lucky brothers' laps.

Right before they were about to sit down to eat, Grand-father's oldest brother, Toots, came in dressed in his army uniform. He was going to be shipped off to Europe in two days, and everyone went wild seeing him. They almost never saw Toots anymore because he was always off gallivanting and pursuing some new girl or money-making scheme. He sang a dirty song he'd picked up downtown and he did his famous impersonation of James Cagney.

The table was covered with food. The turkey was so enormous that you couldn't put your arms around it if you tried. There were mounds of sweet potatoes and cranberries and corn and sweetbreads. And then there was round after round of cakes and cookies. You couldn't possibly imagine how much his family ate that day. They ate like the big bad wolf in fairy tales, who could swallow whole families.

And the house, which was usually so cold and bleak, was filled with cigarette smoke and laughter and yelling and tears and accusations. And everyone telling the same favourite memories that they would tell every Christmas. And they laughed about jobs they had lost, and girls who had gotten away and pets that were in heaven.

Even though Grandfather sometimes felt left out during the year and like nobody on earth loved him, everyone remembered to bring him something so lovely that Christmas Day. He suddenly felt like a regular Little Lord Fauntleroy, what with all those gifts. He got teddy bears, mittens with snowflakes on them and a little tin fire engine.

That night seemed to last and last and last. No matter what was going to happen, if Toots never came back from the war, which he never did, and some of the girls grew fat and unhappy with his brothers, which they did, they would always have this night when everyone was happy and worry-free.

It seemed like with everything Grandfather recalled,

he imagined it bigger and better and stranger than it could actually be. But this Christmas Day, to our surprise, seemed like any Christmas Day in any household. It was as if he couldn't imagine anything grander than the typical Christmas that people were having. It was magical enough on its own and couldn't be improved upon. This sort of made my brother and me feel very warm inside.

But then, after his fourth glass of eggnog, Grandfather told us that later in the evening, Toots took off his jacket and his mermaid tattoo started flirting with one of the cousins. At which point Toots threw the cousin right out the window and into the backyard, where, to everyone's amazement, they discovered a tipsy reindeer with a bright red nose, throwing up.

"Excuse me," the reindeer said. "I get motion sickness with all this spinning around the world on Christmas night. Not to mention I had a few too many with the elves before leaving the North Pole."

Then the reindeer staggered up into the sky, skirting past the girls leaping out of windows, and circling around the wayward air balloons whose passengers sat in the baskets, singing Christmas carols.

Then Grandfather's mother noticed that the reindeer had left behind a package: a little bundle wrapped in fish paper. She opened it and found Jeannie, Grandfather's youngest sister, who happened to have been born on Christmas Day, curled up and sleeping inside.

"And that," said Grandfather, "was what Christmas miracles were like before the war!"

THE WOLF-BOY
OF NORTHERN QUEBEC

Two years before we met and fell in love, Pierre-Loup was discovered in the north of Quebec, half-naked and covered in filth. It was the newspapers that nicknamed him Pierre-Loup, a name he told me he could never stand. At the time of his discovery, his identity was confirmed as that of Pierre Normand, who had gone missing from a campsite eighteen years earlier. Everyone thought the little Normand boy had long been murdered or had starved to death, but this was not the case. Pierre had been living among the wolves.

Sightings of the legendary wolf-boy had been common in the north of Quebec for years.

"There's Pierre-Loup," high school boys would tell their girls, pointing into the woods, and the girls would clutch them tighter. People would occasionally claim to have seen a naked little boy running out of their yards with strangled chickens in his hands, laughing. When he was seven, the wolves found him red rubber boots, a pair of shorts and a brown sweater in a garbage dump. As a clothed little boy, Pierre-Loup was able to venture into parks and super-markets and steal whole barbecued chickens to bring back to the pack. The wolves had never eaten so well in their lives, and in this way, Pierre and the wolves lived their lives hap-pily, with Pierre becoming a valued member of the pack.

But then at twenty-three, Pierre-Loup was apprehended running out of a supermarket with an armful of raw ham-burger meat, as a pack of wolves lay waiting in the parking lot.

"Unhand me, varmints," cursed Pierre as the wolves scrambled over parked cars on their way back to the woods.

In the hours that followed, the world learned of Pierre-Loup's history. Sociologists and linguists rushed to meet him in the hotel where he was sequestered, to learn how a feral child could have grown up to speak so well.

Pierre-Loup told them he had learned English by over-hearing as he rooted through garbage cans behind people's houses and reading the labels on beef jerky wrappers.

"I've always been a fast learner," he said. "The only one in our pack who could peel an orange."

The authorities made an attempt to contact his parents, but as it turned out, the grief over his childhood disappear-ance had driven them both to despair, and five years earlier, after coming home from an evening out with friends, they had sealed up the windows, laid themselves down in bed and turned on the gas.

And so Pierre-Loup was left without a human soul in the world.

* * *

Pierre was unexpectedly charming, not at all what you would expect from a feral child, and people couldn't get enough of him. He did the talk-show circuit, regaling interviewers with stories about his wolf family.

"I had one cousin who was always trying to pass himself off as some sort of 'lone wolf,' but then around mealtime, he'd always creep back, pretending to have forgotten something."

When asked if he'd always felt like an outsider among the wolves, he sneered, "Why would I? I am a wolf."

And he did vaguely resemble one. His mouth was huge like Mick Jagger's and his face almost seemed to split in two when he smiled. Although he was only twenty-three, his messy black hair was going prematurely grey, and from out of it, his huge ears stuck out, accentuating how narrow his face was.

"Didn't you ever feel there was something different about you while growing up?" Barbara Walters asked.

"Well, my mother did lavish an inordinate amount of attention on me," he said. "I *did* mention the red boots I was given, did I not?"

You could see Barbara Walters looking a little flustered. Seeing that he had missed her point, she continued.

"You must miss your dead parents terribly." She said this with her trademark empathetic squint—the look that cues her producers to zoom in for the guest's tears. But Pierre-Loup was nonplussed.

"My wolf family is my only family," he said resolutely, and rather than cry, he pulled out some beef jerky from his pocket and sucked on it contentedly.

* * *

Pierre-Loup continued to perplex and surprise many more hosts on many more TV shows. When it was time to walk on stage for *The Oprah Winfrey Show*, he was so excited that he ran out on all fours and collided into the couch, knocking over most of the set and scaring Oprah very badly. To make matters worse, during the commercial break, he relieved himself in a rubber tree plant beside his armchair. And then, back from the break, he pulled out a goldfish from a Ziploc bag and poured it into his bottle of beer. He called it his "protein shake."

He then spent the remainder of the interview talking about his dislike of "Pitou," the hairdresser's lapdog, which he'd met backstage.

"That little jerk would stab you in the back! A real vainglorious runt. He couldn't take down a rabbit with a broken leg, so why is he so full of himself?"

In spite of his shenanigans, Pierre-Loup was TV magic. He was recruited by a touring agency that booked him on a speaking tour of Europe, where he became as beloved a North American export as Jerry Lewis and Twinkies.

He was a particular hit with the French intelligentsia, who wrote essays about him, holding him up as a symbol of our primordial spirit and all that we have lost. Also, they loved when he performed La Marseillaise and begged him to howl it every chance they got.

Pierre-Loup became notorious for being thrown out of a hotel for swimming naked in the pool, peeing off a balcony, eating tropical fish out of an aquarium and murdering a guest's Pekingese. He befriended a stray German shepherd from the pound who had a missing eye and broken tail, and together they toured around France, the two of them riding first class and drinking champagne. The French media began to call him a *poète maudit*.

These were very good times for Pierre-Loup. He enjoyed seeing the world and seemed to thrive on all the attention. Because of his popularity, feral children became all the rage in Europe, and so, to draw even bigger crowds, the tour organizers decided to pair Pierre-Loup with George LeCurieu. While on an Indian safari with his parents, George had fallen from a jeep and, subsequently, had been raised by macaque monkeys.

A new poster was hastily prepared in which George was shown laughing, with a banana peel on his head, as Pierre-Loup stood beside him scowling, with a dead rabbit in his mouth.

From the very first moment that Pierre met him, he hated George LeCurieu's guts. The two feral children were complete opposites. Whereas Pierre was aloof and imposing, George was always trying to put everyone he met at ease. In fact, when they first met, George was riding a tricycle around and around in circles. He handed Pierre a red balloon, which Pierre quickly popped on his thumbnail.

George had been mentored by a showbiz chimpanzee who had done a lot of film work. He had instructed George in what he believed impressed humans the most. George could barely even talk, but being so desperate for love, he would roll his lips under his gums, puff his cigar and smilingly wait to be applauded, and when he was, he would tip his pink-and-purple party hat.

Pierre-Loup was sickened by George's complete lack of dignity. When George clumsily tap-danced to "Tea for Two," Pierre would bite his knuckle until it bled.

"I refuse to tour with that imbecile," said Pierre-Loup to the tour manager.

"We can filter that aggression back into the act," the manager assured him. "Maybe start each show with a fake sword fight. Monkey versus wolf!"

Pierre-Loup wanted to quit on the spot, but the truth was that he had developed quite a taste for expensive wine and fine clothing. In fact, when asked by reporters if he still felt the call of the wild, he said, "Not really. It's just too bloody difficult being hungry all the time."

* * *

For Pierre-Loup, the bottom finally fell out at the now-infamous lecture that he and George gave at École normale supérieure, during the question and answer period. It seemed that some of the professors wished to challenge Pierre's assertion that he was in fact a wolf.

"You don't have a tail, monsieur!" Professor Monpetit exclaimed.

"How dare you!" Pierre-Loup retorted. "My brother had his tail cut off in a mink trap. Does that make him any less of a wolf? If a man loses a leg in the war, is he not still a man? You cannot reduce my essence to a body part!"

"But you can speak several languages, monsieur!" Professor Delinelle yelled.

"Wolf is my mother tongue, and even you, sir, will concede that it is superior to English."

All the French philosophers chuckled at this one, but still they were not deterred.

"What wolf would wear Yves Saint Laurent suits and a diamond pinky ring?"

Calmly and rather menacingly, Pierre-Loup explained that, despite appearances, a wolf could never be domesticated. Because, he argued, if you offered a wolf a milk bone, the wolf would bite off the entire hand. The milk bone, he said, would just be the cherry on the cake.

The audience looked skeptical. George LeCurieu twisted nervously on his tricycle seat.

"I am a wolf," Pierre-Loup said, pounding the lectern. But still, a trace of uncertainty had crept into his voice. Just the same, he continued: "I am an outlaw—a metaphor for death and destruction. You humans are programmed to be instinctively terrified of me. There can never be any true love between our species."

With these final words, he walked past the podium over

to the edge of the stage and glared into the audience. Everyone felt the hairs on the backs of their necks stand up. With shaky hands, the philosophers lit up their Gauloises. There were no further questions.

In the silence that ensued, George LeCurieu grew uneasy, and so to diffuse the tension, he began to pull on the suspenders attached to his diaper. As he did so, he blew into a slide whistle.

Pierre-Loup focused his rage on the poor monkey-boy.

"You are not an animal," Pierre-Loup yelled at George. "If you were a real monkey, you would be throwing your feces at this crowd! You'd be pounding your chest and making war cries. You are a man imitating a monkey imitating a man."

The philosophers liked that line a great deal. Some of them even jotted it down in their notebooks for use as a possible title for a later treatise on postmodernity.

No longer able to bear the spectacle of it all, Pierre-Loup leapt at George and almost bit off the ear of the security guard who tried in vain to pull him off.

* * *

After that event, Pierre-Loup was judged uninsurable. He returned to Canada, depressed, lonely and detoxing from expensive French champagne. He continued to search for his wolf family in the north and finally discovered, to his dismay, that the lot of them had been captured and put in a Montreal zoo. He went there every day, gripping the bars of

their cage and swearing to get them out as soon as possible—
he just needed to find a big enough apartment for them all
to live in. He described how beautiful St. Denis Street was
and he assured them that they would all be strutting down
it soon.

It was there at the zoo that I first saw Pierre-Loup, squat-
ting beside the wolf cage. There was something about the way
he was whispering so tenderly between the bars, the way the
wolves were all gathered around him, that attracted me right
away. I was never the love-at-first-sight type, and yet what I
experienced that day was unlike anything I'd ever felt for a
man I'd only just met.

"They'd better be treating you guys well," he said, "or
they'll be hearing from me."

It was an incredibly odd thing to be saying to wolves, but
I lived in a Bohemian neighbourhood and so I figured he must
be a poet.

When he turned and saw me staring at him he smiled,
and I recognized that smile from countless newspaper articles
and TV appearances. He bared all his teeth and tilted his face
downwards while looking at me. He kept this expression frozen on his face as he made his way over.

"Yes, I am the infamous Pierre-Loup," he said. "And you
are an absolute vision in that little red coat of yours. The
moment I saw you I said, 'Why, that girl's so cute, I could eat
her up.'"

He threw his head back and laughed.

That first night we spent together, there was a full moon
out. He said he couldn't stay in on a night when the moon

was full. We went to the social club down the street from my apartment and danced all night. It seemed that no one had ever taken poor Pierre dancing. He rolled around on the dance floor in delight, overturning chairs and tables until finally we were thrown out.

At the end of the night, he carried me up the stairs of my apartment building and onto the roof. He tried to get me to howl at the moon with him, but when I tried I only ended up giggling, and once my giggles had faded to silence, very slowly, he leaned in and we kissed. It was Pierre-Loup's first kiss ever and it was so sweet—so small and yet filled with so much promise. It was the kind of kiss that little boys make when they kiss their mirrors alone late at night and dream of being men one day.

THE CONFERENCE
OF THE BIRDS

The whole lot of us are at the rental board: my mom and my dad and my three brothers. We are all dressed up. I have on a black sweater dress that is too hot. There is a big hole in the butt of my underwear, but no one can tell. We all sit in the blue plastic chairs while the landlord's lawyer explains why we deserve to be evicted. We have been going to the rental board for as long as I can remember. The landlord is always trying to get us OUT. We are always so nervous, but the judges always give us another chance no matter what we do, because nobody likes to put a family out on the street. If we are evicted, then other landlords don't have to rent to us, and they for sure never will. And then if we are homeless, child protection will put my brothers and me in foster homes. And we will all be separated. We will be doomed!

The landlord's lawyer keeps listing all the things we have done this time. In the tiny courtroom, the landlord makes a lot of accusations against us. He says that my brothers and dad pee out of the window. This is true, because it is hard in the morning for everyone to wait their turn to get into the bathroom.

The landlord says that we destroy mail from the mailroom. This is true too. Once we took all the circulars and made them into paper crowns. That had been such a fun afternoon. All the other kids came around, and they all wanted to be able to make themselves paper crowns as well. We had all been kings.

He says my dad set some fireworks off behind the building. There were only actually five fireworks. He had made a big deal about buying them too. There was a Native who was selling them out of the trunk of his car. The rockets made soft popping noises, just like a bird being shot in the heart with an arrow. And then all this silver fell. It was so pretty. I put my hands out in case the silver would come all the way down to the yard. I would have pools of silver in my hands, like Jesus, kind of.

The landlord complains about my brother's snow woman. He made her with really big breasts and then used buttons as nipples. Plus he used a pinecone as pubic hair. And he put an old wig that he found in the basement on its head. It caused a car accident when someone slowed down to look at it. It was a work of art.

The landlord says that we played racquetball against the building wall, making everyone who lived in the apartments annoyed. We don't remember this ever happening. Another tenant comes to testify that we poured pink food colouring on their white cat. Which, actually, we had done, but I regret it to this day.

From the other side of his big white desk, the judge tells us that he has had enough.

He says that he has been looking through our files and that he has decided that we have been warned plenty of times. That it just isn't fair to the landlord and the other tenants around us. And that the next time we are brought in for disturbing the general peace of the building, he will evict us.

As we ride the subway home, we vow to ourselves that we will change the way we act.

"Turtledove," my dad says to me. "It's your job to keep an eye on all of us."

We get on our knees on the seats to look out the window. We almost never go anywhere, so the ride is like a vacation and we are carefree. My dad puts his arm around my mom.

* * *

My mom has a scrapbook filled with some newspaper articles about when my three brothers and I were all born at the same time. On that major day, my dad told a doctor that he was out of work and he didn't know how he was going to afford all these kids that had shown up on his doorstep, so to speak. The doctor had been really nice about it and suggested that we call a local newspaper. The newspaper set up a hotline so that people could send money and stuff to help us out.

My dad had always wanted to live in one of the project buildings. But he couldn't until we were born. When we came into his life all at once, he moved right to the top of the list.

He climbed up that list exactly like when you land on a ladder in that board game.

We still have too many stuffed animals left over from when we were first born and people sent us gifts after reading the paper. They are always piled up on all our beds and I have to tunnel under them to go to sleep. They are so dorky. There is an alligator that wears a tuxedo, for instance. I don't know why we didn't throw them away, but we never really throw anything away. There is even a broken television on top of our fridge.

We love our small apartment because it is on the ground floor and we don't have to climb stairs, and we're lazy in that department. There is always this sound of rumbling from inside the walls. We are not sure what it is. My dad says that he thinks it is actually the sound of the boiler in the basement that we are hearing. We can't complain about it because the landlord will tell us, well then, go on and move. The landlord hates us because we are on welfare and are doing nothing about it. Also, once my dad was drunk and told him that he was a blood-sucking slumlord and threw a beer can at his head, which for some reason he took to heart.

My dad said that he stays on welfare because he gets more money with four kids than he would if he still worked for the sales company that he used to work for before my mom got pregnant. He said that looking after us is a full-time job. He also said that he has Type 2 diabetes. He doesn't want to have a diabetes attack, so he can't do anything too strenuous, like putting on shoes at seven in the morning.

* * *

We always say that I am the baby, even though we have no idea who the baby is. When you are a girl, you are always going to be littler than boys. Sometimes it is annoying to have so many brothers. Like, let me tell you this: I like to wear lollipop rings. They always grab my hand to suck on the ring, which is gross and nasty and against my rights.

It's Friday after school, and my mom pushes us all in a grocery cart at the same time. But we get into a fight because nobody wants to carry the piece of ham on their lap. Then the manager comes to complain to my mother about it and to say we can't all be in the damn basket at once. Maybe it's a fire hazard, because almost everything good in life is a fire hazard. Anyway, we climb out, one by one.

My brothers and I are very lucky that we were all born together, because nobody else will have anything to do with us. All the kids think that we are weird. Like my brother Sparrow, who wears the participation medal that he won in day camp around his neck every day, will show anyone his penis if they ask him.

Robin got to take the hamster home for the weekend. The hamster escaped and it most likely got accosted and murdered by some rats in the alleyway. On account of that, none of the other kids would talk to him after that.

The science teacher is always picking on Robin. He gave him a zero on his assignment about his favourite animal, and he said that he wished that he could have given him less. My mother said that chicken pox affected him harder than it had the rest of us.

Jay threw a ruler out the window in math class and even

he had no idea why in the world he did that. The teacher told him to go sit outside the class until he figured out why he did. He sat there for three hours and he still didn't know.

The teachers in our school give my brothers a different diagnosis each month, it seems. For example, once Robin had ADHD and Jay had something called dysgraphia, and then the next month they swapped. Sometimes they all have the same diagnosis and sometimes they have different ones.

I guess I am the smart one. I base that in part on the fact that I like to read a lot. I don't only like books though. I like to read things like the backs of cereal boxes and the warning labels on bottles of poison. I love reading the IKEA catalogue. I enjoy discovering new words too. But most of all, I like to smell books. You know, I can stick my face in the spine of a book and leave it there, breathing in and out, for hours. Despite my extra knowledge, my mom loves us all just the same though. That's the way that she is.

My mother starts singing along to a song on the loud-speaker in line at the grocery store. But she sings it too slow. So she is still singing once the song is over.

On the way home, the garbageman whistles at all the women. But he doesn't whistle at her. I ask my mother how in the world she got so fat.

Was it because she had eaten too many cupcakes? Was it because when she was little, her own mommy had only ever given her hamburgers and milkshakes from McDonald's?

She says no. She says that the reason she is so fat is that she always held so many things in. She was so shy when she was little that she was afraid to express herself. She would never put her hand up in class, so she kept all these ideas inside of her. And each one popped like a kernel of popcorn, until she was like a big bag of microwave popcorn.

My mother says that there are all sorts of opportunities that I have that she did not have as a girl. She says that she always had to stuff her bra when she was little. She says that she had to laugh at all the boys' jokes all the time, even if they weren't funny at all. She says that she wishes she hadn't, because she wouldn't have as many wrinkles now and her teeth wouldn't be so yellow.

When she won an award for her handwriting when she was in Grade Three, she thought that for sure after that happened she was going to make something out of her life. But she didn't. She decided to have a boyfriend instead.

On account of the general conditions of the kitchen, we eat the ham in the living room while watching TV. My mother does not know how to clean up a kitchen. She has been trying to straighten up ours for like eight years, but the more she goes at it, the messier it gets. It is impossible now, 'cause there are too many dishes. The counters look like a landing pad for all sorts of dirty spaceships. We don't know why there are more dishes in our sink than in any other place in the world. Sometimes we all pitch in to wash the dishes, but then we get bored and we go do something else.

After we eat and we're all crammed together on the couch, we don't pay attention to the TV that's still on and we beg our mother to read to us from *The Guinness Book of Records*. I think that it must be so lonely to be the world's tallest man, with your head way up in the clouds like that.

We all feel so sorry for the tallest man that we all start to cry. We hope we never grow like that. It is much better to be ordinary.

My mother lies about what our first words were, when we ask her. But I can't blame her. She does it to make us happy. She tells my brother that his very first words were, "Beam me up, Scotty." His face gets red because he's so proud of himself.

We beg our mother to count our toes. We don't know why we like it so much, other than that it reminds us of having been born.

My mother didn't throw out those little tiny jars of food that you buy when you have babies. They were too cute to get rid of. And if you don't ever chuck them out, you would not even begin to believe how many little baby jars you will have. I am so glad that she kept them all because we keep everything tiny inside of them. Like one bottle is for buttons and one is for thumbtacks. We are like scientists, because it is in the nature of scientists to collect tiny things.

When we were tiny little babies, we were all inside her belly and it was like we were all inside of separate baby jars. I was mushed-up peaches. Jay was mushed-up peas. Sparrow was mushed-up pears. And Robin was beef stew melee.

My favourite time of the night is when after the news they let the balls fall out of the lotto machine. That means that it is time to go to bed. The boiler is making a gurgling noise, like your tummy makes in class before lunchtime. It doesn't keep me up for long, though. We are so happy here, I have to make sure that we don't leave.

* * *

I have to garden today. I have a little square at the community garden right behind the Children's Library. My brothers did not understand why I wanted to sign up for that type of thing. But I always have to have a project. I cannot keep still. I audition for all the plays at school even though I never get a part.

"Goodbye!" I scream again at the front door, but nobody answers.

I find a Virgin Mary statue sitting on one of the window frames in the hallway. She just sits looking out of it like a sad little old lady. I decide to bring her to my little garden. She's actually kind of heavy and she keeps being asked to be put down to walk. Most of the other gardens don't have statuettes or things like that in them. The gardeners are too busy using all the room that is there to grow all sorts of vegetables and things to eat. I gather up some broken bricks and carry them over to place them around the rose.

I have a rosebush that has no flowers on it. It is nothing but an ugly little shrub with thorns on it, but I believe in it. I know that it will be beautiful someday. I sit on an upside-down laundry bucket and read *The Little Prince* to the rosebush.

I till the soil for an hour. My favourite thing is to look underneath the rocks and see everything that lives there. The soil is crawling with worms and earwigs and centipedes.

You would not ever believe how many different species of beetles there are. They have these entire complicated cities with their own miniature subway systems and roadways and underpasses. They have mossy little condominiums where they can have babies. It's really like another Tokyo under my bare feet. They do so much work! They are busybodies. They are just like me: too busy to make trouble.

* * *

When I get back to the apartment, there are a bunch of naked people drawn in chalk all over the cement in the front of the building. Jay must have drawn them. He isn't a very good artist or anything, like he can't do animals or horses, but he is very gifted at drawing naked people. The drawings are doing really dirty things too, like oral sex. A man who lives across the hall from us shakes his head when he steps over them. I rub out the chalk people with the bottom of my running shoes as fast as I can.

As I walk into the building's cement courtyard, I see another one of my brothers. Sparrow has a black nylon sock tied around his forehead. He is practising kung fu moves, which involve kicking his leg up as high as possible in the air and yelling, "Assassinate!" and then standing straight, putting his hands together in prayer and making a bow. An old lady walks by him nervously, afraid that he'll karate-chop her, I guess. But it's Sparrow who screams out, because an empty plastic bottle hits him on the head out of nowhere. I look up to see Robin throwing garbage off the roof of the building. When he sees us noticing him, he yells out, "Assassinate, my ass!"

"Get down from there!" I call up.

"Assassinate, my ass!" he yells back. I have to run for cover, with some other people who live in the building, as an empty tin of beans comes out of the sky like an asteroid.

Robin only comes down when he runs out of garbage. Then I can finally get all my brothers together to tell them off at once. After I'm done yelling at them that they are scaring and seriously disturbing all the neighbours, the sun has already gone down and it's chilly. The night sky is an air conditioner.

I say we should all put some turtlenecks on and pretend to be worms. We stand outside in the yard with the necks of our shirts pulled all the way up over our heads. We wander around yelling that we lost our heads, until someone calls from a window that if we don't shut up he'll call the police.

* * *

It's early Saturday morning and we all get woken up by the landlord banging on the door. He is mad because we keep our shoes lined up in a neat row all the way down the hall-way past everybody else's doors. He throws a pair of shoes at my dad. My dad catches it and, before thinking too hard about it, throws it back at the landlord and pings him on the head.

"I'm taking you to court again. You're a lazy, filthy welfare bum."

We all eat breakfast really quiet. Nobody wants to think about going to court again. Nobody wants to think about how bad my dad's feelings have been hurt. It always makes us really sad that our dad doesn't have a job. We don't like to bring it up to him. We like to pretend that we have never really noticed that he doesn't go to work every day. If ever he gets into an argument at the grocery store or with one of the neighbours, they just tell him that he is a welfare case. Then his cheeks get all purple and you can see all the red squiggly veins in them, and he feels ashamed and, right away, he wants to go home, where he sits in his bedroom with the door shut.

My dad also makes us go to the food bank for him because he is too embarrassed to go himself. We pull the grocery cart down the street and present the welfare stub to the woman at the front table. We don't mind.

Sometimes when he is awake, my dad puts on his fur hat and gets on his hands and knees and snarls like a wolf and chases us around the apartment. We always play the big bad wolf and the four little pigs. Even though there were only three in the original story. We are never sure whether we like this or not. When he catches us, we are always laughing and crying.

My brother fell over a chair while my dad was chasing him. He ended up with a bloody nose and a black eye. Child services came over and we had to reenact the whole game for him.

* * *

Later that day, to make things more cheerful, we beg our dad to see his bow ties. My dad says that when he was a young man, he used to work as a salesman, but he never liked to wear ties. They always made him feel like he had a noose around his neck and that he was strangling himself. So he would wear bow ties. I think that he has the most top-notch collection of bow ties in the world. He has them all laid out at the bottom of a drawer that he sometimes pulls out for us to see. There is a red one with white polka dots. There is a yellow gold–coloured one. I don't know what bow ties look like anymore, but they can't still be making them like this. They look like the world's most gigantic wrapped candies.

He worked for a company that made fancy silverware. There were little roses carved into the handles of all the spoons and there were forks that had handles that were shaped like leaves. We love hearing stories about our father's magnificent cutlery.

One other thing that you should definitely know is that he used to play the trombone. When he was at elementary school, he won a medal for being the top player out of all the students. He had wanted to be in the International Symphony Orchestra, but he wasn't quite good enough. So instead he got a job in sales.

Finally he takes out his bow ties and he lays them on the bed like they are exotic butterflies. We spend half an hour trying to decide which one is our favourite.

My brothers beg and beg him to let them wear them. But my dad says that they each have to wait for their first office job and then he will give each one of them a bow tie.

I'm not sure what I am supposed to wear to my first day. My dad is really old fashioned. I don't think he thinks that a girl is supposed to work.

Maybe I was the last of the four of us that was born. It was as though there wasn't enough material left to make another boy and so I got made. I'm like the last funny cookie on the tray that there wasn't enough dough for.

* * *

Now it is Saturday afternoon and time to go out. My dad always has sore feet because, like I said, he has Type 2 diabetes. The other day he found a wheelchair in the basement and now he wants us to push him around in it when he goes out. He says that he doesn't have to stop at red lights because he is handicapped. He yells at us to push him right out into the middle of the street even though the cars are all honking at us.

We push our dad around to see all the different people who will listen to him when he talks. My dad has a friend from the bakery and he is able to get my dad really huge jars of maraschino cherries for cheap. We cover our ice cream in maraschino cherries. It's like clowns were caught in an avalanche and all you can see of them is their noses. We have maraschino cherries in our orange juice in the morning. We often think that we are so lucky that our dad is likeable.

He knows the owner of the little pharmacy. We like stopping there okay. When we do, we read all the different Hallmark cards. We especially like when one of them happens to be a little bit dirty. And we like to read the backs of all the paperback murder mysteries.

But our very favourite place is the pawnshop! That is

where we head today. There is a bookshelf and, instead of books, the shelves have tiny teacups with flowers painted on them. We kneel on the floor and look into the glass cabinet. I always like to look into glass cabinets because it is similar to looking into an aquarium of amazing things.

We have to get off our knees and move to the back of the store when a real customer comes in and wants to sell their crappy television set. One thing I learned from hanging out at a pawnshop is that people all think that their television sets are worth more money than they actually are. The reality is very hard for people to accept. Especially since they have spent so many happy hours with their television set. And a television set is really so much like one of the family.

Today the owner of the store, my dad's good friend, says that a trombone came in just the other day. He goes to get it. My dad has always bragged about being able to play the trombone, but now I am worried that he has made the whole thing up. I don't like finding out when people are lying to me. It makes me feel like I am spying on them or that I am reading their diary or that I am watching them undress through a tiny hole in the wall. It's rude of me.

My dad picks up the trombone. And he tests it out to see if it slides up and down easily enough. He seems to be satisfied that it is oiled to his liking. My brothers and I stare at him, so afraid. But then he puts it to his mouth and he plays the *Star Wars* theme song. That is our favourite theme song! In fact it is one of mankind's most remarkable inventions, I'd say. It's like all the delivery trucks stuck in traffic are honking their horns, but in harmony.

Who you are is not what country you are from, or what religion you are, it is what your parents' jobs are. You can be a plumber's kid or a lawyer's kid. But it sure doesn't work to only be a welfare case's kid. Today we are a musician's kids. In the dark alcove at the back of the shop, my brothers and I keep looking at one another and smiling, just like when we were all together in my mom's great belly.

* * *

Are you who you are when you are a teeny fetus? There are some people who will say that you aren't properly you yet. But of course you are.

You are you even long before that. You are you when your parents begin to get dressed in fancy clothes one Saturday night. You are you when your mother, who is barely twenty-one years old, puts on a pair of yellow lace underwear. When she plucks her eyebrows in the mirror and when she puts on a red dress that is cut really low and burgundy lipstick: that's all about you, baby.

You are you when your father, who is also twenty-one years old, pops a pimple on his forehead. When he puts on his fancy shiny shirt that was made by children in a sweatshop in Indonesia. When he isn't sure that he actually looks good—but he has been lucky twice before when wearing it.

They are both riding the subway in opposite directions to meet each other and you have already begun. That is your beginning. You have just as much right to be as anybody.

* * *

But my dad is in an even worse mood after we get all excited about him being able to play the trombone. It probably reminded him of being things that he doesn't get to be anymore. He tells us to stop at the liquor store. We all beg him not to go in and Robin even gets on his knees in front of the wheelchair. But he shouts at us to push him inside. He gets a bottle of whiskey and they put it in a paper bag for him, even though our lives are now going to be hell!

We push him down the street as fast as we can and he keeps yelling at us to slow the fuck down. But he keeps taking deep gulps and we have to get him home before the liquor hits his heart. I hope that people don't see us behind the wheelchair. Maybe they will think it is an electric wheelchair and that it is rolling by itself and we just happen to be walking behind it.

My dad points to a man who is passing by and he says, "Hey you, you fucking cowboy. I'm sick of your ugly face. I don't even know you and I know that you won't get married."

We don't even stop to see the poor man's reaction, and we keep right on going. Unfortunately, we have to stop at a red light because it's a busy street. There is a woman standing next to us, also waiting for the right time to cross.

"Hey, skinny," he says to her. "Do you think that men are attracted to chickens? No? Then why in the world do you have those skinny chicken legs exposed? No man wants to see that. I can assure you."

As soon as the light changes, we take off. We are pushing

him so fast that we almost run into a middle-aged man who tells us to be careful.

"You inconsiderate bastard," my dad yells. "Can't you see that I'm a cripple? Can't you see that I'm being pushed around by a little girl? You know what you are? I'll tell you. You're a fucking pimp. That's it. You don't like me to say the word to you because it rings a bell. Well, my brother. Pimp. Pimp. Pimp."

We push him as fast as we can into the building and lock the front door.

* * *

My mom is fixing my hair on Sunday morning so that I can look so good like all the pretty black girls do. While she braids my blond hair, my mom explains to me that men get more hurt than girls. And they get more upset about being out of work than girls do. In that way, she says, it's easier to be a girl. I don't think this is true, because of my projects, because of my garden! I like working a lot.

Whenever we are in court, my mom always speaks with a teeny-weeny high-pitched voice. It's as if she inhaled helium, for some weird reason, and it makes her sound like a baby. She wants the judge to feel sorry for her. This is her defence mechanism. It's a little bit like when bugs play dead so that the birds won't muck with them. But I don't think that is the way I want to act just because I'm a girl.

My mom only does cornrows on one side of my head. Then she says that she has to stop because it's giving her arthritis and that having to concentrate like that is giving her a migraine. I beg her and beg her to do the other side, but she can't. She has to lie down and take a nap.

The cornrows on the side of my head are too beautiful to undo, so I go out later with only half my head braided. I get made fun of by all the kids that I pass. None of the black girls at the park will have anything to do with me. They look at me like I'm crazy, like they always do.

On the way home, this man drives up alongside me in this shitty gold car. The back window is made of cardboard and duct tape. And he asks me if I want to sit on his face. I don't know what that means but it makes my heart bang so loud that it's like a basketball smashing up against a wall. I decide not to tell anyone in my family.

* * *

Sometimes my brothers and I drink lemonade out of a tiny tea set. None of them mind playing games that are supposed to only be for girls. We all liked to take baths together for the longest time. But then my mom said one morning that I was too old to take baths with everybody else.

I have to take them all by myself now. I feel so alone when I am in the bathtub tonight. I feel like I am ten thousand miles from my family. All the toys are covered in soap grime. They are all inside of the soap dish and in the gargling glass. They look like they escaped from the sinking *Titanic* and are now dealing with shock.

I am so skinny that I think I will slip down the drain and

I will go down through the pipes like I am going through a monster's intestines. I do not at all like the way that the drain sounds like it is swallowing and swallowing my bathwater. Like it cannot get enough of it. Like it has an unquenchable thirst. Like it just had a huge meal and is trying to get rid of the hiccups. Something has got caught in its throat.

I look down the drain to make sure there is no long tongue that will come out of it and lick me.

The towels don't match. But it is easier for us to be reminded of which one belongs to who: mine has purple flowers on it; Robin has one with tiny red berries; Sparrow owns the one with little brown pansies all over it; Jay's is a really old one with a tree with pink blossoms on it. They make up a whole natural world. We don't really get to see all those sorts of flowers outside, since we live downtown.

* * *

Human beings have destroyed the whole island of Montreal. In class we go on a field trip to the Natural History Museum. In the back there's this diorama that has all the taxidermied animals that used to exist in Quebec. You would not believe it. There were like wolves walking down the street. Can you imagine what it would be like to look out your window and see wolves walking down the street? It would be terrifying, but then at the same time you would like feel so freakin' alive.

And the birds! Did you know that at one time there were so many passenger pigeons that when they flew over in a flock, the whole sky would grow dark and there would be a shadow cast over the whole island? And you only had to reach your hand up in the air to grab one. You could hold up a pot and some birds would fly in and you would seal the lid on it.

There is a tree outside our building that tried to fight back. The roots of the tree reached out from beneath the sidewalk like a giant squid underneath a boat and broke through. When I get home, I wrap my arms around the tree and tell it that I understand. That it had been really, really angry. And it had all these big ambitions and the city had got in its way.

Its roots look like an elephant that is drowning in quicksand.

* * *

My brothers have no idea what they want to be when they grow up. Sparrow says that he wants to be an opera singer. I don't think it's because he likes to sing, but because he wants to get fat. Robin got a detention for writing an essay about how he wanted to be a pimp when he grew up. It made everyone in the class laugh though, so he didn't care.

I want to be a scientist. But instead of telling anyone, I decide that I will have to prove it.

Walking home, I find an old bulletin board in the trash and I get an idea. I go out at night so that I can collect a jar full of moths. I stand under a lamp that is lighting up the back exit of the Chinese restaurant and I jump about capturing the flittering creatures.

How amazing. They think that they are somewhere way, way up in outer space. They think that they have flown all the way up to the moon, but really they haven't gone anywhere at all.

Two policemen drive up next to me in their car and one of them tells me that I shouldn't be outside. He says that it's too dangerous for girls to go out at night.

I have enough moths anyways, so I take their advice and hurry home. All the rapists are two inches behind me. They are going to catch up with me any second and they will rape me and then I will have to go home and tell my parents that I have been raped.

I tried to imagine what it would feel like to be in the jar, trapped and banging on the glass, trying to be let out, like the moths. I remember when Tinker Bell was trapped in a jar in the movie. I had really felt for her. I really had! Nonetheless, I put the jar in the back of the freezer, behind the bag of pierogies that has been there for seven years.

And in the morning I pull out the jar and all the moths are dead and still beautiful. I stick the jar under my nightgown and run back to my room. I pin them all to the bulletin board one by one. One of the moths has round spots on its wing that look like cigarette burns. When I am finished I step back and look.

I wonder if I could take it to school and show the science teacher. I had a fantasy of the science teacher looking at my bulletin board and being amazed. "Aren't you clever, Turtledove? Aren't you my most brilliant student?"

I say it under my breath so I can hear what it sounds like

to hear a compliment like that. I pretend that I am presenting my bulletin board at a conference for butterfly experts all over the world. I imagine myself travelling to Brazil to catch a rare butterfly and name it after myself.

I also think that my moths look so much like my dad's bow ties in his drawer. I decide to wait no longer and unveil my project to my family. I can't wait for them to be struck by wonder and amazement.

My mother screams when I show her the board. My whole family runs in to see what the commotion is and they start yelling about it too.

My dad says that if the landlord were to make an inspection of the living quarters and saw all those bugs, then we'd get evicted right on the spot.

My brothers say that no man in their right mind would go out with me when they learned that I like to touch bugs.

My mother throws my whole lovely bulletin board in the garbage. I will never become world famous for my moth collection. For a second, I hate all of them. For a second, I do not want to be a part of this stupid family at all. I feel as though they are going to ruin my whole life. I don't care if we get evicted. I so want to throw all my clothes into a pillowcase and get the hell out of here.

"At least I only had one girl," my dad says, and they laugh and laugh and laugh.

I wonder whether every little girl feels as though she is the only little girl on the planet.

But then by dinner, I feel bad that I had wanted to leave everybody. Sometimes I think that it is my job to worry about the family. If I stop believing in them, they will cease to exist, like a bunch of fairies. I am always worried about their feelings, but I am not sure whether or not they are worried about mine.

* * *

Since it is Tuesday night we take our Tuesday night stroll. We all push our dad down to the riverbank in his wheelchair. You can see the amusement park on the other side of the river. I can see the coloured lights across the water. It is like there is a galaxy all the way over there. What are things like in that galaxy? I wonder. Are the laws of physics different? Is nighttime daytime and is daytime nighttime? Can you breathe underwater? Are paupers kings and are kings paupers? I want to go all the way over there.

There is no way that we can afford to go to the amusement park. But on the sides of Coca-Cola cans there are one-dollar-off coupons for the park. If I get enough of these together, we can go to the amusement park on the other side of the world. My brothers aren't allowed to drink Coca-Cola because of their ADD. And both my parents have Type 2 diabetes on account of being so fat, so they aren't supposed to have Coca-Cola. So I have to find the cans lying around the city.

I am happy to have a new project. I will always need a project in life, that is who I am. I go to all the festivals that month because that is where the most cans are at. There is a festival for wiener dogs. There is an Orchestra in the Park festival. I get into a fight with a junkie wearing nothing but jean shorts and beige sneakers when we both go after the same can under a bench. I go through every garbage can trying to see if there are cans inside of it.

I collect 170 cans. I shake the bag and the bag makes the sound of a marching band with skinny, handsome musicians playing my favourite instruments. All my family is amazed and my dad promises that we will go to the amusement park that weekend.

That night as I am trying to sleep, the boiler starts making more noise than usual.

* * *

But the next day, the celebrations are over because we get a letter in the mail saying that we have to go to court because the owner of the building wants to evict us.

We sit around the kitchen table, sick to our stomachs. Now it is for real and we can't even eat our Cheerios. My mother says that this is going to make her hair fall out. We want her to hang on to the little hair that she has because we surely don't want a bald mother on top of everything. Our dad says that he doesn't know what we will do if we get kicked out. We can't afford to live anywhere else. We will be homeless.

We will have to live inside of grocery carts forever and not just for a joyride down the grocery aisle.

My dad spends the day in bed because he is depressed. We don't talk about the amusement park even though I have all those cans under my bed and they are trembling with excitement.

* * *

My dad says that we should all go to court again, so that we can elicit sympathy from the judge. He tells us to put on our fancy clothes.

He is wearing a tweed jacket and some grey pants. He wears a brown V-neck with little diamonds on it. He has a white shirt underneath. The collar coming out of it is kind of yellow. It is the colour that white things turn when they can't handle being white anymore. He puts on one of the bow ties, but I don't think that it helps him. He just doesn't look employed. It's one of the strange facts of life that you have to have a job to look like you have a job. Nobody knows why.

My mother is wearing a dress that makes her look all bulgy, like a melting candle. Her tiny heels look like they will break every time she steps. Her makeup is all half a centimetre higher than where it should go.

I am wearing a pair of burgundy tights that have really big holes in the toes, but you can't see these when I wear my loafers. I wear a grey wool dress and it feels like there are two thousand ants going up and down my arms. My brothers have to wear what they ordinarily wear, because they have nothing fancy.

It costs us a fortune to ride the subway all at once.

* * *

In the tiny courtroom, the landlord makes a lot of accusations against us once again. My brother Sparrow tied a toddler to a telephone pole. Robin peed in a squirt gun and fired it at the janitor. Jay scratched his initials into the window of the front door of the lobby. My dad stole everyone's shampoo samples from their mailboxes. I hung some dolls by their necks from the jungle gym in the courtyard. We all look at one another. What the hell is so wrong with hanging dolls?

The landlord says that we stole a wheelchair from the basement. We thought it had been abandoned. We hadn't even really needed it. It was only for my dad's convenience. If we had known it was stealing we wouldn't have taken it.

Things do not look good for us after the trial. We know that they probably have us with the theft of a wheelchair. But there is nothing for us to do but wait for the results of the judge's decision to come in the mail in two weeks.

That night I know I am going to have trouble sleeping because of what happened. But I really can't sleep because the boiler is bubbling and burping all night long. Like it had a huge meal and now has indigestion.

* * *

My dad says that we should all go to the amusement park, to get our minds off things.

What a clamour all those cans make coming up the stairs of the subway! We're like wasps coming out of a nest that has unfortunately been disturbed. The cans say that we have arrived.

The park is more amazing than I could have ever imagined. There are airbrushed waves on the sides of the little ships, and statues of mermaids on the back of them. There are dragons that you can climb into. There are swings that swing out from a giant post that has paintings of shepherdesses laughing on them. There is this strange imaginary hand that pushes your swing.

We ride all the rides and we make sure to scream louder than any other family in the park. I love the bumper cars the most. What would it be like to steer the bumper car out of the way so that no one could hit you, and then to drive it right out of the park? Wouldn't it be wonderful to ride the bumper car right down the highway and forever?

We are too afraid of the haunted house. There are papier-mâché witches hanging out of the windows, and a giant snake coming out of the chimney that keeps exhaling smoke. And you can hear children screaming inside, all terrified, but they come out laughing with tears in their eyes. What is nice about the amusement park is that it makes it okay to be afraid all the time.

Robin and I sit in the Ferris wheel cage together. We rock back and forth. And then we start to slowly climb up and up. I can hear my other brothers screaming in their cage. Saying things like "Oh no, oh no, oh no!" I can hear my parents laughing in their cage.

All the bright lights from every ride at the amusement park are all around me: orange and red and yellow and green and blue, as if we are in a meteor shower. And as I look out onto the city, all the little streetlights are like strings of pearls. All the windows are lit up. We are right in the heart of the Milky Way.

We cry on the way home from the amusement park because it has been such a fun day and we are sad that it is over. We know that we might never get to go again. Not as kids anyways. And when we are old enough to finally afford tickets, the magic will be all gone.

Now it is night and the boiler is making a kicking sound. It sounds like there is someone trapped inside it. They have pretty much given up and reconciled themselves to their fate, but every now and then they give a violent kick to the side of it with their boot.

ACKNOWLEDGEMENTS

Thank you most of all to Jennifer Lambert.

Thanks to the great team at HarperCollins Canada: Cory Beatty, Kelsey Marshall, Noelle Zitzer, Leo MacDonald, Iris Tupholme, Kaiti Vincent, Shannon Parsons, Suman Seewat, Stacey Cameron and everyone else.

Thanks to everyone at Quercus in the UK and, in particular, to the wonderful Rose Tomaszewska and Jon Riley.

Thanks to everyone at FSG in the United States: Mitzi Angel, Will Wolfslau and Sarah Scire.

Thanks to Courtney Hodell.

Thanks to my agents and everyone at WME: Claudia Ballard, Jennifer Rudolph Walsh and Cathryn Summerhayes.

Some of these stories have previously appeared on CBC radio and *This American Life* and in the *National Post* and *Rookie* magazine.

Research for this book included in part the following works: Julie Kavanagh's *Nureyev: The Life*; Robert Gildea's *Marianne in Chains*; Richard Vinen's *The Unfree French: Life Under the Occupation*; Susan Zuccotti's *The Holocaust, the French, and the Jews*; Tom Douglas's *Canadian Spies: Tales*

of Espionage in Nazi-Occupied Europe During World War II;
Mark Zuehlke's *Juno Beach: Canada's D-Day Victory*; and
Angelo Jo Latham's *Posing a Threat: Flappers, Chorus Girls,
and Other Brazen Performers of the American 1920s*.

Thanks to the Conseil des arts et des lettres du Québec
for a writing grant for this book.

Always thank you to Paul Tough.

And a special shout-out to my favourite human being:
Arizona O'Neill.